OFF THE ICE

JAQUELINE SNOWE

PUBLISHED 2022

Published by: Jaqueline Snowe

Copyright 2022, Jaqueline Snowe

Cover Design: Dany Snowe

Editing: Katherine McIntyre

Formatting: Jennifer Laslie

All rights reserved. No part of this publication may be reproduced, stored in a retrieval system, or transmitted in any form, or by any means, electronic, mechanical, recording or otherwise, without prior written permission from the author. For more information, please contact Jaqueline at www.jaquelinesnowe.com.

This is a work of fiction. The characters, incidents, dialogue, and description are of the author's imagination and are not to be constructed as real. Any resemblance to actual events or persons, living or dead, is completely coincidental.

ACKNOWLEDGMENTS

This series wouldn't have happened without Sarina Bowen and her call for proposals for her World of True North. The summer of 2020 was rough for so many reasons and writing became *hard*. Finding joy at that time was hard. But writing Holdout and living in Ryann and Jonah's world became an escape. Fast forward, I was able to write Michael and Naomi, then Cami and Freddie, then Gabe and Dani, and now Cal and Elle. I am in love with this friend group and the Central State series.

Another huge thank you to Kat McIntyre. She kicks my ass with edits and revisions (and sends nice emojis to make it nicer, lol) but I am SO damn thankful for you. I love working with you, hearing your thoughts, and hope we get to do more work together!

In Take the Lead, I thanked Sil (@thebookvoyagers) and Nick (@romancefiend) because their posts helped me find new readers and there are not enough words of gratitude for both of you. Because of your posts, I've gotten to get wild amazing messages from Ale (@latinasmoak) and Sarah T Dubbs and Courtney Michael Clark. Getting DMs and chaotic messages are my FAVORITE thing ever so thank you all so, so much. Also a HUGE thanks to @booksandbeyonddd @rrbookreviews @ashleyanreads and @paperdreams.x @eleanorlynnreads for all the tags and support. I don't often get emotional but… I *might've* when you've shouted out about some of my books. I am not a hugger but I would for real hug all of you.

Thanks to my husband who not only combines his sports graphic design skills with my romance covers, but also lets me talk about romancelandia all the time. We have a family motto of doing what you love, and love what you're doing and he never lets me settle.

Lastly, a huge thank you to you, dear reader. Thanks for giving me and this series a chance. It's been a dream come true. I hope you enjoy Cal and Elle's story. It is the most emotional story I've ever written. Please note the content warnings below.

Content warnings: talk of parents death, depression, anxiety attack, bar fight

OFF THE ICE

Elle Van Helsing wants to start her life away from home. Constantly living under the shadow of her brother, she plans to find romance and survive on her own: even if its financially harder than she thought. Getting a job at a dive bar three doors down from her new place is the perfect solution. Well, it was, until the owner has a family emergency and asks his nephew to help out in his absence. The guy she *used* to have a crush on until he ruined it.

Cal Holt might be a legend on the ice, but off it? He's alone and likes to keep it that way. It's easier to protect himself when he's always a jerk, but the *one* person who gets under his skin is Elle. Torn between wanting to get to know her and pushing her away, he's surprised when he learns she hates him. She looked at him differently the year before, and now that they're stuck managing a bar for a few weeks, tensions rise.

She's a hopeless romantic who wants grand gestures and sees the world through rose-colored glasses. He's a grumpy cynic with a permanent scowl. She dreams of love, and he wants a one-night stand. She plans to build a life on campus, and he plans to leave and head to the NHL Complete opposites in every way, they shift from enemies to friends…but Cal refuses to fall in love, and Elle deserves more. For the girl who never felt enough and the guy terrified to feel, fear might ruin their chance at finding *love.*

To found families and finding your people, who accept you as you are.

CHAPTER
ONE

Elle

Jonathon Jackson quickened his pace, desperate to get to the love of his life. His feelings gripped him, almost magnetic in how they pulled him toward Fern. His pulse raced like a river, his heart thumping a deep vibration with each beat. She must say yes to his proposal, or he'd forget his purpose.

"Eleanor Van Helsing?"

I shut my laptop way too fast, hitting the tip of my finger as the voice startled me. My finger stung, and I hid my wince, forcing a smile as I glanced up to see Charlie Miller on the other side of the bar top.

"Elle, hi, yes. This is me." I hated the immediate flush of embarrassment at getting caught up in the moment. It happened whenever I read or worked on my secret novel. I forgot where I was, what I was doing, and escaped. My family joked about my daydream situation, and while they *meant* well, it tended to minimize what I wanted: to live in my writing. My face burned, but I masked it as quickly as I could. "No one calls me Eleanor unless I'm in trouble."

"Noted." The large, beefy man placed the flats of his palms on the wooden bar. "Welcome. I'm the owner."

"Nice to meet you officially." I held out a hand and shook his. He had a firm grip and didn't have sweaty palms, thank god. Sweaty palms were the worst. "Thanks for taking my resume—I really need a job."

"Don't we all, sweetheart." He rocked back on his heels before pulling a sheet of paper from under a stack of pens. "You've waitressed for five years?"

"Sure have. Also helped behind the bar on busy nights. I have the best *customer is always right* face. Try me."

His lips twitched, and he ran a hand through his extremely long beard. I imagined he lived in the woods, in a log cabin and wore plaid a lot. Definitely chopped his own firewood and had at least four tattoos. Totally used beard oil too.

"Good to know," he said, pulling me from my momentary blip of creating an entire backstory for him.

I smiled, leaned onto my elbows, and tilted my head to the side. "I'll be here whatever hours you have available. Do any side work. Cleaning toilets doesn't faze me."

"You able to stay until close on weekends?"

"Yes. I live less than two minutes away." Hope sprung alive like flowers after a storm. *Please, please, please.* I wanted the money, and I knew I'd make good tips here. I refused to admit to my *perfect* brother or my parents that I needed help. I'd work twenty-four seven if it meant I was on my own. It was close to campus, one of those hole-in-the-wall bars that alumni always came back to. Hockey posters covered the wall. I avoided *a certain someone's* poster because ugh, what a disappointment, but the vibes were what I wanted. Busy, chill, and safe.

Charlie squinted at my resume, his bushy brown eyebrows hiding his expression. I desperately wanted to know what the holdup was. I had experience, could handle myself, and would work my ass off.

I mean, I had no choice. This was the deal with my parents—I did community college for two years, then I could transfer. They'd pay for tuition, but all living expenses were up to me. They valued education but thought it was silly to not live at home for free…and they didn't love the fact I wanted to be a writer. With both of my parents still paying off student loans, they refused to let my brother and I get them.

Of course, Gabe received a scholarship, so that bitch was here all four years, living my dream.

Charlie's hand was covered in tattoos—I freaking knew it—and he ran it through his hair, gray spotting both temples. He had to be mid-forties, around there. Chubby but cuddly. I could picture him with twin daughters driving him wild at home.

Focus. Get the job.

"Sir—"

"Oi, none of that sir shit. That'll get you fired immediately." He guffawed, putting his hands in the air and shaking his head so much his beard wiggled. "Charlie. Chuck. Those are the only two names I answer to."

Excitement shot through me like a firework. "Wait, *fired* implies I'm *hired*."

"Well, yeah." He scrunched his face like I was absolute bonkers for suggesting I wasn't given a job. "Alex and Tina hold the bar down, but Tina's having a baby and will be out. That'll leave me and Alex, and I'm getting too old for the weekend shifts."

I made a fist, punching it into the air like the ending of The Breakfast Club. Gabe made me watch it last weekend, and not only had the music stuck with me, but John Hughes' storytelling captivated me. How he nailed teenage experience… I wanted to study his screenplays to make myself a better writer. Hell, I hoped I had an assignment this fall that required a deep study of a writer.

"Score!" I slapped the bar top, making my laptop almost fall off. I caught it and beamed at Charlie, my new boss. "When do I start? What's the dress code? What are the hours?"

"Alright, you're a little hyper, but this place could benefit from it. With Callie-boy always here moping around and Tina bitching about her pain… plus, Alex is… well, they're broody. Has a wonderful sick sense of humor. Yeah, we could use your energy."

"Honestly, hyper is one of my good qualities."

Charlie studied me for a bit, shaking his head and laughing. "I admire your confidence."

I flipped my hair over my shoulder. "Thank you, Chuck."

"Jesus." He snorted just as the front door opened, letting some of the afternoon sunshine blast into the bar. Now that I noticed the beams, it was obvious how dark this place was. No windows, dim lights. It was moody as hell, and I dug it.

Charlie nodded at the guest but then snapped his fingers. "Perfect. Alex, meet your new bartender."

I spun around super-fast, smiling and ready to befriend my new work buddy. *God,* I wanted a friend here. Someone who wasn't from my hometown who didn't know my entire life story or parents. Who wasn't in awe of my brother and viewed me as an afterthought. I loved my brother, but it was hard always being in his shadow. He was always exceptional, and I was always average. "Hey, I'm Elle."

Alex had short hair, buzzed on one side while the other hung down. They had tattoos covering their left arm, with the right completely bare, which gave them a wicked cool look. They wore all black—tight black shirt, black jeans, black biker boots. Their lipstick was bright red though, and I grinned. "Oh my god, I love the lip color."

"Her? No." Alex shook their head, frowning at Charlie. "Look at her in her sunflower dress. Do we look like the place where people wear *sunflowers*?"

"I asked Chuck here about the dress code, but he laughed at me. You want me to dress in all black? A slutty top to get more tips? Tell me."

Alex's tone or comment didn't offend me in the slightest. I knew I was an acquired taste and wouldn't settle for half-friendships. People either loved me or hated me, and that was okay with me.

My best friend Daniella thought I was hopelessly romantic, saying I expected nothing less than one-thousand percent investment from a partner to sweep me off my feet, loving me for all I was. Maybe it was true, but none of my insecurities stemmed from *who* I was. I generally liked myself. I spent most of the time in my head, daydreaming and creating stories, and I realized one day I was pretty damn awesome. If anyone else didn't get that memo, like my parents or brother, then that was *their* fault, not mine.

"Don't judge me until you see my skills." I got off the stool, placed my laptop in my backpack, and hoisted it on my shoulders. "I can memorize orders without writing them down, can charm the pants off a real dick of a human, *and* I'll clean the silverware without complaint. I actually find doing dishes comforting, isn't that weird? It's the repetition I think." I was blabbing way too much, but I swore I saw Alex's mouth twitch.

"You're exhausting." They sighed.

"Oh, I know. But I'm worth it."

"When does she start?" Alex asked Charlie, their hands moving through their jet-black hair. "We're gonna have a rush tonight with the Bulls in the playoffs."

"I was just asking about that! They play tomorrow at seven, but pre-game starts at six thirty. I have the cutest Bulls jersey I can wear too. I actually have two if you want to borrow one?"

"Fuck." Alex pinched their eyebrow just as the door opened again. "Oh, great. My favorite person."

"Shut up, Alex. I'll spill bleach on all your clothes."

"You wouldn't dare."

"Watch me."

The glare hid the person's face, but I knew *that* voice. It belonged to the face on the wall I'd avoided staring at because a girl couldn't just erase raw attraction. I'd crushed—from far away —on Cal Holt for two years, only to be deflated when we actually spoke. My left hand curled into a fist, and my heart punched my ribs. *Why is he here?*

"Elle," he said, his deep timbre a damn string, yanking me toward him. I kept my feet firmly in place, digging my toes into my matching flower Vans.

The door shut, and I blinked. The light settled, and now I could view him in entirety. I hadn't seen him since he oddly helped us move a couch into our apartment, but I would've been okay *not* running into him again. I nervously swiped a hand over my neck, hiding the way my pulse raced just from his presence.

He wore a simple black T-shirt and dark jeans, the fabric stretching over his toned muscles. Drafted at eighteen yet choosing to stay until he got his degree? A body of a Greek god? The crooked nose that made him slightly more rugged than handsome? I cleared my throat, forcing myself to remain cool. He might've got me revved up before, but he was an asshole.

"*What* are you doing here?"

"Wait." Alex full-on smiled now. "Do y'all know each other? Do I sense a tone?"

"No," I said.

"Yes." Cal narrowed his eyes at me, his lips curved down like he was upset. His glare and frown were famous, from what Dani told me, so there was no reason for him to be stressed at seeing me.

I wasn't the one who'd ruined it that night.

"This is my nephew, Elle." Charlie's voice was strained, like he too was trying to piece together why the bar had gotten so hot and filled with tension.

Not the sexual kind. Anger tension. Smack Cal with my notebook tension.

Charlie coughed into his fist when no one said anything. "Elle's gonna bartend here."

"Tomorrow," I added, grinning at Alex. "Alex is showing me the ropes. Can't wait. We're gonna be the best of friends."

Cal ran a hand over his forehead, pushing back his

obnoxiously great brown hair. "You're working…here? In this shithole? Why?"

"Shithole? Fuck off, Cal. You're on the damn stool every day." Charlie shook his head.

"What?" He shrugged and stepped closer to me, his mouth parted. "It's true, Charlie."

"Well, thanks for hiring me, Chuck. I can't wait to get started. You won't regret it! And Alex, I'll see you tomorrow." I knew it was time for me to go before Charlie changed his mind or Cal tried to talk to me.

I shouldered my bag and walked right to the door, moving around Cal so our bodies wouldn't touch and breathing the fresh humid air the second I could. It was humid and muggy outside, a little early in the summer. But it was better than the tension inside. If what Charlie said was true and Cal was there all the time, I'd have to deal with that.

Surely it'd be so busy that it wouldn't matter if he was there. I'd find things to do rather than serve him. The list was always endless. I got about ten steps away from the bar before Cal shouted my name.

Damnit.

"Elle, wait up."

I walked faster, but I had nothing on his thick muscly thighs that helped him skate like a god. Yes, my crush was half to do with looks and half to do with his talent on the ice. I'd watched my brother the last two years and had fallen in love with Cal's skating and aggressive play. People who loved what they did and were good at it sparked something in me. Observing him on the ice replicated the feeling of when I wrote.

He caught up to me, gently tugging on my elbow. When I moved my gaze toward where his fingers touched my skin, he dropped his hand and stepped back. "S-sorry, wanted to get your attention."

"And I attempted to ignore it."

He frowned again, deep wrinkles on his forehead and around

his mouth. The lines showed so easily that it briefly made me sad that he never smiled. I already had crow's feet at the corners of my eyes, and I was barely twenty-one.

"Are you all moved into your apartment? Do you need any more help?" His deep, gruff voice was two octaves lower than you would think. It reminded me of the old blues music my dad listened to on his vinyl.

If I removed his face and attitude, I could write stories about that voice and the epic love story it sparked. *Can it sing?* Oh, baby, I bet it could. The voice, not Cal. I separated the two in my head.

"We're all set, thanks." I continued walking, hoping he'd get the hint to leave me alone, but he kept pace. "Can you not take a hint? I don't want to talk to you, so why are you following me?"

"I'm not. I live in the building you do and am heading back. Just happens to be on the *same* sidewalk at the *same* time. Don't assume things."

My temper flared, but remaining quiet was the better move. For me, arguing ended up with me sounding like a fool, eyes watering out of embarrassment or anger. A good comeback would hit me in three days from now, and it'd be a real zinger. But ugh. *Me* not assume things? From the guy who told me my *blonde* ass didn't know shit about hockey and chose the easiest major to skate by? *Creative writing* was a fast way to unemployment and a joke of a career choice, according to my parents and brother. Everyone, from my teachers to my parents, told me I would never survive off it. That'd I'd be on my parents' couch in a year. Cal had pushed the sensitive button that kept me up at night, knocking my already thin career confidence. Yeah, the comment was half a year ago, but it had stuck in my head, rooting and growing into a forest of distaste.

He didn't even realize what he had said or how the words resonated with me. It had been hard to acknowledge a guy I had major respect for and a huge (secret) crush on had been so cruel to me. Avoiding him was for the best, but it might be a challenge at my new job.

He stayed by my side the entire time, not saying another word. We got to the main doors, and he went toward the stairwell while I headed toward our unit. Dani and my brother were hanging on the couch, both looking up at me expectantly.

"Well? Did you get the job?" Dani asked.

Focus on the positive.

"Sure did!"

I smiled and gave two thumbs up.

Gabe frowned. "At *that bar?* The shithole place next door?"

His tone bothered me. "Yes."

"Elle, you can find a better spot than there." He scratched the back of his neck. "What would Mom and Dad think?"

My face heated. "It's not their business."

Nor was my choice in major. Creative writing was what I wanted, even if it wasn't as splashy as business or hockey or all the things Gabe did. Our parents never compared us or made me feel less loved, but living in Gabe's shadow seemed unending.

I adjusted my hair and stood taller. "I *want* to work there. It's perfect." *Despite Cal being there a lot.*

Gabe huffed, and Dani patted his thigh. I *loved* them separately and together, without question, but sometimes my brother annoyed me with his unwanted opinions.

"I think it's a great idea." My best friend winked at me.

That helped settle the growing tension in my gut, and I plastered on my fake smile. "Two against one. Told you this would happen."

Gabe muttered some reply, but I didn't catch it. I grabbed my laptop out of my bag and escaped to my room. Writing was where I reset my soul. I pushed all thoughts of my brother, my choice in career, and Cal out of my head and let the words flow.

I'd gotten a job, and I was thankful.

CHAPTER
TWO

Cal

Days like today made me pissed off at the promise I made to my parents. *Get a degree, so you always have one to fall back on. You're a single injury away from ending an NHL career.* I could still hear my mom's voice when I focused. It was getting harder each year, but I had videos. They were tough to watch and usually sent me in a tizzy where I drank too much, fucked too hard, and made more enemies.

But today had me feeling antsy. If I'd chosen to head straight to the NHL, I'd have a schedule, a nutritionist, and a team of guys who I could work out with or bother. There'd be more of a purpose besides eat, sleep, and work out on repeat. Summers sucked on campus, but it wasn't like I had anywhere else to go. My parents left me a shit ton of money, so a job seemed useless. I had the gym and the bar. Things had been better with the team, but it was tough to let anyone in.

God, my life sucked.

Charlie was my only family left, and call me sentimental, but I liked being around the guy who grew up with my mom. He looked nothing like her, thank god, but had her same calming energy. He was one of only two people I could stand being around without getting angry. Michael Reiner, the assistant hockey coach, was the second.

That was a lie. There was one other person, but she hated my guts.

I couldn't believe Charlie hired her. Elle didn't belong in that bar. Rough people went there. They smoked, cussed, and drank too much. They'd get handsy, and Elle was too…delicate. There was something about her that made me want to protect her.

Her large, expressive brown eyes paired with her straight blonde hair. Her bowed lips, her top one almost too big for her face worked for her. Plus, her unsaid confidence captivated me. Her two birthmarks right under her left eye. God, they did something to me. I rubbed a hand over my chest, staring out my apartment window and wishing I had a different life.

An easier one.

One with family and laughter and smiles. I'd even settle for boring instead of this bullshit cycle of sadness, anger, and pain.

The sun hit my row of plants, and I *almost* smiled at the aloe. I bought it half-off a few weeks ago assuming it'd probably die, but seeing new stems grow filled me with pride. No one knew my secret, and no one would. I loved buying plants half-off, half-dead and trying to nurse them back to life. My entire YouTube history was filled with hockey plays and plant tutorials.

I bent low and studied the other flowers and succulents. Two of them were browning, and I adjusted them in the pot so they wouldn't get the full sun. A small coffeepot of grinds sat to the right, and I put a little bit in the soil

Ironic? Sure. I felt half-dead too somedays. Would a therapist suggest I saw myself in the plants? Possibly. I picked up the leather journal off to the side where I jotted observations and progress. My plant health tracker.

After tending to the rest of the succulents, I realigned the porcelain pots so they were in a straight row. Clutter and disorganization physically bothered me, so my spotless apartment felt empty but was always clean.

My phone went off, and for one second, I was excited. *Someone to talk to.* But then I shut that emotion down. Might be hard for some to understand why I welcomed the pain and anger and pushed people away, but it was safer.

Reiner: Bulls play in an hour. Wanna watch it?

Cal: Your girlfriend too busy for you?

Reiner: Oh, you took your dick pills today. Great. I'll see you there, and first drink's on you.

I huffed out in amusement. Reiner had a unique ability to call out my bullshit. Every single time I tried ending our friendship, he held on tighter. He too had lost both of his parents and was left an orphan at a young age. But a flicker of jealousy wedged its way in my soul at the fact he had a sister.

Charlie was family, but we didn't talk about feelings or goals or shit like that. He made sure I was alive, and that was about it. Most days it was enough, but some, I wanted more.

Watching the game would be nice, *and* visiting the bar meant I could see how Elle was doing. Content and almost anxious, I showered and dressed in a T-shirt and shorts. The quick walk was way too hot and muggy, a sure sign of a summer storm coming, and I pulled my shirt from my chest to get some airflow in there.

Cold and ice were some of the reasons I loved hockey. It felt good to have the sting in my nose and chill in the air. This Midwest humidity bullshit was the worst.

Yells and groans greeted me once I walked in. "Pass the fucking ball!"

Ah, home. I loved chaos. Hockey fans were chaotic as hell, and I almost smiled as a group of men stood up, arms in the air, yelling at the TV in the back. Sports fanatics were fun.

There were about forty people inside, nowhere near capacity, but my gaze moved through every face until I found hers. My chest got tighter as I watched her. Elle wore cutoff jean shorts with strings hanging down, a tight Bulls jersey, three necklaces, and high-top black and red Chucks. Her hair was in a ponytail, and were those Bulls earrings?

She was so out of place here it wasn't even funny, but no one else seemed concerned. Charlie stood behind the bar, chatting with customers on stools. Alex, well, they were doing whatever they did. That moody asshole was fun to poke at, and they loved riling me up.

My usual spot was empty, so I sat down and watched her. Before Elle hated me, we'd talked for about twenty minutes that night months ago. She mentioned she wasn't athletic in any way, that all the athleticism all went to her asshole brother, but how she moved between tables holding drinks seemed hard. She swayed her hips, not spilling a drop as she smiled at everyone.

But then her gaze landed on me, and that smile fell.

My stomach soured at the hatred on her face, and she looked away, a slight redness to the upper part of her cheeks. I had no idea what I'd done to get her to hate me. I was used to people thinking I was a dick, but that was different. The hockey team knew my value on the ice so they put up with it, and with Van Helsing's help last year, things were getting better. I was even in two separate group chats. I responded a handful of times too. That was growth.

Women? I was a free ticket to the NHL. I could blink and say bedroom, and they'd jump on me. Elle though… I fucking hated how she dismissed me.

She took her sweet time returning to the bar, a tactic, I was sure, and when she did, she served everyone else besides me. She finally approached me, face flat, no sparkle in her eye. "What would you like?"

"Is your first night going okay?" I asked, gripping the edge of the bar and hoping she'd stay for a conversation. She didn't seem flustered or put off by the interesting clientele. "Everyone treating you well?"

"Besides you? Yeah. I can manage this." She waved her hand in the air in a circle, then pointed at me. "It's you I can't handle."

It's you.

Those words hurt more than I cared to admit, but I didn't give anything away. Just like Michael and Van Helsing had said, calling me out and forcing me to accept I was a shit person, her insult stung and plucked at the part of me I thought I'd buried deep: the need to be wanted. I kept my face neutral despite my heart speeding up. Instead, I leaned onto my elbows to get closer to her. She smelled like vanilla and cinnamon and spice, and the combination was delicious. I breathed it in, jutting my chin toward the line of beers on draft. "312."

"Tall or short?"

"Tall."

She gave me a pinched smile before grabbing a glass and rinsing it with the spicket Charlie installed last year. Without looking at me, she tilted the glass and started pouring. A ticket that was at least ten inches long printed from the register, and without removing her hand from my drink, she tore it off and put it in her mouth.

There was something sexy about her handling shit. A quiet confidence. She set my glass down to settle, then retrieved seven more glasses with a finesse I only had on the ice. Two dark lagers, a Guinness, a black and tan, two pale ales, and a Bud Light. She even picked up a tray, spun it in a circle, and had all the beverages on there just as Alex stormed behind the bar.

"I need those drinks! This table is a fucking menace." They huffed, and Elle winked.

"Already done, Darkness."

"Lux, I swear to gods, those better be for me." Alex walked by in their all-black outfit, their usual uniform, and they grinned. Full-on smiled. Wow, seeing them smile was different than the usual expression. And, *of course,* Elle would get them to do that.

"Not bad," Alex said.

"How about *nice job?* Would that kill your soul to say it?" she fired back, already tearing off the next ticket and grabbing glasses.

Her arm muscles clenched and bulged as she hoisted a glass rack up onto the bar.

"Blondie, we need shots."

"And I need a foot massage. Pipe down for one second, Mac Attack." She put the dirty glasses in the empty rack, throwing a smile over her shoulder to one of Charlie's gruffest patrons.

Macintosh Sawyer was a grumpy old man. But here he was, grinning at Elle like she hung the moon. I took a long drink of my beer, in a terrible mood. She could smile at that piece of shit but not me? Why? I wanted to know so damn badly.

Elle hadn't looked at me once, but I couldn't stop watching her. By the time Reiner sat next to me, she'd been called so many nicknames, I couldn't keep track. Lux, Blondie, Ellie Bellie, Sunshine. It was the damn white-blonde hair. It stood out.

"Hey, Charlie hired himself someone with actual charisma." Michael nudged my shoulder and lifted a hand in the air. Elle saw, and I swore her eyes flickered with heat.

Figures. Michael wasn't an ogre.

"Hi, what can I get ya?" she asked, smiling at my coach. She had a dimple on one side, and I found that even more charming. Not two, but a little asymmetrical.

"Well, what would you suggest after someone spent all day looking at rings?"

She sucked her lip into her mouth, tapping her fingers on the bar top. Each nail was a different color, and I was annoyed I noticed. She still wouldn't look at me.

"Depends on the types of rings. Are we talking championship ones? Engagement? Olympic?"

"Ah, excellent question. In this case, I'm talking engagement rings."

"Dude." I hit him. "You're gonna propose to Naomi?"

He beamed so wide that something plucked at my heart. That utter delight on his face wasn't something I'd experienced since my parents died. It was almost painful to see how happy he was.

He shrugged and let out a huge sigh. "Yes. I'm asking her to marry me."

"Congrats!" Elle clapped and wore the same big grin. She didn't even know Michael or Naomi, but glee radiated from her, like other people's joy actually made her happy. "This is a time for shots. What will it be?"

"Fireball."

"On it!" Elle floated to grab the whiskey bottle, and I stared at the way her calf muscles came out when she stood on her tiptoes. She returned with two shot glasses, and Michael frowned.

"Oh no, you get one too. This is a celebration. I never thought I'd be in this place to ask someone to marry me. Thought it was for other people." Michael stared at me when he said it, his words hitting something deep in my mind. I knew what he meant. I felt that every second of every day.

When you lost the people you loved most in the world, why would you even attempt to love again? Grief was lonely and terrible, but it was safer than ever experiencing those feelings. I wouldn't recover a second time—hell, I never did the first.

"Love is for everyone. Just looks different for different people. That's what's so beautiful about it." Elle poured the shots, slid one each to Michael and me, and held up her glass. "Congrats to you and to your lucky lady!"

"Hear, hear!" Michael said.

We took the shots, and I swore Elle's throat bobbed when she looked at me. Her brown eyes were a sucker punch to the gut, so deep and beautiful. But the three seconds of truce ended, and she went back to hating me.

Other patrons needed her, so she picked up our glasses before darting off somewhere else. That left me and Michael. His joy radiated off him, and I wasn't a complete monster—I was excited for him. Saying it though was difficult to articulate. I wasn't expressive or charismatic or peppy. I grunted and hated talking because I had nothing important to say ever. But the thought of letting him down caused heartburn, so I forced my voice to rise an octave. "I'm really happy for you, Coach."

"Did it hurt to say that?"

"With every ounce of my body."

He tossed his head back and laughed. My own lips twitched, but I hid my own amusement. "So, how are you asking her?"

"Not sure yet. Something with numbers? Data?"

"Romantic."

"Hey, she's weird, but she's my type of weird, you know? Likes what she likes and is okay with it. Fuck." He rubbed his chest, a serious expression on his face. "It's moments like this that I wish they were alive. It eats me whole."

I closed my eyes, understanding what he meant. How were we expected to grow into adults without having parents to call and ask questions to? My *parents* were YouTube and the internet, but you couldn't really google *how to propose* and get good advice.

Without overthinking it, I put my hand on his shoulder and squeezed. "Do what feels right. That's all you can do."

"Yeah." He nodded a few times and shook his head. Just like that, Michael Reiner the upbeat guy was back. It was incredible how he could do that, shake off his grief and be happy. It made me envious with how he'd moved on, healed, and found someone to make his life better. Every time I tried being happy or trusting another person, it backfired.

A loud cheer startled me. I'd forgotten the game was on. The Bulls were down at the end of the first, but that wasn't what caught my attention. It was Charlie. He was a gruff man, but his face was pale and his eyes as wide as hockey pucks.

My skin felt too tight in my body, and I clenched my jaw. He stood toward the back office, his posture rigid.

"Be right back."

I slid off the stool and pushed people out of my way to get to him. I knew that face, that panic. It was the same one my high school coach had when he told me about the accident. My pulse raced. "Charlie, what is it?"

He stared up from his phone, blinking way too fast as he opened his mouth a few times. "I have to leave."

"To where? Do you need me to drive?"

"No." He ran a hand over his face. "I need to travel to Indiana."

"Why?"

"Apparently, I have a daughter I know nothing about, and her mom just died."

CHAPTER THREE

Elle

Chuck looked serious. His bushy eyebrows were drawn together, his left eye twitching every other second. My mind spiraled into what this emergency meeting was about—he won the lottery and was buying a boat and peace-ing out?

He was harboring a fugitive?

He found out his girlfriend had three secret families? Whoa, that was dark. I shook that thought away and yawned. He'd shut the bar down early, the second the Bulls game ended, and demanded everyone get out.

All except Alex, Cal, and me. Alex had to use the restroom, so here we were, waiting in silence.

Cal sat to my right, his left knee bouncing up and down. It wasn't egotistical to say that it felt weird to not see him staring at me. All night, I'd felt those intense blue eyes on me. I swore his gaze prickled my skin as he constantly watched me. But now, they focused on whatever captured his attention on the top of the table where he sat. He scratched it with his long fingers, and the muscles along his jaw clenched.

He seemed to be in a mood too.

Alex returned after a tense two minutes, and Charlie pressed his hands together like he was praying only to release them with a soft exhale. "There's no easy way to say this."

Oh no.

No winning the lottery and buying a boat.

I placed my hand on my chest, rubbing small circles at whatever news he was going to share. Even though I hardly knew him, I only wanted the best for him. We all held our breath as Charlie ran a hand through his beard, clearly disgruntled.

"I have a daughter."

Alex sucked in a breath, and Cal didn't seem surprised at all. I wasn't sure if this was good news or not. From Charlie's stressful reaction, I gathered it wasn't.

I traced a crack on the table with my pointer finger and waited for more.

"She's in Indiana."

"Jesus, Charlie." Alex inhaled loudly. "When did you find out?"

"Two hours ago."

"You *just* found out you had a daughter? Two hours ago? Oh my god. Are you alright? How old is she?" I blurted out, trying to imagine a world where one just discovered they had a child. Maybe... yes, maybe he had a passionate lover, and she'd left him.

Yes, that's it. She left him and had a baby but changed her mind and wanted him back. It'd be a passionate second chance, secret baby romance. She pined for him, and he regretted never going back for her. He was too attached to the bar, but now, he realized he needed her to be happy!

I had their whole story formed in my head just as Charlie swallowed hard. "I guess her mom died and left a note with my information. She's four, and... I have a four-year-old."

Oh no, no, no. My eyes stung; my created fantasy crushed. It wasn't a second chance romance. It was tragic. I squeezed my eyes shut, hoping to prevent tears, but it was too late. One slipped out, and Cal narrowed his eyes at me, the familiar frown lines forming on his face. I angled my body the other way. He didn't need to see me cry. He'd probably tell me it'd make me dumber or something.

"What are you gonna do, boss?" Alex asked, the question hanging in the thick air for a moment. It smelled like beer and popcorn, and the humidity snuck inside even though there were no windows.

Then Charlie placed both palms on the top of the bar, and he leaned forward, resting his forehead on them. "I don't fucking know. I can't stop thinking about this little girl who lost the only parent she'd known. Lizzie. Lizzie Swanson. That's her name."

"You need to get a test done to be sure," Cal said. His tone was brisk and to the point.

I flinched.

"Obviously that would happen," Charlie said. He stood up and looked at each one of us for a beat. "I need to go there. It could take a while to get things sorted out."

"What does that mean for us?" Alex asked. "Are you closing the bar?"

"No!" I shouted. Heat flooded my face, but I backtracked. "You can't close it with hockey and basketball playoffs. Plus, it's baseball season!"

"I could be gone for weeks."

"So? We'll manage."

Charlie eyed me, his dark hair falling over his face. "You that desperate for a job?"

"Honestly? Yes. Tonight was the best I've felt in months. Plus, if your daughter comes to live here, you can't be working all these nights anymore. You'll have to pass it off, and what better time than now? Alex and I can handle it. We might have to close during the day, but we could adjust our hours."

"She's not wrong, Charlie." Alex nodded and met my eyes. Their dark brown ones had a hint of gratitude in them, but they blinked it away. "Lux and I could figure it out. My roommate needs a side job—"

"And mine could also help! She's on the dance team with me, and hell, we could get the whole dance team in here volunteering."

"Okay, Barbie, calm yourself. I'm not working with *dancers*."

"Why? Because their glitter would clash with your skull earrings?"

Alex barked out a laugh before masking their face. "We got it. I need the money, and Sunshine over here clearly needs something to do."

"I do! I could create a spreadsheet with hours and extra shifts."

"I can help."

We all froze, Charlie's eyes widening as he stared at his nephew. "What was that, Cal?"

"You need more people. The two of you can't run this place alone." He stood up, putting his hand in his pockets, and he shrugged. "I'm a quick learner. Good on my feet and I have exceptional balancing skills."

"Yeah, yeah, we know you're fucking drafted." Alex groaned. "Don't love this idea, but it's not totally garbage."

"Yes it is," I blurted out, drawing all the attention. My face flamed, and I quickly came up with a hopefully valid reason why I said that. "He needs to uh, focus on Charlie. And his cousin! That's right! You should go with!"

"No."

"No."

They both disagreed, which okay, guys, come on. But I chewed my lip and switched to another tactic. "But hockey practice!"

"Summer schedule. Nice try." He met my eyes, and one side of his mouth lifted up. "I'm actually bored out of my mind, so yeah, working here and helping my uncle sounds great."

"It's not a shit idea." Charlie looked at Cal for a full minute. "You do need to do more than sulk around and hit a puck."

"Fuck off, I don't just sulk." Cal stood, his arms wide like the evidence of his words was hanging in the air.

"Right." Charlie's face relaxed as the idea seemed to take root.

"This could work with you three, *if* you modify hours. I don't love the idea of shutting the place down for a few weeks."

"Then don't." Cal pointed at Alex. "We're all capable."

"You up for this, Elle? You've been here one night, and shit can get busy." Charlie stared at me, a spark of hope behind his eyes.

"Yes. Hell yes, I am." I smiled, putting my hand in the air palm down. "Team on three?"

"Put your hand away, you fucking weirdo." Alex's lips quirked as they said it. "When do you leave for Indiana?"

"The email said tomorrow." He shook his head, the dazed look returning. "What am I gonna do with a fucking daughter?"

"Be her dad." Cal shrugged, his jaw flexing on both sides. "What time are you leaving? Maybe we can meet here first and go over the plan?"

"Great idea. I need to get air. Go smoke." Charlie fanned his shirt and jutted his chin toward the door. "All of you, go home. Be back here tomorrow at eight am. And, if you have any reservations about this, bring them. Once I leave, I'm not changing the plan."

I nodded, hoisting my small bag over my shoulder and already moving toward the door when once again, Cal was right there. "If I'm going to be working with you every day, we certainly don't need to walk together."

"It's almost midnight."

"Thank you, I can tell time. Analog too. Shocking for a blonde, hm?" I flipped my hair over my shoulder, enjoying how his frown deepened. The shock of Charlie's news, the high of earning two hundred dollars in tips, and the full moon had me in complete sass-mode.

"Elle, please." He gently touched my elbow with two fingers, stopping me for a second. His touch sent shivers up and down my arm.

"What did I do for you to hate me?"

"Aren't you used to being an asshole? Isn't that your entire persona? The hotshot future NHLer with a chip on his shoulder?

A dick to everyone but no one calls you out because you might *make it big?* Well, I don't give a shit." I tugged away from him, the adrenaline from the first night waning. Plus, my feet ached. I wanted fuzzy socks and pajamas and to maybe re-read what I wrote earlier. Escape into my fictional world where I could control the happy endings. Where I didn't have to answer to anyone else or defend my choices. A world where guys like Cal didn't call me stupid or tell me that my goals were dumb and that creative writing was a joke. I would never be Gabe or a hockey player, and comments like *his* just reminded me of the fact.

He winced and stepped back.

I never thought I'd have a comeback witty enough to wound someone, let alone Cal Holt. His face contorted into pain for one second before he shook his head, and the mask was back in place. The emotionless, hard expression he had every time I saw him. Even on the ice, it was the same.

"Whoa, that was a step too far," I said, regret forming low in my belly. I twisted my fingers along the strap of my bag and exhaled. My mind went right back to that night, where he'd made me feel even smaller and had gotten my parents to laugh, but being cruel wasn't who I was.

Cal remained where he stood, his face hard. "No, you're right. That's me."

"I shouldn't have said that. I'm tired and crashing. I forgot to eat dinner because I was so excited to start. I'm not *me* when I'm hungry. I'm the Snickers commercial." My words came out too fast, too slurred together in haste to get Cal to forgive me. I might be right and feel that way about him, but I had no business saying it to him. "I'm sorry."

"It's alright."

He didn't look fine, but that wasn't my problem. Did he deserve my forgiveness? Probably not, but I wasn't raised to be an asshole, ever. Neither Gabe or I were. Maybe it was the Catholic guilt that never went away. My stomach soured, and I tried to stop myself from feeling so terrible, but my mind wasn't that strong.

"I'm making a frozen pizza. It's not fancy. Just a Jack's pepperoni. Want some?"

He blinked, his eyes widening for a second before he slowly said, "Yes."

Damn. The invitation was an olive branch, but never did I think he'd accept? My teeth pressed down over my bottom lip as I tried to smile, but it came out weird, and I ducked my head. "Alright, let's go. I'm starving."

"You should eat before your shift. Or tell Charlie, and he'll give you a break."

"I know. It's always been a thing with me. My friends, parents, family all give me shit for it. I can get caught up in my head at times and forget to eat. Which, honestly is wild because I love food."

"You *forget* to eat?" He opened the doors to our building, motioning with his left hand for me to go first.

I did the good old Midwestern head nod of thanks before answering. "I get busy, and time jumps."

"God, I'd love for time to jump for me." He sighed as he let his arm hang down. The movement caused his cologne to waft toward me, and I tried not to breathe it in. Scents were dangerous for me because it was my strongest sense.

As humans, we had thousands of associations with smells, but I always felt like I had twice as many. His clean, soapy smell with a hint of evergreen was damn good. Made me think of cardigan sweaters, dates at a bookstore, and late-night coffee. Said coffee would keep us up all night, talking about our dreams and wishes, which would lead to a morning date.

Damn. I did it again.

Cal stared at me as I got my keys out of my bag. I avoided his eyes but felt his gaze. He might've said something, but I certainly didn't hear it. I was too busy imagining a late night with him all because he smelled good.

No more dinner invites.

"Sorry." My face heated, and I tossed my keys on the counter as we walked in. "I was doing it again."

"Doing what?"

"Getting lost in my head. It's a character flaw." I preheated our oven and set the pizza on the counter. Cal stood awkwardly near the door. His body was so built, and his biceps in his T-shirt were taunting me. *Look at me! Look at me!*

Muscles didn't talk, but if they did... his would be all attention-seeking. I figured he was a gym rat, but he seemed even bigger than when I saw him last fall. And his hair was longer, like he hadn't cut it in months. It worked on him. Him being in my place though...I shouldn't be thinking about his hair or muscles. Not at all.

"What do you think about when you...get lost?" He crossed his arms over his chest and lowered his brows. The stance and expression were a tad intimidating, but I refused to let him belittle me again.

I mirrored his stance and arched a brow. "I create scenarios that wouldn't happen."

"You daydream?" He laughed.

That chuckle caused my gut to tighten with embarrassment. I looked at the ground and focused on the crack in the tile. Daydreaming made me sound childish, stupid even. Like when I told my family I wanted to publish stories for a living. *It's a fun daydream, Elle, but you need a solid career.*

My throat got tight, and I shrugged. "You know, maybe we could do this dinner another night."

"Whoa, hey, what's wrong?"

His voice was closer. His scent was stronger. His body radiated heat onto mine, and I put more distance between us and sat at the kitchen table. He sounded concerned, that was for sure. But it didn't forgive the way his comments hurt people.

Okay pot, meet kettle.

"Never mind. So, you have a cousin." I changed the subject,

determined to get through this and then go back to only seeing him at the bar.

He followed my lead and sat across from me, his large fingers resting on top of the table. Those were firewood-cutting hands, big and capable and *not again*. My mind needed to chill with Cal thoughts.

"Yeah." He exhaled, and I studied the tension in his posture.

It'd be weird to find out if my uncle had a kid somewhere, to gain a cousin. The oven dinged, and I placed the pizza in there. "Are you excited?"

"Why would I be?"

The *anger* in his tone had me turning around in shock at his answer. "Are you kidding? Charlie's your uncle, right? You have a *cousin*."

His brow furrowed deeper. "She's four and lives in Indiana. I'll be going to the NHL soon on the West Coast. I'd see her maybe three times ever. No point to get enthusiastic." He scratched the table with his nail, his posture so straight it looked painful.

"What the actual fuck, Cal? She's family? I thought the rumors were exaggerated, but are you that heartless?"

He pushed back in the chair, the legs making an awful sound grinding on the floor before he faced me. "I should go. You're right. Another night."

Without looking at me, he walked out of my apartment, making me regret ever inviting him in. Cal and I might be co-workers for a few weeks, but that was it. Who was so unfeeling that they weren't excited about having a cousin?

No friend of mine. That was for damn sure.

CHAPTER **FOUR**

Cal

Ty had grown stronger. That was the only reason he almost beat me during drills. He must've doubled his workouts or protein intake because my competitive side flared when he shot me a grin.

"Slowing down, Cap."

"Fuck off." I shoved his shoulder, earning a loud laugh from him. Sweat fell down my temples, and my lungs burned. On the ice was where I felt most alive. Like my sole purpose on earth was the skate and to hit the puck in the opposite net. My heart raced from adrenaline after doing our push-up start sprints. They were something I saw in my deep dive YouTube nights, and I asked some of the guys still in town if they wanted to do them once a week in the summer. It started with Jenkins and Ty, and now eight of us met to do them.

Feeling *proud* was a new thing to experience, but it was the only thing that made sense when I watched my teammates push themselves. We started on the ice in a push-up, then launched up and exploded down the ice. We repeated it eight times, and by then we were all gassed.

"Push up, and *go!*" I shouted. This was round six. Jenkins, Ty, Eddy, Paxton, Eric, Erik, and Brandon all jumped up and burst off the line. I still led everyone, but Ty kept inching closer. That was unacceptable. I panted and took my time skating back to the starting line. I'd allow us thirty seconds to catch our breath before doing another one.

"What happens if I beat you?" Eddy asked. The soon-to-be-sophomore had really large teeth and bright red hair. He'd transferred and clearly didn't know the team dynamics.

"You won't."

"But what if I do?" he asked again, smirking.

"Then we get Holty here to do something dumb." Jenkins skated up to us, breathing heavy and smiling. He was always fucking smiling.

"No. Wrong."

"Nah, them's the rules. Ain't that right, Ty?"

"Sure is."

"If you can plot and chat, then you're not pushing yourself hard enough," I said, narrowing my eyes. They *used* to shrink back when I did that. Now, they laughed. Deep down, I loved it. I loved that they gave me shit and had my back and included me, but I didn't know how to express that besides pushing them to be better on the ice. "Ten seconds, then we do it again."

"We hear ya." Ty hit my back.

My watch counted down, and everyone lay on their stomachs. It chimed. "Push up, go!"

The clash of skates on ice echoed in the rink. The swish and swoosh of the blades was my favorite sound. It was home. All thoughts left me, and it was just the team and the ice. The cool air hit my face as I gulped to breath, and I grinned. *I win again.*

"That a smile I see? Who is she?" Erik with a k asked.

"He sleeps with his hockey stick," Ty panted. "We know this."

"Fuck. Off." I gasped for air as we all did, but my lips twitched. "I do keep one under my pillow."

"Fucking knew it." Jenkins barked out a laugh, and the guys

followed. It was amazing to be *in* on the joke instead of the brunt of one. I clapped Jenkins's shoulder, embarrassed at the surprise on his face.

"One more. Then we take a break."

We finished the drill and rested before doing another. Practice in the off season felt so different than before. Instead of the nagging dread that I made everyone worse or the weird headspace that turned me into an asshole, the jabs and laughter seemed inclusive. Planning the holiday party with Gabe had changed things a little bit, and they'd only gotten better. With him gone, I was captain now, and it kinda sorta felt like it.

I didn't hate the responsibility or the way the guys looked at me. If anything, it made me feel wanted, and *that* was a sensation I knew very little about.

Incubus played from my phone as I tended to my plants a few hours later. The band was older, and few people knew or listened to them my age, but they were my parents' favorite band. They saw them live four times and would blast the angsty jams around our house when I was little. It helped form my intense appreciation for alternative music.

Three Doors Down, Audioslave, Hoobastank…they all filled my playlist, even if they didn't pump me up or calm me down. Instead, they made me feel like my parents were still alive, even if for a few minutes.

As I changed out the soil on the worst-looking succulent, my heart raced. *A cousin. A little girl who lost the only parent she knew.* It was too much. It hurt too fucking much to imagine it. She'd never get to share moments with her mom, and my chest ached for her.

How could I be excited about that?

Elle's question had thrown me off. I wanted to ask her a million things, like how she got caught up in her head but seemed happy about it. I always got lost in mine, but it was dark and sad and horrible. She enjoyed the thoughts in her mind; it must be a wonderful place to be. I'd stopped daydreaming or wishing for things after my parents died, but she was so damn joyful.

Sunshine.

It really was a great nickname for her, but *fuck*. Was I excited to meet a four-year-old who was related to me? No, because her life would be turned upside down if she moved here. Maybe there was another family member who she knew well to take her in.

I certainly had no one besides good ole Charlie. He wasn't warm or fuzzy, but he let me hang out at the bar every night when I couldn't stand being alone. He wasn't emotionally capable of being a father.

My pulse had picked up at Elle's tone, how she didn't understand a single thing going through my mind. I was an asshole, and maybe it was time I accepted she hated me. I trimmed the brown ends off another plant as the song changed to Blink-182. My mom would be fucking thrilled they toured again and were making a comeback.

She'd also be so excited and happy for Charlie. Sure, the story had to be all sorts of fucked that this woman never told him about his daughter, but my mom would find the good in it. *Kind of like Elle, it seemed.*

Charlie wanted us at the bar in fifteen minutes to go over the plan, and regret formed deep in my gut. I needed to apologize for bolting out on Elle. Even though she'd tried to end it early for some reason, I shouldn't have done that after she put the pizza in.

God, I hope she ate it.

Did she remember to have breakfast? There was a small café at the end of the block that had the best fucking croissants, and without thinking about it, I left early to go and purchase a few. It'd be weird to just get her one, so I bought four.

We could have them as we figured out the bar situation.

The sun hit the back of my neck as I approached the bar, and it felt nice. Almost like dethawing the negative thoughts rooting in my head. I faced the midmorning light and took a deep breath, letting the beams touch my face. It felt good since we worked out that morning. They were texting about plans and working out harder to prepare for the season. It was weird to be thrust into leadership when I never felt like I deserved it, but Reiner never let me have a pity party for long. Oh, I could call him too, see if he proposed yet.

Yeah. That sounded like a plan.

"Praying for a new face?"

Alex.

Their quip made me grin though, and I faced them. "Nice one."

"Thanks, actually just thought of it." Their lips almost smiled before they nodded toward the bag in my hand. "Tell me those aren't for you."

"We all get one."

"Thank Christ. My roommate ate my stuff again, and I need carbs." Alex opened the door to the bar, and I followed them inside. Charlie and Elle sat at a booth, both of them looking at her phone as he wrote stuff down.

Alex didn't even say a word before plopping on the other side of the table, but Elle smiled at them. She did *not* smile at me.

"I brought food." I tossed the bag in the center, tensing and waiting for her to take one. She didn't *seem* hungry, but what if she was daydreaming about killing me all morning?

"Gimme." Alex shoved napkins to everyone and reached for one of the raspberry ones. Elle waited for Charlie to take one, and she hesitated.

"Go ahead. That one is blueberry and the other is chocolate."

She narrowed her eyes at me for a beat, then reached for the chocolate one. Her middle finger had a small silver ring on it with a red gem. That little ring charmed me. I wondered if someone gave it to her or if she'd bought it for herself. She grabbed a napkin and bit in, letting out the littlest of moans.

No one else heard, but they weren't paying attention to her like I was.

"You eat breakfast?" I asked.

Her gaze turned to a glare, and she ignored me. I got a little zing of pleasure at knowing I was right and able to feed her.

"I was just showing a list of what Charlie should buy if his daughter comes home with him. We're almost done, then we can get started." She leaned closer to Charlie and pointed to her phone. "You'll need a toddler bed. Four is out of a crib, I know, but she might have a twin bed too?"

"Cal."

I met my uncle's eyes. "Hm?"

"I'll send all this stuff to your place. I might need your help getting it ready so when I get back it won't be all in boxes. The guest room is a hot mess and needs…kid-proofing." He rubbed his forehead so hard there were indents from his nails.

"You want *me* to set it up?" I asked, the blood leaving my face because I knew just as much about four-year-olds as I did about nuclear energy. Nothing.

"We'll pitch in. All of us." Elle flashed an evil look at me, daring me to disagree.

"That would be great. Actually makes me feel better knowing you'll pitch in. You seem…prepared."

"Because I identify as a female? Wear pink and yellow?"

"Yes."

We all laughed at Charlie's blatant honesty, and I wasn't even a little offended that he didn't trust me. Hell, I could open boxes, but getting a room ready for a child? I'd probably ruin it somehow. Elle looked pleased, and that made my chest feel a bit weird. She could totally handle a little girl.

"Okay. Sending all this shit to Cal's place. Elle, Alex, you'll help Cal get the guest room ready and put it all together." He swallowed hard and looked at Alex, then me. "Thank you both. This is a lot, and I appreciate you willing to help."

"Don't mention it. Just know, if I'm decorating, there will be something black in her room."

His lips twitched, and he nodded. "Fair enough."

"Scheduling. I have a life outside of this shithole, no offense, so I want to know the hours." Alex got right to it, and I choked back a laugh.

They were so full of shit. They acted so tough, but they loved Charlie and had even spent Christmas with us last year. But, like me, they rarely said nice things. I wasn't the only one emotionally stunted.

"I'll adjust the hours from four until ten Sunday through Wednesdays. Thursdays through Saturday, you'll stay open until two." He paused and looked at all of us. I nodded, then Elle and Alex followed.

"I need two of you here at all times. Not sure how that works with your life, but I'm so used to it being three or four of us that I don't have anyone else to call in. Fuck, even Elle is so green I'm nervous."

"I can handle the work. Maybe not the manager stuff like inventory and ordering what you need, but service? Cleaning? I got all that." Elle hit the table with a fist.

"Great. Elle is charge of cleaning before and after her shifts. Done."

Elle blinked and nodded at the same time. It was cute, and I could picture her as a front-row type of student, always answering questions and ruining the curve on tests. I smirked, and she caught me staring at her.

I wiped that smile off my face.

"Alex or I will always be here with her," I said, gesturing my chin toward her.

"Why? Because I'm a *blonde* woman?"

"No." I swallowed down the comment about wanting to make sure she was safe. "Because you're new."

Her lips formed a pretty little *oh* shape. "Hm. Fine."

"I like it. Plus, this place gets rowdy, and no offense, Sunshine, you couldn't throw someone out. Alex and Cal definitely could," Charlie said.

Elle looked at Alex's arms with half a smirk, and they raised a brow in response. "Sweetie, you know nothing about me. My arms might not be beefsticks like this shithead, but I have my ways," Alex said.

"They have a black belt in karate and collect knives," Charlie said.

Elle smiled. "That's awesome. Can you throw knives?"

"Oh yeah."

"Sick."

Alex almost smiled at Elle, and I rolled my eyes. Elle thought *knife* throwing was fine but hated me. Cool, cool.

"Alex, you've been around a while. Could you deal with inventory for the next…two weeks? Might be longer, but we can start with that."

"You got it, boss."

"And making trips to the bank?"

"Sure can."

Charlie sighed and gained a little color in his face. "This is crazy, right? I shouldn't leave."

"No." Elle spoke before anyone else. "You absolutely have to go. We can handle it. If we can't, we'll close it for a day."

Charlie looked at me, his eyes wide and worried, and I nodded. "You gotta go, man. It's your daughter. She lost the only parent she knows. She'll be thankful to have a parent left." My voice shook, and I hated the momentary slip of vulnerability. I wiped that shit away and refocused. "Don't be a fucking dick of a dad who sends a check once a year."

Charlie stared at me a long time, his emotions clearly on his face. He was thinking about me, my parents. He opened his mouth to say something, and I cut him off. "No. Let's talk business. What else do you need?"

"Maintain a good atmosphere. There have been a few fights lately, but luckily, the college kids aren't back yet. Stop any aggression and underaged kids from entering."

"So, basically I'm the muscle?"

"Yes."

"I'm good with that. Can't hold a tray worth shit."

"Yet you can hit a dumb puck." Charlie barked out a laugh and relaxed into the seat. "This might work. It's not forever or ideal, but maybe this will be okay."

"It will." Alex's voice got more intense. "Not everyone is accommodating in the world, so Charlie, any child will be lucky to have you in their life. Even if it's messy. Acceptance and love and safety are all kids need."

"Alex is right." Elle blinked back moisture, and it made her eyes sparkle.

Charlie hit the table with his fist and jutted his chin toward the bar. "Let me out, would ya, Sunshine?"

"Sure thing." Elle got up, her stomach on display with her black cropped shirt. A bolt of lust hit me so hard I leaned forward, like her skin tugged me closer. She was tanned and had a birth mark right below her belly button. I wanted to touch it.

My entire body tensed with a pull toward her, and I closed my eyes, took a breath, and leaned back. How uncharacteristic of me. I'd hooked up with women, obviously, and attraction was never an issue. But this was *intense.*

She didn't notice a thing and had already sat back down when I gained my composure. She finished her croissant and took out a sheet of paper. "Okay, team, how do we want to divide up the nights since two of us need to be here at all times? Anyone have any nights that are absolutely a no for you?"

"Wednesdays are my karate classes."

"Okay, Cal and I on Wednesdays." She wrote our names with pretty handwriting, looping her letters to the point it looked like a font. It totally fit her.

"I'm free every any time for the next month."

"No pucks to hit?" she asked.

"I'll go during the morning if I have to."

"Alex, any other days that are a no for you? I want us each to have at least one night off. We should all probably be here Fridays and Saturdays." She sucked half her bottom lip into her mouth as she filled out the three of us for the weekend.

"Nope."

"Okay, let me write this down."

Sunday: A, C
Monday: C, E
Tuesday: A, E
Wednesday: C, E
Thursday: A, E
Friday: A, C, E
Saturday: A, C, E

"No—you're working six nights, Elle." I shook my head. "Let me do the Tuesdays."

"I don't mind. I have no summer classes and sit around all day."

I took the pen from her hand, her fingers brushing mine, and I sucked in a breath at her touch.

Our eyes met for a second but then she frowned. "You're not here Tuesday."

I adjusted the schedule and gave her my best, *don't fuck with me* face. "Fight me on it."

She rolled her eyes and glanced to Alex. "You already working with him for a night?"

"I can handle him, Barbie."

"Good. We got this." Elle smiled and leaned closer to us. "Are you kinda excited? This is a big project, and we're gonna be so tired, but I love this stuff. Once, I organized this charity drive and was on my feet for twenty-seven hours straight. It was exhausting but the best kind?"

"You talk way too much for it being ten-thirty," Alex said.

"Time doesn't play a role in my chattiness," Elle fired back.

"I'm looking forward to it," I said, wanting to see her goofy smile again. She eyed me before shaking her head, like she didn't believe me.

"Anyway, if Charlie is leaving today, we should relax before coming back, huh?" Elle stood and stared at both of us, her cutoff shorts a danger to my libido. Her legs were long and smooth. She had to put lotion on, and fuck, I wanted to know what type.

She backtracked. "It's Tuesday, so you're off tonight, Cal."

"I'll come anyway. It's the first night and game two of playoffs." Even though I hadn't worked here the last three years I came here, I knew the crowd and just about everything one could without receiving a paycheck. "You'll need an extra set of hands."

"Fine. You can be a busser." She pinched her lips. "Unless, hotshot Cal is beneath bussing tables."

"Nope. I can do it. Hell, if we need a couple, I know a few guys." An idea hit me hard and fast, like a slapshot to the gut. Van Helsing—the senior co-captain from last season—was on me to be a better leader. Provide more team bonding experiences. Be emotionally available.

Fuck the last one.

Bussing tables at a bar? That could be an experience some of us could do. At least the older players on campus. "Could we tip anyone who comes to help us bus?"

"Without question." Alex eyed me. "Who are you thinking? I didn't realize you had friends."

Ah, another shot at me. Elle met my eyes, guilt written all over her face. The sting of her words last night hadn't quite left yet, and I worked my jaw a few times before responding to Alex. "I'm captain of the hockey team. They'd be willing to help a campus legend."

"Interesting." Alex smiled. "I wouldn't mind the guys working here."

"Van would love that," Elle said, grinning, but *not* at me. "Okay, well I'll see y'all later. This girl needs a nap and food."

Alex waved as she left but then they stared at me, a smirk forming on their red lips. "Watching you pine for her is better than all the trash TV there is."

"I'm not *pining* for her, fuck off."

"Oh, but you are." They stood and headed to the back office, but not before turning around again. "Seeing you fall in love will be my reason for living."

And with that, they left me alone.

Fall in love? Ha. As if. That shit would *never* happen to me. Elle was hot, that was all. I would never *love* her.

I'd never let my heart care for anyone again.

CHAPTER **FIVE**

Elle

My best friend in the entire world *might* be dating my brother, but that hadn't changed a single thing about us. We laid in her bed, our arms touching, and she tossed a stress ball up and down.

"Every night?"

"I get two nights off, I think." My face warmed at Cal's determination to let me rest. I didn't understand his motivation or why he cared, but I appreciated it. Just a little though. "I need the money." Especially if I had to prepare for a career in writing, where I *would never make a comfortable living.*

"But you have enough saved up for three months right now."

"True, but I need a nest egg." Daniella might know my parents weren't paying a cent to live here, but she didn't realize the fear they'd instilled in me.

You get one shot, Elle. Could you choose a more financially stable option? You're so smart—could you go into education instead? We want what's best for you, and that's to be independent. We don't want you starting life in the hole without a career.

They supported me and loved me unconditionally, but they

were obsessed with Gabe and I being successful, and to them, that meant traditional careers. Not creative writing, and not being a romance author. They wanted it to be a hobby.

"You think working yourself to death to save a few hundred dollars is the answer?" Dani tossed the ball too far to the right, and it hit the ceiling fan. "Shit."

I pushed up onto my elbows and laughed at her. "Did I tell you the part where I maybe sort of volunteered you to help too?"

Her eyebrows disappeared into her hairline. "Say what now?"

"If Charlie is gone for a month, we'll need more hands, and who better than campus's dance team?" I batted my lashes at her, smiling and being extra cheesy. "It'll show leadership, and your coach would love to see y'all work. You could make posters and host a fundraiser. Oh, yes! Sell shirts or coasters or pinup shots of you all."

Dani laughed. "Ah, right. The topless photoshoot we did. How could I forget?" Sarcasm dripped from her tone before she sat at her desk chair. "I'll try my best, but this kids camp starts at six am, and I'm not one of those early risers. You know this."

"Yes, yes, but even a dinner shift here or there would be appreciated."

"Fine. Of course I'll do what I can. But only if you tell me about why you went from wanting Cal Holt's babies to hating him."

Damn. She went there, fast. My skin burned with embarrassment and hurt, since his comments had been living rent free in my head for months. It was absurd. I didn't know him. I just really liked his face. And yet, those comments stuck with me. I grabbed her pillow and put it over my head, screaming into it without real anger.

"Nice." Dani snorted. "Helpful."

"He insulted my intelligence and motivation and major in one breath."

"Okay, but he's an idiot?"

"It was a lot to have the player you had a huge crush on say you were dumb and creative writing is a joke, making your parents laugh at you. He said it was a joke of a major and an easy choice for blondes. That's all. Doesn't help that he's an asshole. He told me he wasn't excited to learn he had a cousin? That's an asshole flag right there."

Dani winced. "Van hasn't shared a lot about their chats, but it seems Cal is going through some stuff."

"Doesn't give him an excuse to be a dick though." I sat up and stretched my arms over my head. "Working with him is gonna be a real joy."

"Stay busy." Daniella smiled at her phone, and an odd sense of envy went through me. She had a great relationship with my brother. They truly were a fit—them bringing out the best and making the other's life better.

I wanted that. The romance. The swooning. The grand gesture. Gabe had *killed* it when he asked Daniella to go from fake girlfriend to real, and they'd been together ever since. I dated a guy named Jenson in high school for six months and then some artist in community college freshmen year.

My past boyfriends were lukewarm. Fine. Medium. Like eating leftovers that you heated up in the microwave but weren't in long enough but you were too lazy to reheat it so you ate it kinda cold. They were like that. They filled the role and did the job, but the relationships weren't *romantic*.

Putting myself out there in my hometown was rough. Too many connections but here? Clean slate for my romantic endeavors. Now, I just needed time, which… I wasn't gonna have for a while because of the bar.

"Will I find love?"

"Obviously." Daniella set her phone down and rested her elbows on her legs. Her red hair hung in two braids, and she frowned. "Don't like that you asked this question after talking about Cal Holt."

"No, it was seeing you grin at texting my brother." I had a half smile. "I want that."

Her features softened, and she exhaled. "It's the best thing ever. You'll discover your person Elle, but don't rush or force it."

"I've read all these sweeping love stories about couples meeting in college and then getting married, traveling. Maybe pop out a kid or two. I want that." My life was fulfilling, but I never had a partner. Again, I loved Daniella, but she didn't fill the void that seemed to ache in my chest. I wanted what the main characters had in the books I read and stories I wrote.

When good things happened to me, there wasn't that one person I couldn't wait to share it with. Yes, I'd call my parents and my brother and Dani, but I wanted the one, the person, the supportive partner. Maybe it was a pipe dream.

"I must be hungry again to get this sappy." I pushed up and walked toward our kitchen. One way I'd passed the time when living with my parents the last two years was to cook and try new recipes. It was ironic that I forgot to eat when I was lost in a manuscript, but when I listened to audiobooks? Cooking it was.

I put on the latest story from Chloe Leisse and pulled out the dishes I'd need. I could totally make enough to share with Alex and Cal tonight or give some to Charlie for the road. It wasn't the first time I cooked shepherd's pie, but changing up the spices or amount of flavor I put in the mixture always made the taste different.

"Anxious chopping?" Dani came out, smiling at me. "Need help?"

"No, you know I zone out when I do this. Writing and cooking are what dancing is to you. Let me be, woman." I pointed the knife at her, and she laughed. Daniella went back to her room, and I turned up the volume. There were some authors who wrote so well, so consuming, that it made me pause and wonder if it was worth it to even try.

But then I stared at the tattoo on my left forearm: 26 letters, endless stories.

It was pretty incredible we had 26 letters and were able to create millions of words and stories and screenplays and poems.

The same with music. There were only so many notes, yet music was limitless. I got lost in Chloe's world and focused on cooking. There was no sense getting caught up in my head this time, not when tonight was going to be wild.

Chaos. Beautiful, noisy chaos, but still. My feet ached, and my arms hurt, but my smile was real. The place was packed for game two of the Bulls playoff run, and drinks were flowing. Alex seemed like a hot mess, with their hair undone and the red lipstick completely erased from their face.

Cal too looked hot. Not physically. But red face and sweat beading on his brow as he roamed through the crowd and picked up dirty glasses. He hadn't stood still once since the game started, and a part of me was impressed. I wasn't sure why I'd assumed he'd be lazy working here, but he wasn't.

Probably because he cared for Charlie.

"Another round of shots if he sinks this three." A tall, rowdy man with a handlebar mustache hit the bar top hard, shaking some glasses, and bam. The up-and-coming point guard made a three-pointer at the end of the third quarter, and the place vibrated with cheers.

I poured seven shots of rum and slid them to Handlebar. He passed them to his friends as I added drinks to his tab. The tips had been incredible. Thank god for the Bulls winning because their success meant more drinks, and more drinks meant more tips, and here we were. Orders flew up and down the bar, and I raced to each one.

Lagers. Whiskey. Shots. Wine. Cocktails. Mules.

I poured and smiled and accepted their cash. I cleaned dirty glasses and restocked them, and I dripped with sweat. My mouth was dry, and I took a deep breath, needing two seconds of rest. It was that moment Cal came behind the bar, his navy-blue T-shirt sticking to his chest and his black jeans resting on his hips. I was hungry and weak, and that was the only reason I admired his pecs and forearms.

"Hey, take a breather." He walked so close our feet touched. "You've been running around like mad."

"So have you and Alex," I fired back, even though a break sounded really nice. "I'm fine."

"Elle." He gently touched my elbow again and pulled me toward the office. My feet kinda went with it because I saw a chair in there, and oof, I wanted a chair. "Five minutes. I brought energy balls."

"Wait, what?" I eyed him, suspicious of his intentions right now. "Are you offering me your balls?"

One side of his mouth quirked up, and the half-smile changed his entire face. He was *gorgeous* with that grin. Fuck, I did need food. He pushed me, softly, into the chair and shut the door. It blocked out the noise from the game, and it was just us in the small space. Him being gentle messed with my anger. Staying mad at him was safer.

He smelled like laundry and sweat, and his breath hit my face—minty and *why is he leaning toward me?*

I froze, unsure what I wanted him to do. Kiss me? Leave me alone? I gripped the sides of the chair as my heart raced. But Cal only grabbed a bag of treats that rested on the table behind me. I exhaled, feeling silly for even thinking he was going to kiss me. All that talk with Dani about romance had gotten to me.

"Your balls, I take it?"

"It's granola and peanut butter and a little bit of chocolate. Chia seeds. Protein powder. I eat them before a hard practice. Eat three, then you can come out."

"Are you the boss of me?" I said, sounding mature as hell.

"I'd like to be," he said, heat entering his eyes and sending an SOS to my lower parts.

A tug plucked down there, and I wanted to see what else he had to say. But he blinked back, almost like he surprised himself, and he pointed a finger at me. "Eat three."

He shoved the door open and left, leaving me alone with the balls and my confused, pounding pulse. He wanted to boss me around? Was that... sexual? Like a dom thing? To each their own, hell, if it's consensual who the fuck cares what people are into, but *boss* me around? A hint of shiver tickled my spine at the thought of Cal Holt telling me what to do in bed.

He'd be firm but soft, aggressive but tender. His hands had to be talented, and that jawline was meant for face-sitting. We wouldn't talk, no. That would piss me off, so it'd be an anger bang. Oh, one of my favorite tropes. The *get it out of our system* one. Then, after nights of passion, he'd realize he was a dick and change. Oh, I could see the entire story playing out—

"Stop sitting on your ass. We need help!" Alex poked their head in and screamed at me. "Come on, Barbie."

I shoved the third ball in my mouth, chewing fast as an embarrassed blush covered me head to toe. I didn't want Alex thinking me lazy or not helpful. Damn Cal and his balls. I'd gotten caught up in my head again and ugh. *Focus.*

Throwing myself back to it, I hated to admit Cal was right. I'd needed the extra fuel. The shepherd's pie was great, but that had been five hours ago, and I wasn't someone who worked out a lot, (meaning ever) so the calories I was burning far outranked what I ate, and the balls did the trick. I felt stronger and less attracted to Cal. High five, me.

The Bulls won, making it 2-0, and everyone went bananas. Drinks spilled (aka were tossed into the air), and I was sticky everywhere. And not in a fun way. I listened to older folks go on and on about the Bulls in the 90s and how it was their year, but I was not prepared for this wildness on a Tuesday night. It wasn't even the finals!

"More beer!" A large man dressed in a red polo approached the bar. His face was stern and unsmiling as he waved a twenty at me. "Each second it takes you to pour my drink is one dollar less of a tip, Blondie. Now hustle."

My jaw clenched as I forced a tight smile. Fuck that guy and his attitude. We made enough tips already that night, so his precious twenty could suck my ass. Instead of rushing for him, I took my time cashing out the latest patron.

"You dumb or what? Pour my beer."

"Enough." Cal appeared, his face twisted in fury. He had an inch or two above the man in red, and I wasn't kidding about how mad he looked. My stomach flipped over, and I sucked in a breath as Cal gripped the guy's collar and yanked. "Get out."

"What the fuck, dude?"

"You have three seconds."

"Oh, like I'm a toddler? The blonde took too long getting my goddamn drink. Charlie wouldn't allow this shitty service. Where is that fat fucker anyway?"

A deafening silence roared in my ears as everyone looked our way. Men like polo guy weren't uncommon, but the anger and aggression of him scared me. I gripped the glass tighter, ready to throw it at his face if necessary but then Alex appeared on the other side of him.

"Let's go."

"Okay, Marilyn Manson, you going to *fight* me?"

In a span of two seconds, Alex had red shirt guy on the ground, and Cal dragged him to the door. My gasp caught in my throat, my hand over my erratic heart, and I watched Cal pick up the guy and toss him outside. Alex helped, and when they came back in, the bar cheered.

"That guy is a fucking dick!" someone yelled.

"Fuck him!" mustache man cheered.

"You okay, honey?" A very old and wrinkled man leaned forward on the bar and spoke to me. "He didn't rattle ya, did he?"

"A bit, yeah." I cleared my throat, thankful for both Cal and Alex. I wasn't some weak woman who couldn't handle herself, but there was nothing I could've done that would've helped the situation.

The older guy patted my hand before going back to a conversation with his seatmate, and I took a deep breath. Rattled was the right word. Not put off or upset. Rattled. I didn't mean to search him out, but I found myself staring at Cal, who stared right back and mouthed *you okay?*

I nodded and mouthed *thank you.*

Then, of all the things he could've done—he winked.

CHAPTER **SIX**

Cal

It was two in the morning before we got the place cleaned up and not smelling like piss and beer. We were all exhausted. Alex kept their mouth quiet as we worked in comfortable silence, and even Elle lost some of her sunshine.

This bar stuff was no joke. My body ached in places it shouldn't with how much I worked out, but I welcomed the burn. Made me feel like I did something and was alive. "Charlie texted me three hours ago, but I didn't see it. He arrived and will meet his cousin tomorrow."

"How nice." Elle lifted her head up from doing a final wipe down and smiled. It didn't meet her eyes, and there were shadows underneath them. I hoped that fucking asshole didn't scare her. Just thinking about how he'd yelled at her had me cracking my knuckles.

He seemed like the type to get revenge, so if Elle thought she was walking home alone, she'd have to fight me on it. Alex called a rideshare and waved goodbye, but Elle stopped them.

"Alex."

"Hm?"

"Thank you for tonight." Her hand gripped the base of her throat, her cheeks flushed. "I really appreciate it."

Alex's face softened for one second before nodding. "Anytime, Barbie."

Elle smiled for real and then turned to me once Alex left.

Before she opened her mouth, I barked out, "I'm walking you home every night. I don't care if you don't like it."

She slammed her lips shut, blinking back in surprise. "Wow, uh, I was going to ask if you didn't mind."

"Oh."

"Yeah." She bit the side of her lip and smiled at me. It was a sweet, adorable little grin that had me feeling weird inside. There wasn't an ounce of hate in her gaze, and I felt two inches taller. I liked how she looked at me right then. Like I mattered. Like I wasn't a fucking angry asshole who lashed out all the time.

"That kinda freaked me out. Not that I can't scream really loudly or break a glass on his face, but these noodles?" She held up her arms and shook them. "They are great for typing or pouring but not much else."

"You have great arms," I said, silently hating myself. *Why* did I say that? "They're fine, for arms."

She snorted and shouldered a mini backpack. I had no idea what she could even fit in there. Two cookies? A bottle of water? One hockey puck? It seemed impractical when she should fill it with snacks. She headed for the door before hitting her forehead. "Oh, the shepherd's pie. I don't want to leave it here."

"It can wait, right? You're exhausted."

"Why thank you. You give the best compliments." She shook her head, but the sarcasm was noted. I hadn't meant it in a bad way. Fuck.

I ran my hands over my face, groaning. "I didn't mean... you look fine. Just bags under your eyes."

"Again, stop it. You're making me blush." She waved a hand in the air and laughed. "Just give me a minute. I'll get the pans, and we can head out."

She disappeared for a second and returned holding a large, empty glass dish. Immediately, I walked toward her and grabbed it. "Let me take it home and wash it."

"What? No." She tried yanking it back, and I held it higher. "Cal, what are you doing?"

"You cooked for us. I can clean it for you."

"But it's my pan!" She jumped, trying to reach it, and let out a cute little grunt. "I like my dishware and wash it a certain way."

"Yeah, with soap?" I teased, really admiring her face with how close she was. Her two moles under her eyes just about killed me.

"Fine. *Fine.* Scrub it. If you ruin it, you'll buy me another one." She settled down from her jumping but lost her balance for a second. She put her hand on my chest, just as I used my free hand on her hips. "Whoa."

"Alright?" My voice came out all low and breathy. My fingers grazed her skin where her shirt rode up, and oh my god. It was like fire. I let go immediately, her nails digging into my chest for a second before she too stepped back.

"Tired. That's all." She ducked her head but not before I caught a slight pinkening of her cheeks.

Interesting.

"Come on, let me walk you home."

She nodded, and with her pan securely in my arm, we locked the doors and stepped outside. Crickets and lightning bugs paved the way on the short walk, and *if* life were different, I'd say it was pretty outside. If it were a date, I'd kiss her slowly before letting her go inside.

But my life wasn't that.

We got to the door, and I swung it open, letting her go first again. She smiled, quickly, and beelined it for her door. She wore black high-tops tonight, and I loved how she tied the laces around her ankles.

"Goodnight, Elle." I waited for her to go inside, but she stilled and slowly turned around. Her expression was sweet, shy even, with her smirk and open eyes. There wasn't an ounce of hate blasting from her, and while I knew it wouldn't last long, I loved it. It made my insides feel strange.

"Thank you, for tonight. The guy... the protein balls... walking me home."

"Sure."

She chewed her lip before pointing her thumb over her shoulder. "I should head in."

"Get some sleep. I'll see you tomorrow."

"Just you and me on the schedule." She played with a loose string hanging from her shorts, her purple and yellow nails catching the overhead light. Her brown eyes met mine, and I wished my life was different.

That this was a date and I could kiss her.

"Yup. See you." I had to move away from her, get a hold on these feelings of regret. I knew better than to hope for things. Made shit harder when dreams didn't come true. I didn't look back at her as I took the stairs. Despite the ache of my muscles, I needed an outlet for the emotion.

Four flights of stairs did it.

I googled the best way to clean cookware, set it in the sink, and passed the fuck out.

The discounted plants at the hardware store were my favorites. I wasn't a DIY guy and knew jack shit about tools. Could I skate faster than anyone on the team and get a six-figure dollar signing bonus? Sure. Could I tell you what drill was best? Nope. But I enjoyed seeing all the other people who came in with a mission. The dads with jean shorts and white tennis shoes. The moms in tight pants who strutted straight to the right aisle.

The walkers who clearly had no idea what they were doing.

The people grabbing every single paint swatch and holding them up like cards.

I preferred the outside section, and I inhaled the soil smell and almost smiled. There were four plants with brown stems that needed a home.

I figured it'd be a great way to break up the day after my workout and before heading to the bar for the night. The plants were annuals, but it was summer. They had three months to live their full life if I nursed them right.

A familiar laugh caught my attention, and I whipped my gaze toward it. *Elle. What is she doing here?*

Fuck. Her brother was with her. Gabe Van Helsing was great as a teammate on the ice, but he made it quite clear to stay the fuck away from Elle. Something I really didn't want to do for reasons that made no sense to me. I could get with any puck bunny, any time, so it wasn't *that.* But just like my knowledge of power tools, I had no plans to figure it out.

"Start with two. Not a whole shelf."

"But it would look cool!"

"I thought you were getting all weird about your money. Dani said you're working too much at that damn bar. That place is a shithole, by the way."

"Sure, but it's awesome."

That pleased me. Charlie worked hard to get *Jags* to be a home on campus. But why would Elle be getting weird about finances? I didn't like that. She didn't need to be spending money on food for us if she had issues. Without being a total creeper, I placed the half-dying plants in my basket and maybe followed them.

"Okay, so your patio dream plant stand. You want wire shelving?"

"Yup, And all sorts of colors. Pots and flowers and succulents and spices. I want to add lights and everything. But today, it's just pots and flowers."

"There are such things as houseplants. Get one. *One.*"

"If you're gonna rain on my parade, why did you offer to drive me? I could've taken the bus."

"I have a car, and I was already at your place. Does Dani know about this idea?"

"Oh, don't even start."

I kinda loved how she didn't let Van Helsing give her shit. I pretended to admire the snapdragons when suddenly, Van Helsing said my name. *Busted.*

"Cal Fucking Holt."

My face flushed when I tried to think of an out. He saw me, which meant Elle did too. I couldn't pretend I didn't hear him at this point, and fuck, the silence went on too long. I nodded at him, unsure how to explain myself.

"You doing community service or something? Why are you buying plants?" He jutted his chin toward the basket. "Ones that look like shit, no less."

Right. He didn't know I was listening. I relaxed and lifted a shoulder in a shrug. "Getting them for someone."

It felt too personal and real to tell him the truth. Exposing a part of myself no one knew about. Elle joined at his side, her face lighting up for a split second. That moment of joy was enough to fuel me the rest of the day.

"Hey, Cal. Nice flowers. Not bad for discounted ones."

"Thanks." I cleared my throat and hated the awkwardness. Van Helsing stared at me, then his sister, then pinched his nose.

"Are you two friends now?"

"No," I said, just as Elle said yes.

The joy was gone, and she almost seemed hurt. Which gutted me. "Well, we're not *not* friends," I said, frowning and hating the defeated look in her eyes.

If she knew the real thoughts I had about her, she'd laugh in my face.

"Oh, that's perfectly clear." Van Helsing stared at his sister. "Ready to move on?"

"Yeah." She ran a finger over the handle of the cart, this nail orange, and she sighed. "See you later."

"Right."

My throat felt too tight, and my feet were rooted to the cement floor as Van Helsing and Elle walked away. Her shoulders were slumped as she glanced over at me, her frown still very much in place, and I hated that I'd done that by saying we weren't friends. Fuck! If she thought we were friends, then that meant she didn't hate me anymore. Well, at least until five seconds ago.

I needed to apologize and get back to the moment where her eyes lit up when she saw me. Frantically glancing around, I knew what to do. She wanted a wire shelf of spices? I could get her seeds and a little potting soil. Yeah, and maybe a book on how to grow them. No, that could be insulting. Just the seeds and pots.

A purple watering can was right there, and it was so bright I had to get it for her too. Content with my apology gift, I checked out with my new additions and her present. Where she talked about money being an issue, it was one thing I never had to worry about. My parents left me quite a bit, and with my signing bonus? I was set for ten years, even if I never played in the NHL.

This small gift wasn't even a tiny dent for me. If anything, it got me excited to give it to her. My mood lifted as I ran a few more errands and headed home. I could picture her smile when she saw the gift, and it almost made me smile.

I set everything outside her unit when I heard her voice. *Shit.* I didn't want her to see me leave it! I stepped back, almost tripping on my feet when the door opened. Her soft brown eyes landed on me first, her lips parting in an O. *"Cal?"*

"Hey."

"What are you—what is this?" She stared at the items on her welcome mat and then back to me. "Did you...get these for me?"

I gripped the back of my neck, hating how fucked up I was that even saying yes took so much effort. I nodded.

"But why?" A worry line formed between her brows, and my finger itched to trace it. I kept my hand firmly at my side, safe and away from her.

"Because we're friends. Friends help each other out."

She pressed her lips together, the worry line still there. "I don't understand."

"Your brother said you had money issues. I don't. I bought you this gift."

Her worry line disappeared, and instead, fire danced behind her eyes. "So, this is a pity present?"

"What? No!" I held up my palms. "You said we were friends and got a hurt look in your eyes when I said no. I wanted to make you smile, so I brought you spices."

This was an epic failure. She wasn't smiling. She also wasn't picking up the gift. If I left, maybe she'd take it then. "I gotta go. See you later."

"But Cal—"

I pushed my way into the stairwell, my emotions warping into a major ball of *everything*. Like an everything bagel where one flavor didn't dominate the taste but they all mixed together. That was how my feelings worked. Just one big one.

I needed to shower and tend to my plants and listen to Blink-182 and stay busy. That would help with the confusion and inability to be a normal human.

Fuck, why did I think my gift would make her smile? Why did I have to say we weren't friends? I ruined *any* and all progress we'd made. This was why I didn't bother with feelings.

CHAPTER
SEVEN

Elle

Torn between being angry and grateful, I stared at the spice seeds and little pots to start them in. But more, the purple watering can. That surprised me. I chewed the inside of my cheek, eyeing my watch to make sure I had enough time to get ready before heading to the bar. I had to say something to him.

Better here than the bar.

Set on a mission, I got into the elevator and went to the top floor. I wasn't sure if I wanted to yell at him or not. I kinda planned to start talking once I saw him and hoped my mind would finish the thoughts.

You have money problems.

Ugh. It sounded so condescending. *I don't.* Well, not all of us are NHL draftees, mister. I had the entire convo in my head, so by the time I pounded on his door loudly, I had a couple of sentence starters queued up.

He answered, his bare chest coming into view, and all those practiced words evaporated. My mind was kaput. Dead.

It was skin and muscles and hard lines. Oh shit. A towel. His hand gripped the side of the towel, resting so low on the hips I could see his hip bones. My mouth dried up. Desert style. My mind got fuzzy from lust. I was in a full-on lust haze where speaking was asking too much.

The heat from his shower clouded me, and his soap? Fuck. I inhaled, so caught up in all of *him* that I might've blacked out.

"Are you coming in or what?"

Right. I should say something. I nodded, breathless and feeling my entire body blush with what I wanted to do to his stomach. I wasn't an overtly sex-crazed person. It was medium the few times I'd had it, but right now, I wanted to *bite* into his skin and taste him. I floated, because I was totally having an out-of-body experience, into his apartment, and he shut the door.

"What's up?" he asked, all casual, like my insides weren't roaring with lust.

"You're in a towel."

"Yeah, you were banging like wild on my door." His lip quirked up on the side for a second, and I curled my toes into my Birkenstocks.

"Because I was mad." I looked at his TV, white walls, one couch.

"Why?" He stepped closer.

"Reasons." I swallowed hard and avoided staring at him directly. It was like looking into the sun, only if the sun was your secret crush for three years and your dream star.

"Oh. Right. Sure. Well, I'm sorry for *reasons*."

I snapped my gaze to him, unsure if that was a joke. It was. He beamed, full-on, and *oh baby.* Yup. Sun. I was a little planet orbiting him, pulling toward him. "Jesus, put that away." I covered my eyes and stepped back.

"Put what?"

"Your smile."

"What?"

I cracked an inch between my fingers and found him grinning even more at me. "Stop. Your smile is too much."

"Are you saying you like it?"

"It is very clear that's what I'm saying. Now put on a goddamn shirt so I can yell at you properly."

Cal laughed. Cal Holt, serious grumpy-ass Cal, laughed. The sound was magical. Could probably solve world hunger with it.

"Could you yell at me improperly?"

I picked up a couch pillow and threw it at his face. "Shirt. Now. Or I'll get pissier."

"Sorry my chest is so distracting to you, *friend*."

I refused to take the bait and felt my way toward the couch, never opening my eyes. It was for self-protection, and I didn't care if he realized I thought he was hot. He had eyes and a mirror and lived in a gym. Of course, he knew how he physically looked. It would be absurd if he didn't have self-awareness. Scientifically, he was attractive.

Yeah, go with that one.

After a minute, he cleared his throat, and I chanced a peek. He wore loose gray shorts and a Central State shirt. Much better. He sat on the other end of the couch, feet away from me.

I relaxed and stood up, ready to complete my mission. "How dare you get me those spices! And gorgeous watering can! And soil!"

"I'm sorry?"

"You're not!" I pointed a finger at him, hating the way his lips curved. "Stop laughing at me."

"Sorry. You're kinda cute when you're trying to be angry."

He thinks I'm cute. HE THINKS I'M CUTE. My skin flushed, and my heart beat twice as fast. It felt like my soul floated in the air for a second.

Focus.

"I'm not trying to be angry. I am. I don't have *money* problems. You misheard. I don't need a charity gift or a pity present or anything."

He sighed, opened his mouth, and closed it before rubbing his hands on his knees. "I thought you'd like them."

"I do. I love them. But—"

"Then what's the problem?"

"Because you got them for me, and you didn't need to."

"That's the point of a gift, Elle." Heat flared in his eyes, and his deep tone got even lower. "I upset you, and I wanted to make it right."

"You've upset me multiple times." I ran a hand through my hair, flustered and out of sorts, and it was his chest's fault. "I don't—"

"Will you ever tell me what I did?" He softened his tone and scooted closer toward me. "The first time we spoke, you had this look of awe on your face."

"Yeah, because I loved watching you on the ice." Oh, so apparently I had no filter and was laying it all down for him. "You were my favorite guy to cheer on. I loved your passion and aggression and focus. I watched every game you played from freshmen year. Even bought a shirt with your name on it when I streamed games at home."

Cal's mouth dropped open, and he blinked a lot. His chest heaved too. "What?"

"It doesn't matter. You said I was a dumb blonde without a real career and only an idiot would choose to be a writer." I huffed and put my hands on my hips. "This is stupid. I came up here to give you the gifts back, but in my tizzy, I forgot them."

"Elle. Elle." He shook his head, his eyes closed and his jaw tight. "I never... what?"

"Yes, I'm attracted to you. That's obvious. You're hot, but nothing will *ever* happen between us. Not saying that you'd want it to anyway. God, that was presumptuous. I just meant... fuck." I took a breath. "You don't want to be friends, and you've hurt my feelings so many times that maybe it's best we're just co-workers."

"Hold on." He stood up and paced, his breathing quite loud. "You've shared so much that I need a minute."

"There's nothing more to say."

"Yes, there is," he snapped. "You said a lot of things, and they are untrue, so give me a second so I can think because I don't appreciate you telling me I hurt you."

"But you did."

His eyes flared, and his throat bobbed as he swallowed. "If I did, it was a complete accident. I wanted to see your smile; that's why I bought you the spices. I made you frown when I said we weren't friends, and before I fucked it up, you almost seemed happy to see me. No one looks at me like that, and I needed to get it back." He ran a hand through his hair, pulling on the ends before staring at me again. "Keep them. *Please.*"

No one looks at me like that.

The utter heartbreak and sadness on his face was almost enough for me to forgive him. But I couldn't. Not when he didn't even remember what he'd said to me. I jutted my chin toward his window ledge filled with pots and greenery. "You clearly like plants. You can use them."

"Elle," he said, the magnetic pull drawing me toward him once again. I remained a good distance away, but I kept my arms crossed for some protection.

"What?"

"I didn't know you wanted to be a writer. I would never say that about you, that you're dumb. Not at all." He closed his eyes and pinched his nose. "Please, believe me."

"I heard you. You said only a dumb blonde would choose creative writing as a major, that it was a joke of a career choice, to my face, alright? That night in the car with my parents? It crushed me. Now, I need to go. Let's keep it business tonight, okay?"

His face paled, and a part of me felt validated. Good. Maybe he finally remembered those hurtful words. He swallowed hard before shuffling his feet.

"I'm still walking you home." His tone got dangerous. "That's not up for discussion. I don't care if you fucking hate me, but I'm walking you back."

"Fine."

"Fine."

We stared at each other, the air thick with tension, and I bolted out of there. It was too much. His chest, his towel, my verbal vomit, his insistence that he hadn't insulted me. Cal was a headcase, and I didn't want to get caught up in it. My pulse raced, and my body was too hot as I got back to our place. Dani was gone at camp, and that left me with my spices and can.

He wanted to see me smile.

That was what he said.

But that contradicted his horrible comments all those months ago. He didn't refute them or acknowledge how he hurt me. And for that, his insult made me feel small again. Like wanting to be a writer was *dumb*. I needed to cook. Yup. Stress cooking was the best remedy, and with that, I forced myself to follow a recipe and not think about my co-worker.

Last night's chaos was a complete one-eighty to the slow, almost boring Tuesday night shift. No big games that benefitted central Illinois were on, and it was bitching hot outside. Even with the air on full blast, the humidity was awful. Cal found a fan in Charlie's office and plugged it in to get airflow moving, but it didn't work that well.

Hell, I preferred the busy to this. Six customers at the bar, two in the room. Cal leaned on the wall, his face unreadable. We worked in a comfortable agreement to not talk. It was great for the first four hours, and now there was only three more to go.

I promised myself I'd bring my laptop with me every shift, just in case it was boring like the present. I didn't care for anything on the TVs, and I'd already done everything I could to keep the bar clean. The bathrooms were the nicest they'd ever been.

I twirled my pen around my finger three times before someone tapped on the bar. Ty Penlow stood there, grinning ear to ear in his hipster glasses. Ty, or Penny, played on the team with my brother, and I'd hung out with him a few times here and there. But there was no reason for that big of a smile. "What?"

"Van said you were working here."

"So is Cal."

"Cal Holt?" He raised his brows. "No fucking way."

"See for yourself." I motioned toward the wall where Cal had been all night, and sure enough, Ty spun around and let out a holler.

"Dude, no fucking way! You're the bouncer now?"

"For a bit."

Ty did the bro handshake thing. Cal looked so uncomfortable it almost made me feel bad for him.

"Why? Not that this isn't awesome." Ty winked at me before looking back at Cal.

"My uncle owns it and had to leave town for a few weeks. I offered to help keep it open."

"Ya need any extra hands?"

"Yes!" I shouted, already knowing Cal would say no. "Ty, we do."

His eyes sparkled for a beat before he hit Cal's shoulder. "You shoulda said something, man. Ten guys would be here in a second if you asked."

He rubbed the back of his neck. "I doubt that."

"They want to support their captain. You can continue the grumpy thing, but we've seen you open up more now, Holt." He turned. "Elle, what kind of help are we talking about?" Ty approached the bar again and clapped his hands. "I'm a great listener. I could bartend."

"Because there's no paperwork, bussing and cleaning the floor would be safer." I pulled out a napkin and wrote down times for Thursday through Saturday. "We'd pay you in cash?"

"Thursday the Bulls play again," Cal said.

"I know. It was insane last night. Fun, but insane. We need all the people we can get," I said.

"I'll be here. Care if I bring some of the other guys?" Ty asked, his question meant for Cal.

Cal stared at me, his eyes narrowing like he was annoyed. Tough titties. We needed more people for the weekend rush, so I narrowed my eyes right back and stuck out my tongue. It seemed like the right thing to do at the time, but I immediately felt silly until Cal's lip curved up.

"Sure."

"Hells yeah. Now, Elle, your brother shared that you're majoring in creative writing. I, a handsome scholar, am also majoring in the great choice to guarantee self-doubt for the rest of our lives."

I laughed, appreciating his genuine humor. "That is true. I think about quitting four times an hour."

"Four? Oh, that's sweet. I'm averaging ten."

We both snickered, and I purposefully avoided Cal. The wound was raw about my major, especially after I'd unloaded all my feelings on him. I cleared my throat and refocused on Ty. "So, no Fortune 500 companies lined up for you?"

"No, but I do run a writing group and host a bunch of online writing prompts. You want in?"

"Are you serious?"

"We always meet at the same time and have a common set of rules to go by, but it's fun. It's supportive. It's a great place to bitch about subjectivity. Plus, we get discounts to writing workshops."

"Fuck yeah." Hope blossomed in my chest, my fingers itching to type at his invitation. "When do you meet?"

"Sundays at noon. The coffee shop right off the quad with the cats."

"With cats? Oh my god, I love this school."

"Sick. Here, give me your number, and I'll text you the details."

I did, and my phone buzzed in my pocket. "Thank you for thinking of me."

"It was Van. Don't get me wrong, I love meeting other writers, but he suggested it."

Gratitude for my brother filled me, and I knew it was his way of apologizing for being so hard on me at the hardware store. I smiled at Ty, truly freaking excited, and did a wiggle. "Do I need to prepare anything for Sunday?"

"Bring ten pages of whatever you're working on. We pair up and critique." He tapped his knuckles on the bar, smiling at me with a little interest. It made my skin prickle a bit, but it was nothing like how I'd felt around Cal earlier.

That was magnetic, raw, and made me want to tear his clothes off with my teeth. With Ty, I was flattered.

"Care if I stick around for a drink?"

"Not at all. This one is on me, friend."

His smile grew, and as I poured him a tall glass, I could feel Ty's gaze on me. But when I turned around, it was Cal who looked at me with a pale face and wide eyes. Like he'd seen a ghost. It got my heart racing, and I searched the bar for whatever made him freak out. When I spotted nothing, I returned to him, but he'd masked his expression and was back to glowering at the wall.

Whatever. I didn't have time to worry about him anymore. I had a new writer's group to obsess over, and I picked up some bar napkins, hoping to jot ideas down. Even as I tried quick plotting a new romance idea, Cal's features kept coming to my mind.

He might look like a perfect romance hero, but he didn't act like one. It was best to repeat that every hour so I didn't forget.

CHAPTER **EIGHT**

Cal

Creative writing major.

I remembered. *God,* it sucked to know you'd been a complete dick to someone. This happened to me often. This cycle of regret. The part where my brain replayed all the asshole comments I made out of pain. It wasn't an excuse, but I remembered what had happened.

We'd been in the car with her parents going to a dinner. I shouldn't have agreed, but Gabe had been all on me to be a better leader, and plus, I had nothing to do after that. Go home and pout? Get drunk and hook up? It was becoming old and made me feel even worse about myself, life. I went with them and was surrounded by parental love and affection. It physically hurt to watch and listen to them praise their kids.

How proud they were and supportive. Elle had laughed with them, and they talked about her coming to school the next year and how she hadn't chosen the major they preferred. I made the comment about not having it be creative writing because that was a joke of a career, that only dumb people went that path. Her parents chuckled, and the tension in the car rose a thousand degrees. I'd tried to be funny, to keep everyone laughing. But I'd hurt her.

She was a fucking *creative writing major.*

She said I was her favorite player to watch.

She was attracted to me.

I wanted to throw up.

She and Ty were getting along so well, and I watched the way he stared at her, clearly interested. *He'd* never insulted her or said the wrong things. He was probably smooth in that hipster way. Plus, she said we could only be friends. Fuck, co-workers. It was my fault. I was the reason she'd never look at me the way I hoped. All because I'd been envious of her parents and opened my mouth to try and be funny.

I was such a piece of shit. Maybe I did need to try that online therapy Reiner was going on about. Said it changed his life after he lost his parents, but he had friends, his sister, a life to get back to. I had... hockey. And some days, that didn't even fill the well. It was what I was supposed to do. It gave me an outlet for my anger.

Did I love it? Eh. Did I need it? Yes. Without question.

"Hey, Cal?"

Elle said my name, and I immediately went to the bar. I scanned her, figuring out if she'd hurt herself or what not. She seemed okay. "What do you need?"

"Could you grab the box of vodka on the top shelf? I can't reach and don't want to balance on a stool."

I'd kill her if I saw her standing on top of a tiny barstool. "Sure."

Ty finished his drink by the time I got around the bar, and I hoped he'd take off. It contradicted the progress I had with the team, but nothing made sense when it came to Elle. A year ago, I would've hidden from a teammate. Now, a small prickle of pride formed when he said guys would want to support their captain—

me. I walked by Elle, breathing in her perfume and noting how delicious she smelled, and our arms brushed. She pulled back way too fast, but I felt the zing too.

We had chemistry. Major chemistry. But I'd ruined any shot of that becoming something because I was an asshole. Sighing, I reached up to get the box as Ty started chatting again.

"So, what are you working on?"

"These two stories. Nothing worth talking about yet. Big contemporary fiction with romance."

"Sick. I'm doing this fiction piece on a cult. Two brothers try and escape, and the backlash affects the whole town."

"Wow." She leaned closer toward him. "How far are you?"

"First draft is done, baby, so now on to betas."

"Ah, that's amazing. I have a few short stories I'm too scared to submit to places. Might bring one Sunday for some eyes."

"Please do."

Elle smiled so easily with him. She lit up talking about writing, and I felt like a fool all over again. Maybe if I asked her about it, she'd tell me. My phone buzzed, and because we now had five people in the bar, I didn't feel bad checking it. I could use a distraction. Maybe it was someone else on the team or Reiner.

It was a picture of Charlie and his daughter.

Holy shit, I have a daughter. Look at her.

She was a mini-image of him. Dark hair, dark eyes, a crooked smile. She was fucking adorable. She was missing a tooth, and pressure grew under my ribs.

My cousin.

I had family. More than just Charlie.

She could need help learning sports or with homework or with playing catch. I could do that. Be there for her. Or if she needed a friend or someone to kick some kid's ass. Fuck. My breathing picked up, and it was too hot in the bar, and I gasped for air. What the fuck? I held onto the countertop, my vision going a little blurry as stars danced behind my eyes.

My cousin.

"Cal?"

Elle's voice sounded from the distance, like she was in a video or something. Fuck, my heart beat way too fast for me. It hurt. Even when I worked out, it wasn't like this. It scared me. I needed it to stop.

"My pulse," I said, swallowing hard, but there wasn't enough air. "Hard to breathe."

"Dude's having a panic attack." Ty hopped over the bar, his legs the last thing I really focused on before I felt their touch on me.

Small, soft hands. Large ones with a firm grip. They each took a side of me. My feet dragged on the floor. All I focused on was getting more air into my lungs to stop the pressure. Was it a heart attack? I was too young. I was healthy. There had to be more in life than anger and hockey. I wanted to experience joy again before I died.

"He needs to sit and take slow breaths." Ty pushed me onto a chair. "Focus on something that you can touch. You can smell. You can see. In and out, nice and slow."

I feel Elle's delicate fingers on my upper back. I can smell her delicious perfume. I see her wide, worried eyes.

"Good. Good. Now inhale and exhale."

I did, repeating it a few more times before the sensation stopped. My pulse was normal, my skin not actively sweating. When I opened my eyes fully, they both stared at me. Ty looked concerned, but Elle seemed upset. Really upset.

"Hey, I'm fine," I reached up and took her hand like it was the most natural thing in the world. She didn't pull back, and I considered that a win. "I'm okay now."

"You have panic attacks before?" Ty asked, pulling me from the moment I shared with Elle. She let go of my fingers, like Ty's words reminded her he was there.

"Been a while. Years, actually."

The first night after learning my parents were gone.

The first holiday without them.
My birthday that year.

I thought I had a handle on the gripping panic that came with losing part of your heart but apparently not.

"Fucking scary each time. You think you remember how it feels but then it happens, and it knocks the wind out of you. Here, let me get you some water." Ty squeezed my shoulder and left the office.

It was me and Elle now.

"Ty should take you home. I can close out the bar tonight. You need rest." Her face was pale and her brows tight.

"Fuck that nonsense." I tried to stand, but she pushed me down. I liked having her hands on both my shoulders. It let me see her lips up close, and god, I wanted to taste them. Feel them for just a second on me. To know what it'd be like to have her kiss me back.

"You need rest, Cal."

"You're not staying here alone."

"I'll call my brother or something."

"No. No." I shook my head, regretting it for a second. The headache started. I hissed but refused to back down. "We'll close. It's slow as fuck."

"You're not doing anything."

"I'm not fragile."

"I know you're not, okay?" Her tone got all soft and sweet, and she cupped one side of my face with her hands. My body tightened, and my stomach swooped when she rubbed her thumb along my jawline. "How about this? I close up, you do the bare minimum, then we all walk back together."

"Send Ty home."

"What?"

"You heard me." I glared at her, needing her to understand that I hated him seeing me weak. That I wasn't in control. That I wasn't a good teammate or captain. He could tell them, and they'd make fun of me or think I couldn't lead us to a championship this year. "The team…"

She nodded, her breath hitting my face. "Tonight's a good night for that pizza. I'll have him leave, but you and I are talking."

"I'd love that." I tried smiling, but I was so tired it probably came out weird. If she was taking care of Tyler, I didn't have to worry, and I closed my eyes. Just a little rest until Elle came back. That was all.

Shit. My neck throbbed, and my head ached from the angle. Where was I?

Right. The bar. Charlie's office. The attack.

Elle! If she'd walked home alone, I was gonna be pissed. I stood and had a surge of adrenaline to yell at her until I saw her at the bar. She had pieces of paper all over it, her arm moving fast as she wrote with a pencil. She'd put her long hair up into a knot at the top of her head, and she sucked the side of her cheek in as she wrote.

She was beautiful.

"No, no, not that." She talked to herself and flipped through some of the pages, her legs crisscrossed on the stool. She tapped the pencil to her teeth before nodding. "Right, because that makes sense. Oh, what an idea, dork."

"Talking to yourself?" I asked, unable to stop smiling.

She turned fast, her eyes widening. "Cal, hey, you're up. How are you feeling?"

"Like shit."

"Panic attacks can make you exhausted. I just read that online. Not that I'm a doctor. Duh. I'm a creative writing major, but I wanted to learn about them." She blabbered and blushed and quickly shoved the papers into a stack. "I'm sorry you're not feeling well."

"It's that but also the angle I slept at. My neck feels like cement." I rubbed it and squeezed, wincing at the pain. "What time is it?"

"One."

"Elle." *Three hours?* "You sat here for three hours?"

"One was spent cleaning, and the others were this." She gestured to the paper. "I can entertain myself anywhere if I have a pencil and paper."

"I'm sorry you waited. You should've woken me."

"No, you looked peaceful. Honestly, that's been the longest you've gone without annoying me."

"Ah, so sleeping me is okay."

"Exactly." She smirked, but it slowly shifted in worry. "What happened? If you want to talk about it, that is. I'm curious."

I held out my phone to the picture of Charlie and his daughter. "He sent me this."

She got up and walked toward me, her long legs such a tease. She squinted at the phone before putting a hand over her heart. "Oh my god. She's so cute. And Charlie looks so happy!"

"That's my cousin."

"The one you weren't excited about?" she asked, an edge to her voice.

That was obviously one of my comments that had upset her, but how did I explain it? I swallowed, taking my time collecting my thoughts. Maybe it was the post-effect from the attack or the fact it was only us and I had a feeling whatever I told Elle would stay between just her and I. No worrying about the team finding out and thinking I was a mess. She'd be kind about it. It was who she was.

My hands shook, and I pocketed them to hide the tremors. It had been years since I'd spoken about their death. Even sharing it with Reiner scratched the surface. A thing we both related to and could talk about. He leaned on me, and I on him.

But to pull the wound open completely…to share *them* outside my mind? It was scarier than a punch to the temple. Elle watched me, her head tilted to the side and her expression blank.

I can do this.

"My parents died when I was eighteen. Three days after I was drafted. Besides Charlie, I have no other family. I went from the best moment of my entire life to the absolute worst in seventy-two hours. I'd trade everything to have them back. Hockey, my scholarship, you name it."

"Cal." She closed her eyes, reached over, and squeezed my forearm. "There aren't words."

"I'm a chickenshit, okay? When Charlie mentioned he might have a daughter, I got fucking thrilled. Another family member? It wasn't just me and Charlie? Another small piece of my mom? I almost threw up I was so happy but then I got scared. What if she has someone else to live with? What if she makes Charlie move away, leaving me alone…again? What if I love her, and something happens to her? I can't… I can't go through it again. The pain."

Elle's eyes filled with moisture, red painting her cheeks before she closed the distance between us and wrapped her arms around my middle. She rested her head against my chest, and I froze.

A full body hug? It had been *years*.

She squeezed me and wouldn't let go.

"Elle."

"Hug me back, damnit."

It took a second to find a natural stance, but I placed my hands around her shoulders, cradling her head against me, and I squeezed her. So many things happened inside my body at once. The increased pulse for entirely different reason. The tightening of my gut because she was *so damn* close. The thrill of touching her, the comfort from the hug, how she smelled, the way her hair tickled my chin. The thud of her heartbeat against me. The pace my heart pounded at how good she felt against me.

I took it all in and breathed.

"Thank you for sharing this with me." Her voice was all muffled from my shirt. She still didn't let go of her grip, and I rested my chin on her head.

Holding her felt right. Amazing. Like the missing piece.

But I wasn't foolish enough to think this meant anything more than a comfort hug. She should be with a guy like Ty, not me. The one who upset her and freaked out from a photo. It hurt, but I accepted it then and there that we'd only be friends.

"Thanks for the hug." I pulled back, removing her from me because it was best, and hated the compassion in her eyes. "Please, don't. I can't stand pity."

"It's not pity. It's hurt. It's pain. I *hate* that your life has bad memories and pain. I don't feel bad for you, Cal. I hurt for you. I am sorry for all that you lost." She squeezed her eyes shut, then opened them. They were a lighter brown, more transparent. "Let's head back. Pizza is on me tonight."

"No, I don't want to eat your food."

"Because of money?" she asked, a slight edge to her voice.

"Yes. I heard you and your brother. Please, I just shared something with you, so don't leave me hanging."

She sighed, looping her arm through mine as we locked up the restaurant. I tried not to overthink why her arm was with mine because it felt damn good to have her touch me.

"It's not money problems yet. It's money anxiety. I get one shot to do this, and I'm terrified of messing up. My parents mean well, but every comment they said about choosing writing… it scarred me. They support me but think my choice isn't wise. It's a contradiction to how they raised Gabe, and I'm learning to navigate all the pressure."

Fuck. "I owe you a sincere apology."

"Don't worry about anything tonight. Tomorrow, you can get me apology croissants." She grinned up at me, leaning her head on my shoulder for a beat. "It's late, I'm hungry, and you need to relax."

We walked the short distance to our building and arrived at her door. She let us in. Her place smelled the same, like vanilla candles and lemon. While she put the pizza on the pan and preheated the oven, I walked toward her patio door. The wire shelves were there and a fresh batch of soil in little pods. *The spices.*

She'd planted them.

It gave me a little buzz of happiness. Maybe I'd buy her a new plant each week so she could add to her collection. With my hands still in my pockets, I returned to the kitchen to find her staring at me. "Do you need help with money?"

"What? No!" She huffed.

"I meant, damn. No, not like that. Like finances?"

She pursed her lips, her arms crossing over her chest. "What are you offering here?"

"I'm really good at budgeting. No one expects that of me because I'm a hockey player, but I had to be. My parents left me… a decent amount. I got the signing bonus. I couldn't just let that sit in an account, so I read a lot about what to do with it. Learned the best ways to track spending."

"Wow." Her lips curved, and she nodded. "That's awesome. Yeah, I bet you learned a lot dealing with that all. Was it hard?"

"It was a distraction. Anything I do is typically just a way to distract my mind from…well, you saw what happened at the bar."

"Feelings?"

"Huh?"

"You're allergic to feelings. I get it. I probably would be too after what you went through. I don't have nearly any of the same trauma you do, and feelings are hard for me too, so I can't imagine." She sat at her kitchen table and pulled her knees to her chest. "Cal, you can't just do things as a distraction. What do you enjoy?"

My plants. Music. YouTube how-to videos. Being on the ice. I itched the back of my neck and yawned.

"Oh, you're exhausted. Please, sit on the couch." She got up and pushed me. Her hands landed on my chest as she nudged me to sit. "What do you want to drink?"

"I'm okay, really, just tired." I sank into her cushions, the feel like a nice cloud. Fuck, I loved her pillows. I closed my eyes and took a few deep breaths. I got that prickly, tingling feeling in my eyes like sleep was gonna come whether I wanted to or not. I could just snooze until the pizza was done. That was it.

Then, I passed out.

CHAPTER
NINE

Elle

I padded outside my bedroom wearing loose Central State boxer shorts and a white tank. They covered all my parts, and Cal was still sound asleep on my couch. What a great night for Dani to stay at my brother's. She wouldn't have cared, but this prevented me from having to explain *why* he was there to both her and Gabe.

My brother wasn't a fan of him, and I was dying to ask if he knew Cal's story. God, my entire soul broke for Cal. I'd tossed and turned all night, trying to even imagine what I'd do in that scenario. I at least had Dani. She'd keep me together, but Cal? The guy who pushed everyone away to avoid feelings?

I rubbed my chest with my hand and willed my heart to stop beating so hard against my ribs. It wanted to escape my chest and go beat next to Cal's, to give him some hope. Because that was the thing I loved most about being human: hope. The hope for a better tomorrow, a better day, a better mood. Nothing was permanent.

I'd started a pot of coffee when he stirred. At some point, he'd fallen onto his right side, and god, he was a sight when he slept.

His features softened. The jaw not tensing like he was holding back screaming all the time. His lips parted, and there wasn't a single line of stress on his face. He seemed content.

Pouring in a little creamer, I stirred it into my mug and set it down to cool. Cal could use another blanket. The fan was on, and it was chilly. Tiptoeing toward him, I unfolded an old quilt made out of T-shirts of mine and set it on him. I tugged the top toward his chin as he moved.

He blinked, his gorgeous wide eyes all sleepy and gentle. "Elle?"

"Good morning." I smiled, realizing I was super close to him. Like, six inches from his face. I stepped back, hit the coffee table, and awkwardly hopped away. "Coffee?"

He groaned, and I chose not to stare at him. It was hard enough being attracted to the guy, but learning his past? Knowing how each day was hard for him? Going through the motions just to survive? I didn't know whether to hug or kiss him.

"Sure."

"How do you like it?" I asked.

"Black."

I poured him a mug and carefully approached him on my couch. The frown lines were back, but his eyes. Oof. They were heated and sleepy and intense as he stared at my legs, traveling up my body and across my neck.

"Here."

Our fingers brushed, and the second of connection had my breath catching in my throat. I brushed it off. This was no time for thoughts like that, no matter how good Cal looked after waking up. "How are you feeling?"

"Hungover." He sipped the mug, his gaze never leaving mine. "I owe you so many apologies Elle. I don't know where to start."

"Stop." I shook my head. "There's no need."

"Yes, there is." He frowned and set his drink down, moving from the couch toward the end where he took *my* cup out of my hand and placed it on the coffee table. So much touching! His hands were so warm, but the pads of his fingers were rough.

He covered my hands with his and squeezed them, the contact a roaring blaze of heat. "I fell asleep on your pizza invitation. I told you we weren't friends. I made fun of your major."

"Ah." My ears burned red. "That."

"I remembered the conversation in the car, and I am so, deeply sorry. There's no excuse. I was trying to be funny, to make everyone laugh because it was clear how much your parents loved you. It was jealousy and me being a fucking asshole." He stared at me hard, the apology evident all over his face. "I wish I could take that back. Then maybe you wouldn't hate me."

"I don't hate you. Not anymore." Oh, baby, his hands were so large and warm and still holding mine. It messed with my focus and made me feel protected. "But thank you for the apology."

"Are you able to forgive me?"

I nodded. "Yes."

"And, the pizza night fiasco? The comment about the friends?"

"Well, you bought my spices and offered to help me budget. I'm pretty sure you do that if you're friends with someone." I grinned, and he blinked slowly before letting go of my hands. "So, yes. I forgive you."

"Good. Good." He yawned and reached for his coffee. "We're definitely *friends*."

The way he said the word friends bothered me, but I wasn't sure why. He gave it more emphasis and had a hard look cross his face. It didn't last more than a second before he gave me a half-smile. When he grinned, I stood no chance against him. It was too much. The final straw. I glanced away and pretended there was something in my coffee.

"This will be great, Cal. We'll see each other a lot, so I'm glad we sorted it out."

He nodded, a sad, lost expression on his face before he smiled. "Me too."

"If you're worried about it, please know your story stays with me. It's not mine to share with anyone else."

His lips lifted on the side as he nodded. "I trust you."

God, those were heavy words.

We drank in silence, the sound somehow louder than our spoken words. It wasn't a bad quiet nor a comfortable one. It was filled with unsaid things, but we were at peace. I could keep my attraction at bay and approach him with more understanding. And he could use a real friend. Someone to be there for him. Friendship and support were my thing. I'd been there for Dani and my brother all their lives. And when they had a tough go, like when Gabe lost a game or Dani had a fight with her mom, a fun activity was needed.

"What are your plans for today?" Energy worked its way into my voice, making me sound more awake than I was. The decision to befriend him cleared up any of the tempting and confusing thoughts I kept having about him. His chest…his hands…his mouth. Nope. Friends. All caps. FRIENDS.

"Work out. Maybe see some guys on the team."

"Okay, what else?"

He shrugged. "That's it."

"So, you'll spend…ten hours at the gym?"

"No. I'll do my workouts, hit the rink. Then head home."

"Where is any fun?"

"What do *you* do for fun?" he fired back, his tone defensive.

I could read him better now that I knew the cause of his wounds. I reached over and squeezed his forearm, hoping to give a reassuring smile. "I'm not pestering you, Cal. I was asking so we could hang out, do something fun together. I think we both earned it after last night."

He swallowed. "Hang out?"

"Yeah. Like watch a movie or play a game, visit the bookstore or library, or hey! You could show me the best places around campus! Or ice-skating!" I clapped, proud of my ideas, but his frown grew.

"Elle, please don't do this." He set the half-drunk mug down on the table and stood. He folded the blanket perfectly before setting it on the back of the couch. There weren't any creases on the material. "I don't need a pity friend."

"Why are you obsessed with thinking this is pity? Are you actively trying to stay miserable? Friendless?" My feelings were hurt, my ego stung. "If you don't want to hang out with me, then say that."

"It's not that." He sighed, put his hands on his hips, and stared at the patio window. "My mood improves when you're around." He ran one hand over his face as his words hit me in the chest.

My stomach swooped. It wasn't the highest of compliments, but coming from him? It felt like the biggest victory. I wanted to smile, but I remained patient. It was clear he had more to say.

"I just… need to go about this slow."

"Friendship?" I said, elongating the word.

"Yes." His gaze bore into me. "I haven't had more than one friend in a long time, and I'm not sure how it works."

"But the team? My brother?"

"Out of duty. The ice changes things. I'm learning still."

"Cal." I stood too, unsure what to do with my hands. It wasn't like I could touch him. No words came to mind, and he remained just as quiet. Three steps forward, two and half back. My stomach growled, interrupting our stare-off, and my face flushed.

"Apology croissants. I owe you some." He walked by me before I could say a word and exited our apartment. His leftover cologne lingered in the air, evergreen and laundry, and I breathed it in for one second.

God, he was complicated. I rubbed my forehead and picked up our mugs, honestly more confused than before. He agreed we were friends but didn't look happy about it, then said we had to go about it slowly. I wanted to respect that, but at what cost? My feelings were real, and it hurt to be shot down.

Annoyed that Cal was taking up space in my head, yet again, I put on Megan Thee Stallion and showered. A clean slate for the day. No more regrets or weirdness leftover from Cal, and by the time I was done, I felt better. Refreshed.

Alex and I were scheduled for the night shift, and I wanted to get more work done on my plant shelf before heading there. I braided my hair, then wore black cutoff shorts and an army green tank cropped just beneath my ribs and even put on hoop earrings. My mom said they were her armor and had bought me a pair before coming here. I loved them, and they made me feel brave. Brave enough to do this on my own, face down grumpy people at the bar and maybe…put myself out there.

Working at the bar gave me the one thing I needed all my life: a place to escape the pressure from my parents and Gabe's shadow. I could be *me* on my own. It was hard to explain the second sibling pressure, even though I loved Gabe. He excelled at everything so anytime I did something, it was old news because he'd already done it. That forced me into a weird position of wanting to impress my parents but not having a way to do it. Writing was so foreign to all of them, that they'd have no idea if I was good at it, and I struggled with proving myself. Jags was for me, regardless if my parents or Gabe approved.

Someone knocked on the door, and my heart leapt in my throat. *Cal.* I opened it, but there was no moody hockey player. There was a bag with my name on it though. The guy had to have dropped these off and run with how fast I answered, so he had to be nearby. "Thank you, Cal."

"You're welcome," he said from the stairwell, then the door to the stairs shut, and heavy footsteps thudded upward. I shook my head, opened the bag, and immediately took a bite. They were so damn good.

Things might still be weird with Cal, but these croissants sure helped. And with that thought, I distracted myself until I had to go to the bar. If I wanted to get more plants, I needed more tips.

Alex had their phone on speakerphone as Charlie's voice carried through. "This is incredible. I don't have words, but fuck, she's... I'm a dad."

"Is she being receptive to you?" Alex asked, dipping chips into ranch. Midwesterners loved their ranch.

"Yes. I guess her mom told her about me after she got sick, so she knew about me a little. This is...how's the bar?"

"Who cares about the bar?" I shouted, leaning onto the table with a huge grin. "Talk about your daughter more."

"I asked because...I need to stay here until the end of the month." He coughed. "Things are still being settled, and I don't want to rush it."

Alex and I locked eyes, and they nodded. "Then don't rush it. We'll figure it out, Chuck."

"That's asking a whole lot for three people."

"We wouldn't offer help if we didn't mean it." Alex tapped their finger on the table. "Elle's getting some people to help bus, be bouncers, that we can pay in tips. Her and I can handle drinks, and even Cal is working his ass off."

"Good, glad to hear that. Is he there now?"

"No. I created a schedule, and tonight's his night off," I said.

"How is he doing, really? I was worried he'd cause more trouble."

"He surprised me, Charlie." Alex laughed. "Very protective of our Elle too."

My insides hummed. He *was* protective of me, which wasn't entirely new since Gabe and Dani would fight anyone for me, but with Cal, it was different.

"*Our* Elle? You threatened to cut off my hair ten minutes ago," I fired back. They laughed, and I even smiled.

"Well, let me know if he gets in one of his moods. The kid has had it tough, but the bar is familiar to him. Ah, she's getting up from a nap. Gotta go. Thank you for... you know."

"We do." Alex hung up, the warmth in their eyes lingering for a beat. "He's a good man."

"Agreed, now, game three is on tonight. Want me to get some extra hands?"

"Cal would come in if we asked, you know. Are you avoiding him?"

"No, and don't bother with your insinuations, punk. He had a rough night, and I want him to rest."

"Rough?"

"Yeah, so about that help?" I didn't want to air his business, and Alex dropped it. Thank goodness.

"Sure, text your people."

And with that, I texted Gabe. Alex could certainly hold down the fort, but I felt better having more people who could take care of large angry men if needed. He responded that he was on it. Getting a few hockey players wasn't a terrible idea.

Ty, Emmett, and Jenkins all arrived, wearing black shirts that said security. They even wore sunglasses. "Are those fake earpieces?" I asked, laughing as they lined the wall. "Oh my god."

"Van said security and muscle. We brought both." Emmett flexed and pushed down his glasses to wink at me. "Boss us around, baby Van."

"Okay, none of that," I said. Emmett charmed me with his antics, and gratitude filled me. "Thank you, seriously."

"We get to help out our captain and baby Van? Not a bad night. You'll pay us in food, right?" Emmett asked.

"Food or tips, whatever you prefer." I pointed to the bar. "I gotta ready the bar, but Alex will go over what we need."

"Got it, boss."

I smiled at them, glad they were there, and prepared the ingredients for the rush. When the pre-game started, the place filled up, and there was already an energy in the air. A fun, rambunctious one that had me in a great mood.

If the Bulls won again, it'd be wild. And all of Illinois would party way into the night and go into work hungover the next morning.

"Alright, why the smile?" Ty leaned up on the bar, his sunglasses forgotten, and in place were his usual glasses.

"Sports are just reality TV for people who like competition."

"Sure. I agree with that." He kept grinning at me, making my stomach get all weird from the attention. He was cute, understood writing, and definitely was flirting with me. It was flattering.

I was eighty percent positive he was flirting.

"Are you into sports?"

"Hockey," I said, winking. He ate it up and leaned even closer to me. He smelled nice too. "Why?"

"Well, if I may. There's a baseball game at the single A field in town. Would you like to go to one with me?"

"As...?"

"A date. As friends. Honestly, you gotta tell me what you're thinking because I'm the worst at reading people. Words on a page? I can decipher between the lines, but humans are more complicated. Like, you're blushing which is good. You're smiling too. But you could be unavailable."

"Hm. Will there be cotton candy or corndogs there?"

"Does your response depend on that answer?"

I laughed, my face warming because he was cute. I didn't get the explosion of butterflies I had around Cal but there were flutters. "It does. I mean business."

"Then yes." He smiled, dimples popping on both sides. "They do have them."

"Depending on the night, I'm in. I have to work here five nights a week to help out."

"Sundays have day games too, you know, if you're so excited to go and can't wait for some time off."

"Are you saying we go from writing group to a game together?"

He nodded. "If you want to. I think we'd have fun."

"Okay then. It's a date."

His answering grin gave me more flutters but then he leaned

closer. "How's Cal doing, by the way? I get why he kicked me out, but he won't answer my texts."

And then the flutters stopped, and Cal's face intruded. Damnit.

Cal was a walking puzzle, and it was foolish to entertain my secret crush on him. I would not be the person for Cal. Not with my hopeless romantic heart. Not with my *flimsy* future. He needed someone sturdy and supportive and confident. I could be his friend, safely, and that would have to be enough.

I sighed and pushed away the pull I always had toward him. "I think he's alright. He settled down last night."

"Wish he'd let someone else in. I hate that he had a panic attack and felt the need to hide from his teammate. I want to be a friend to him, you know? It's just so damn hard."

God, Ty was a good guy. He was the kind of person I should be trying to date, fall in love with, and have the romantic moments with. I squeezed his arm, excited about Sunday even more when the hairs on my neck tingled.

I glanced up, and Cal was there. At the bar. Staring right at me. Looking pissed.

CHAPTER **TEN**

Cal

There were so many things I wanted to say to Elle, some leftover from the morning, some about the call with Charlie. But mainly, I wanted to tell her thank you for taking care of me. She'd inspired me to actually set up an online therapy appointment because one thing was clear: I couldn't freak out every time I saw, talked to, or mentioned Lizzie. My cousin. I owed it to the four-year-old girl whose life had been turned upside down.

I met her on FaceTime. Charlie called and introduced us, and she was…amazing. For a guy whose heart hadn't functioned well in a long time, it burst open to the point of pain. Anything that girl needed for the rest of her life, she had. I'd called my finance guy and set up a college fund for her already, not caring what Charlie thought. I had the money, and he could deal with it.

But Lizzie wanted to ice skate. I promised her we would when she visited. I wanted to tell Elle about it, but she was touching hipster Ty. My face flushed with shame. *Why* was he here again?

Why were Jenkins and Emmett there too?

But mainly, why was Elle looking furious as she left the bar and marched over to me? Her shorts showed off her long legs, but it was the crop top that killed me. Her waist was all curves, and I wanted to see if my hands would fit around her.

"What the *fuck* are you doing here?" she asked, her cheeks red.

"Did I upset you?" I held up my palms, and she pointed at my chest. "I'm sorry."

"You should be—" She paused, noted the hockey guys around us, and moved closer. So close I could smell her shampoo. "Resting," she whispered. "You need to be resting, Cal."

"Did you call them because you needed help?" I asked, a little hurt. "I would've come."

"No. You should relax."

"Don't baby me because of last night. I have it under control." My jaw tightened again, and Ty tugged at her elbow, his fingers touching her bare skin. It was like a knife to the throat. I hated watching him touch her.

"Elle, can I have a minute with him?"

She glanced at his fingers on her arm, placed her own hand on his, and nodded. "Sure, Ty. Yeah."

She glared at me for a second before swaying those damn hips on the way to the bar. I'd fucked up so much with her, and here I was, messing up again.

"Bro, let's go outside." Ty put an arm around me and led me out the doors. I hated his arm around me and the term of bro, but I said nothing. It wouldn't be very captain-like of me to lash out against him, especially after his patience last night. He was a decent guy, and he had no idea the rage I felt when it came to Elle. It wasn't his fault.

"How you feeling?" he asked once we were away from the other guys and outside in the humid air. "Better?"

"Yeah, thanks." I shuffled my feet and swallowed the uncomfortable ball in my throat. Shame prickled along my skin. I bet *he* never freaked out because of a picture.

He cleared his throat. "Look, I know we aren't buds, but we're teammates. If you want to talk, I'm always here for you."

"Right." My face heated with embarrassment.

"Cap," he said, smiling and putting a hand on my shoulder. "You're a legend on the ice and will probably end up in the hall of fame, but *nobody* gets through life alone. Teammates lift each other up. Hockey isn't an individual sport, bro. You're angry all the time, for reasons I don't need to know, but it can't be healthy."

"I'm working on it." I shrugged his touch off, exhaled, and forced myself to relax. Reiner would be pissed and rip me a new one if I didn't demonstrate leadership. Van Helsing had showed me simple ways to lead without it being too fake. I tried to remember his tips, but it was all a jumbled mess. Something about vulnerability, honesty... I swallowed. "Thank you, Ty. You were... great to have last night. I appreciate the help."

"Elle sent me home, which I understand. But if you're worried about me telling the guys, I won't. That's not the type of shit one gossips about. It's your business, *but,* sharing it with all of us won't make you seem weak. Mental health is important, and you'd earn more respect if you shared parts of yourself."

"Thank you." My throat got all tight, and he smiled at me. "Really."

"Sick. Well, I gotta return to my post for the night. Let's meet up at the rink tomorrow and shoot? Jenkins wants to go too and block. You in?"

"Sure."

"Sweet." Ty hit my shoulder before going back inside, and I took a few seconds to breathe. It wasn't the worst thing, having a teammate who had my back. Plus, skating alone wasn't as fun. A flicker of excitement flared inside me at the thought of having plans. I could skate with them and then Friday, I could ask Elle to get together.

Because we were friends and I didn't need to have a freak out about it. I'd meant what I said about going slow, but it was ridiculous that the thought of hanging out made me want to bolt. She scared me but in a good way? It was like I knew with her I couldn't hide anymore. She'd seen it all, and I'd run. Like a chickenshit.

I had to go back inside and make sure she had a snack. Yeah, then I could ask about Friday. Tell her about Lizzie too. I pushed the door open and weaved my way through the tables and cheers until I got to the bar. There wasn't a spot open, and Elle worked like lightning. Hands flipping glasses and pouring drinks and cashing people out. Every part of her body moved as she balanced all the tasks. "Let me help."

"No, go home." She didn't look up at me.

"Not happening."

"Cal." She poured a double Jack and coke. "I don't have time for this. Leave."

"I'm staying until close. Put me to use."

She smiled as she set the drink down but then glared at me. "You are a pain in my ass, Cal Holt."

"He's a pain in everyone's ass, baby Van," Emmett said, teasing her from the other side of the bar. She laughed and winked at him. His grin grew, and fuck, I hated them. How did they get Elle to smile so freely and tease them? I wanted that so damn badly, but I only seemed to upset her.

"Elle," I said, making her glare again. "What can I do?"

"Just give him a chore, honey. He seems beefy and useful." Cindy, a regular with a smoker's voice, patted the bar. "When a man who looks like that offers help, you take it."

"Yes, ma'am," Elle replied. Her lips curved into a smirk before facing me. "Glasses need to be washed, dried, and restacked. That would help me a lot."

"On it."

The dishwasher and sink put me right next to her, and every so often, our arms would brush. It was awkward at first but then I found a rhythm. She'd hand me a dirty glass, I'd pass her a clean one, and she hadn't thrown me a glare once. When there was a lull, I emptied the trash. Replaced the paper in the receipt printer. Took the tips from the jar and put them in the safe.

There were three napkins with numbers on them, all meant for Elle…which annoyed me. What was she gonna do, call the number and be like *hey, yeah, let's hang out* what do you look like? What an inefficient way to leave your number. Idiots.

During halftime, Elle leaned against the wall and yawned. Guilt gnawed at me. She was tired because I'd kept her up. "Hey." I handed her a bag of protein balls. "They'll help. Also, brought you something."

She took the baggie and already shoved one in her mouth. "I forgot dinner again."

"I figured. Sneak in here for a second." I held the door to the cooler, and she walked in. It was small and cold and just the two of us. She ran her hands up and down her arms as I held up the brookie. "It's not dinner, but it's the two best desserts in one."

"Uh, it looks good." Her eyes lit up when I handed her a spoon. "You made this?"

"Yes."

"Why?" She took a huge spoonful and crossed her eyes. "Cal, fuck."

Hearing her say my name like that was a bolt of lust. It was insanely hot. I cleared my throat, glad the air was chilled around us. "Because you asked to hang out, and I bolted. They are my apology and invitation brownies. Friday, do you have plans?"

"Not until here. Why? What are you thinking?" Her sparkled with interest, and I wanted to bottle that expression on her face forever.

"There's a greenhouse I've been wanting to try. Would you like to come with me?"

"As friends?" she asked, a lilt to her voice.

"Yes." I swallowed down any urge to be more. "If you're free, I can drive."

She spooned another bite of the dessert I made, her brown eyes swirling with questions. But she never asked them. She nodded. "Sure, sounds good."

"First plant is on me."

"Cal—"

"You inspired me, and it's a thank you."

"Inspired you?" She took another bite and shivered. "How?"

"I set up a therapy appointment, made plans with the team. I don't know. Talking to you last night opened up something I had closed for years. Plus, I met Lizzie today on the phone, and —" I paused, a lump in the back of my throat. "She's incredible."

"Oh, Cal." She touched my arm just as a huge cheer broke out. "Shit, I gotta get back behind the bar. Do I have anything on my face or teeth?" She smiled wide and cheesy, and she did have chocolate on her face, right next to her lip.

I could've told her, held up my phone or something. Instead, I used my thumb to wipe it off. "There." She froze at my touch, her eyes going large.

"Uh, thanks." She blinked a few times and went to the door. "Thank you, for the dessert too. It seems we keep making missteps, but I think we'll get to a good place, you and me."

A good place.

I nodded, uncertain what a good place meant for her. I wasn't entirely sure what it signified for me either, but it seemed like things were getting better. It made that tiny piece of hope grow bigger, and for the first time in…years, a flicker of excitement burned deep in my stomach. Instead of going through the motions, I was looking forward to Friday.

Friday came fast. There was no reason to feel self-conscious in the GLO mobile. The navy SUV had belonged to my dad, and the license plate read GLO80, a tribute to his grandfather's name, Graham Leonard Owens and year he was born. It was ten years old and had been a part of the family. The GLO, Big G, GLO-seph…I smiled as I tapped my fingers on the steering wheel. We were the worst at nicknames.

"Care to share what prompted that little grin?" Elle asked, pulling me from the nice memory.

I coughed into my fist, my face flushing at being caught. I snuck a glance at her, her legs crossed in a red polka dot dress. She even wore a handkerchief in her hair. Just gorgeous.

"Well, a memory hit me."

"Share it! I'm guessing it's a good one?"

"Yeah. My parents came up with nicknames all the time. This vehicle belonged to my dad, and we referred to it as Big G, Glo-seph. I hadn't thought about those names in years."

"Glo-seph. Well, it's an honor to meet you Big G." She patted the side of the door, amusement in her tone. "I love that. What a nice memory."

"I was Cal-ifornia. Callie-boy, Calzone."

"Calzone." She chuckled. "That's great."

"Our black lab was named Sassy growing up, but we rarely called her that. Instead, it was Toon, Toon-Pie, Saskatoon. Toonifer." I laughed, a genuine cackle deep in my chest. It felt weird yet familiar to laugh about silly things. Rusty, like riding a bike after ten years of it being locked up. "That dog was wild. She'd take our socks off our feet."

Elle's smile took up her whole face, and she let out a contented sigh. "This is my favorite thing you've ever told me. I love people who never use their dog's real names. Oh! And people who have dogs with human names. Like, Adam or Jeremy or Brad. Have you ever heard of a dog named Brad?"

"Can't say I have."

"Roarke. That'd be my dog's name whenever I get one." She hummed to herself. "Definitely Roarke."

"Why?"

"Just a strong name… might be based from a character I really like."

"From what?"

"A book." She lost a little of the laughter on her face, and I poked more.

"Sure, but which one?"

"Some fiction novel," she said, sighing and shaking her head. "No, not anymore," she mumbled. Then she spoke louder. "It's from a romance series written by the one and only Nora Roberts. She is the queen, along with Ms. Beverly Jenkins. I'm trying to not be ashamed of reading and writing romance."

"Why be ashamed? You like what you like, and fuck, writing a book? That's insanely hard."

"Laying it on thick there, Calzone. I've already forgiven you for the comment about creative writing, so no need to sprinkle extra compliments on it." She snorted.

I wasn't doing anything like that. "I meant it. You like what you like, no shame in that." My own face got hot again thinking about my plants and YouTube obsession. *Tell her. Open up.*

"Okay then. It'll be hard when some literary fiction writer tells me its smut or fluff, but like, why is it bad to enjoy something that's about acceptance and love and happy endings? It's so annoying."

"People are idiots."

"Generally, yes."

I glanced at her again as we approached the country road that led to Zed's, the new greenhouse I couldn't wait to visit. They sold organic everything too. Elle wore some color on her lips, and it only amplified my attraction to her. It enhanced her already perfect features. "So," I said, unsure of what to ask. I wanted to hear her speak and laugh and to learn more about her. "What's your favorite book?"

She sucked in a breath. "I don't know."

"I find that hard to believe."

"Really. It's too hard. I have lists of favorites and ones that I'll always reread but a one-time favorite? I can't."

"Top three then."

"Can I get back to you?"

"Uh, sure."

"I need to cultivate the list, and it'll take time. I like different books for different reasons. There are comfort reads, ones I'm saving for a shit day, the 'pull my heart out and stomp on it to piece it back together' reads. There's the angst, the fluffy, the lighthearted. There are my favorite tropes too. Sometimes I'm in the mood for friends to lovers, other times second chance. See? I'm blabbing because there are too many choices."

"Whenever you have something to share, I want to know," I said. Hearing her talk so fast with so much emotion about reading set something off inside me. She loved books hard. Genuinely. So much so that she had *lists of lists*. "I read a David Baldacci book once. My mom loved thrillers."

"Oh, which one?"

"Memory man? The guy who never forgets anything?" *Also, the character who lost his entire family.* The ache in my soul came and went, like it always did. "I'm not much of a reader, but that book caught my attention." I squinted at the upcoming road sign —nope, wasn't this street. It was the next right.

"Not much of a reader means you haven't found something that engages you." She grinned at me, her gaze moving along my face and toward my arms. I snuck a peek at her while driving. She did that sometimes, eyed my arms, and it took all my effort to not flex. "I want to find you a genre that you fall in love with. I bet I can do it."

"Hm. Maybe I don't like reading?"

"Again, I call bullshit. It's because you're not excited! Oh, this is great. A book challenge. Yes! I find you a book that you'll like."

"And what if you don't?"

"Hm, well, then what do you want?"

I chewed my cheek, keeping my mouth shut as the initial answer was to say to *kiss you*. Friends was safe. What she needed from me. But if this was a bet or challenge, then I could provide a dare too. "Okay, instead of wins or loses, I'll create a finance bootcamp for you."

"So, you teach me about money, and I show you the wonderful world of books?"

"Yes. We both gain something then." I turned right, letting my attention move toward her legs for a second. She totally caught me but didn't say anything. "So, what do you think?"

"It's a deal."

A fluttery, almost pre-game type feeling formed in my gut. It was close to excitement, and I fought a grin. This would be fun.

We pulled into the parking lot, both of us wearing our own version of smiles, and I locked Glo-seph just as a familiar voice caught my attention. I turned and found Sherry Wright wearing overalls and a yellow tank top. A former fling who'd wanted more than I could ever offer. *Shit.*

What a way to ruin the perfect moment.

CHAPTER
ELEVEN

Elle

The adorable girl in a straw hat and overalls had to have a cute backstory. Her and her partner opened the greenhouse together. They had baby goats at home and were expecting a daughter, who would wear matching overalls. She preferred iced tea, her partner sweet lemonade, and sometimes they had Arnold Palmers. They totally lived in an old farmhouse that was renovated. They met in college but dropped out to follow their real passion; plants. I could see the entire story unfolding in my head, and I grinned.

She handed another customer a pair of gloves before turning to us with a huge smile. "Welcome to—" She stopped, the cheery face evaporating like someone turned off a switch. She glowered. Red cheeks, narrowed eyes. "*What* are you doing here, Cal? Didn't do enough damage before?"

Oh, shit. I stopped in my tracks and watched Cal totally freak out. It wasn't obvious to anyone but me, since I stared at him all the damn time. I was learning his tells…which, said a lot about me, but he was panicky. His shoulders tensed, his hands forming fists at his sides, and he worked his jaw like he chewed gum.

He'd done something to hurt cute farmer girl.

"How dare you come here?" She marched up to him and flicked his chest. He stepped back, his face paling as he shook his head.

"I didn't realize, Sherry. I wanted—"

"You wanted what? You knew I worked here. You had to."

"I didn't."

"I *told* you I was partnering with Zedd. Or did you not actually listen all the times we talked? Were you just in it for a quick lay? God." Sherry, cute farmer girl, groaned before facing me. "And you brought someone else?"

"Oh, we're not involved. We're reluctant friends," I said, unsure how to handle the situation. These type of things happened with Gabe from time to time, a girl refusing to believe he'd moved on. It was awkward and painful, but it was like a Band-Aid being ripped off. You just had to deal with it head-on. "I'll let you two…talk. I'm here for the plants."

My heart ached at the pain on her face because it was like looking in a mirror that told the future. Cal would break hearts. Maybe not by choice, but by the cards life had handed him. He'd never get involved more than superficially, and I knew that, accepted it, yet it still didn't dampen the little hope that hung around that *maybe* things could be different.

Cal's eyes pleaded with me, but he was on his own. I waved my fingers at him and beelined for the beautiful flowers. I didn't have an opinion on what plants to use to fill my shelving, just that I wanted green. Pale greens, honestly. From the brief research I did, succulents were easier to manage. God, this place smelled so good. Outside, soil, the specific scent of water on cement. I closed my eyes, imagining running a place like this.

I'd wear adorable overalls like Sherry, maybe get a cute hat. I'd meet a sexy landscaper who'd come every week to flirt with me. We'd plant in the community garden and adopt a dog. Roarke would love the dog, obviously. I smiled and looked up, enjoying the sun on my face when a soft hand touched my elbow, dragging me from my imagination.

"Lost in your head?" Cal asked, his fingers lingering on my skin as he rubbed his thumb back and forth. He let go way too soon, his shy smile doing something dangerous to my insides. I thought about cute Sherry, and it settled the butterflies.

"I'm really sorry about that."

"You'll be sharing everything in the ride back." I batted my lashes at him, earning a half-smile. "I'm not judging, but I have a feeling you're at fault?"

"What gave it away?" He chuckled lightly before putting his hands in his pockets. "You've experienced firsthand how I can say the wrong thing. Sherry... is a little more complicated than that, but more of the same."

His cheeks were a tad red, and his eyes kept moving from me to over his shoulder, like he was worried she would come back. Her appearance had definitely flustered him, and I was dying to know more. Maybe for my own sick need to learn everything about him but also to see what would happen to me in due time. But plants were our reason for being here. "I think I want a houseplant."

"A spider plant might be a nice start. Here, they're on your right." He put a hand on the base of my back as he moved beyond me. Warmth from his touch spread up my spine, and I froze, waiting for the sensation to pass.

He squatted and pointed to a couple of the plants on the ground. "This one will be good. Strong." He reached into the dirt and nodded. "Good roots. You could remove it and repot it easily." He picked it up and moved toward the back of the greenhouse. There were a variety of pots in shapes and colors. Cal scanned the shelf and held a copper one. "Here."

He faced me, his expression set in determination. "This one is on me."

"You really don't have to—"

"I owe you from the other night, how you were there for me."

His tone got deeper and rougher. "I'm not...used to people caring for me. Not that you care *for me,* but you helped me. I'm not familiar with others helping me. That's all."

Ugh, the flip-floppy heart of mine would destroy me. I had an upcoming date with Ty on Sunday, and here I was, all flummoxed because of Cal. It was uncomfortable to say the least because back at the bar, I'd been excited to spend time with Ty. Genuinely. But being with Cal was intense and made every other emotion weak in comparison. His cheeks turned red, and he shuffled his feet back and forth, somehow looking more at home here in the greenhouse than he did anywhere else.

I had to remedy this internal battle of mine. "I care for you...in the sense I don't want you to die, you know?"

His lips curved up, and I was blessed with another one of Cal Holt's smiles. It felt like a prize of sorts because they were so hard-earned. I gave out smiles like candy at a Fourth of July parade, free and easy and plentiful. But his were buried down between four layers of grump and pain, and I suddenly had the urge to dig.

"I don't want you to die either."

"See, look at us? Would you have thought we'd be here?"

He snorted, the smile remaining for another few seconds before something caught his attention. Cute Sherry in my dream-outfit wasn't around, and I hadn't forgotten that whole exchange. But I did want to know what had Cal looking hopeful. "What is it?"

He didn't answer. He grabbed a basket with his free hand and swaggered toward another row. He didn't just walk, that was too simple. Cal strode with purpose and excitement, and it got me excited. Had he found a rainbow? A cat? Oh! I loved when places had pets around. I glanced around for a goat or chicken or cat or dog but only found leaves and petals on the ground.

Cal though, he set my spider plant and pot on the cement and bent down toward a patch of plants that had seen better days. One leaf was brown, the soil wet, but it didn't seem to matter. One plant was missing the other half. Cal ran his fingers over the leaves, a dazed, happy expression on his face.

"There we are," he said to the two damaged ones. He put them in his basket before standing straight up. He slowly turned toward me, and I bit my lip to not smile.

Why did he look guilty?

He stared, and I stared right back, unwilling to break our little showdown. I arched an eyebrow and jutted my chin at his basket. He sighed, glancing off into the distance before meeting my eyes. "Okay. The truth is, you have your books. I have my…plants."

"The ones I saw on your window ledge?"

He nodded. "I like," he paused, swallowing hard. He held up the basket like it was show and tell. "I find joy out of buying plants no one else wants. The half-dead ones, the brown ones. I try to get them back to their full life."

"Cal." Emotion gripped my throat, the emotions racing through me almost overwhelming. That was, without a doubt, the cutest thing I had ever heard in my life. *Get them back to their full life.* I couldn't even speak. I needed to wrap myself around him in a hug.

"It's dumb, I know, but I enjoy it." He ducked his head, and I lunged forward. I squeezed his hand with the basket and waited for him to look at me.

"No, my silence was because I couldn't find the words. I wanted to squish you because it was so cute."

"Cute?"

"Yes, oh my god. You nurse dying plants. That is adorable!" I let go of him, and his throat bobbed. Interesting.

"It's not fucked up?"

"Um, no? Why would you think that?"

"Because it could be like I'm finding versions of myself. Half-dead."

"Stop assuming the worst, Cal. Seriously. You're not half-dead. You're sad and in pain. I don't know anything about losing family, but grief isn't linear for anyone. It's messy, and you're allowed to be sad and deal with it how you see fit. But don't you dare pull that self-pitying shit with me. You're healthy, smart, and tender when you want to be."

He blinked, his breath coming out faster than before. My adrenaline surged, and I kept going. "I write all sorts of characters with backstories. Does that mean they're based on me? No. It's because I love writing and people. You caring for plants isn't any different than me writing to show how much I love other people. That means you have a kind heart in that brick wall of a chest."

My skin felt too tight for my body at my outburst. I wasn't embarrassed. I meant what I said. Cal though, he stared at me like I'd grown three heads. That might've been too much for him. He wanted to take it slow as friends, so I sighed, shook my arms out to relieve some tension, and smiled. "Hey, I'm sorry I yelled. I might've gotten a little fired up, but my best friend in the world used to talk negatively about herself, and it made me bonkers. I can't change your mindset, only you can, but I can at least try to point out the bullshit."

"Alright."

"Alright," I repeated, catching my breath. Something flicked my ear, and I jumped. *A motherfucking bee.* My blood ran dry, a paralyzing fear rooting me in place. I *Stay still. Don't bother them. Don't irritate them.* The buzzing roared. I closed my eyes, hating every second of this. *In and out.*

Breathe.

"What's wrong?" Cal's urgent tone sounded closer. "Elle. Tell me."

"Bees," I whispered, like they could hear me.

Wind hit my face, the smell of Cal's cologne growing stronger than before. A warm hand landed on my hip. "Elle. It's gone."

I opened my eyes to find him *right* in front of me. His fingers tightened on my waist, and his jaw clenched. Something deep and needy formed in my gut at the way he watched me, all focused, like I was the only thing in the world. *No.* He wasn't romantic. He wasn't my hero. I blinked and with a shaky hand, pushed my hair out of my face. "So, I have a fear of bees."

He almost smiled and released me. "I found what I wanted. Let's go."

"We drove all this way for two plants?"

He narrowed his eyes toward the front. "It's warming up, and I'm ready if you are."

"Okay, sure." I could've used more air, but the buzzing sound made me jump. It was a fucking fly. "Yeah, I'll be in GLO-seph."

He nodded and went to pay as I jumped back into the passenger seat. The car was steamy, and I fanned myself until Cal returned. He set the plants in the back of the SUV before joining me in the front. "You okay?"

"Yeah. It's so dumb." I laughed. "I've never been stung before, and in my head, it's like I'll lose a limb. I don't know."

"Fears aren't rational."

"Thank you." I shook my body out from head to toe. "I saw a kid in second grade get stung, and he was allergic, so there was stretcher and an ambulance. I still see it."

"That would fuck me up too."

"Like, I don't want to say anything too dramatic, but if I had to sacrifice you to the queen, I would."

"Right, no drama." He almost smiled again. "Good to know though. Bees don't bother me at all. I can get rid of them for you."

"Cal 'Bee Killer' Holt. Nice." I nudged his arm. "Speaking of being a killer…of hearts, what's the story with cute little Sherry?"

He grunted. "I'd rather talk about taxes."

"Ew, no." I recrossed my legs. "Sherry."

He ran a hand over his face, his other relaxing on the wheel. He looked wicked hot like that, his right arm muscles directly in front of me. "We hooked up."

"Yes, gathered that."

He narrowed his eyes at me. "She thought we were together. I didn't. She thought, assumed, misinterpreted what we were. I don't…I fuck around, alright? I don't do emotions or promises.

I'm a three-night guy, nothing more. She wanted to change that about me."

Three-night guy.

Interesting. I chewed my lip, already imagining how that would feel to be his for three nights. Passionate, wild. For sure. I squeezed my thighs together, the scenes flashing in my head not good for being in a car with Cal. I'd seen his chest, his muscles, his arms. His hands were so big and talented… I shivered.

"I can turn the air down."

"Oh, no, I'm not cold." My voice came out hoarse and needy. He snapped his head toward me, and I cleared my throat. "Just thinking about the bees."

More like the birds and the bees.

After a minute of forcing myself not to imagine him in bed, I realized I'd never responded about Sherry. "If you communicated with her about all of it and she refused to listen, then it's not your fault. That's on her."

"I did. I always do."

"Then she chose not to listen to your wants, so don't you feel bad for a second."

"She hoped for more, and I don't do *more.*"

Listen to that, Elle! Doesn't. Do. More. It hurt because that damn little flicker of hope still remained, that he would change… for me… someday, but I'd be foolish like Sherry thinking I could change him. That I'd be enough for him.

He shrugged, his jaw tightening again. "I'm sorry you saw that though. It was embarrassing."

"Calzone, we've both seen each other in a lot of ways." *Not naked though.* "No reason to be embarrassed. I freak out at bees, you at feelings. Maybe this friendship is a great fit."

He nodded, giving me a reassuring smile, even though the words seemed weird to say. It felt like a lie, especially now that I wished my date was with Cal and *not* Ty. It wasn't fair to anyone to have those thoughts. Not to Ty, myself, or Cal. We all were up front about things and to ignore them would be cruel. Rationally, being friends with Cal was the right choice, but a small (opinionated) voice in the back of my head wanted more. I wanted him to *want* to do more with me, but that wasn't how life worked outside of fiction. Cal refused to have feelings, and I was a girl who needed lots of them, which was why we were never meant to be.

CHAPTER **TWELVE**

Cal

Since the greenhouse, things between Elle and I were normal. I snuck looks at her at the bar, made sure to walk her home, and I hadn't done anything to upset her. Three days of peace. I even felt a flicker of excitement at the thought of meeting up to discuss our deal—she'd bring me a book, and I'd give her a money assignment.

I'd spent hours creating a PowerPoint with interactive slides on what she could do first—track her absolute must-spend items, the nice-to-have items, and things she didn't need. She had to write it all down for an entire week and go back three months to see what she'd spent money on. She also had to log the cash tips she made. It was easy to spend cash because once it was gone, there was no trace of it. That was a trick from my mom. She spent all her cash from delivering pizzas on tattoos one summer, and her grandpa almost disowned her.

Another nice memory without the looming sadness. I ran my hand over my left forearm. My mom had sick tattoos, quotes and random images from her favorite albums. I always thought about getting one, but it hurt to think about what image signaled my parents. I couldn't pick one and then I'd spiral. But now…I could find a song lyric or an album they liked. I shifted nervously in the chair at the café with the croissants and watched the time. It was a minute until ten, and she wasn't there.

She might've forgotten. Which was fine. It was Monday morning, and she probably wanted to sleep. It wasn't like I could text her since we'd never shared numbers. How was that even possible? She meant more to me than almost everyone I knew, and I'd never bothered to ask her damn number? What if something happened to her and she couldn't tell me? What if she needed me? I itched my chest and bounced my knee up and down.

The door opened, and she strolled in. Relief flowed through me. *She's okay.* She was better than the sunrise in the morning. My pulse sped up, and I had the strangest urge to stand up until she sat down, to show respect. I hadn't seen her since late Saturday night, and I missed her smiling face.

I had Elle withdrawal after one day.

"Hey!" She held four brown packages against her chest and wore an old baseball cap with a hockey logo. Her plain white shirt hung off one shoulder, and a yellow strap teased me. God, was she wearing a yellow bra?

I had to fucking know.

She tilted her head, brows scrunched. "You alright?"

"Yeah, sorry. Sit." I gestured to the chair, and she plopped down, pushing her long hair over one shoulder. The movement let me smell her shampoo, and I breathed in the floral scent, discreetly. We were in a good zone right now, and I refused to ruin it. "I ordered four flavors for us."

"Oh." She set the packages on the chair between us and clapped her hands. "Want to go splitzees? Half of each one?"

"Sure."

She dug into one and did the whole cross-eyed moan thing. "Raspberry? My goodness, it's delicious."

"You've said that about every croissant you've tried."

"Well, each one is better than the last. Now—" she paused, tapping the table. "Are you ready for a blind date?"

"A date? No. No way." I shook my head, my instinct shouting at me to get out. "I told you, I'm a *three-night* guy."

My palms sweated and my chest ached at my inability to do what she said. Dating meant feelings and feelings meant eventually pain. "Elle, I never date. Ever."

She wiggled her brows, not getting the level ten panic going on inside me. "You might need three nights to really enjoy what I'm talking about."

"What—"

She plopped the packages on the table, spreading them out and making sure to not knock the croissant plate off the edge. There was writing on each package, and the shape hit me. They were books.

"Four blind dates with books, Cal. Books. Not a human. So, stop coming up with ways to run."

Not a human. She wasn't talking about someone else. Thank god. I had nothing to offer another person except three nights in bed.

I let out an awkward chuckle. "Was I that obvious?"

"Mr. Allergic to Feelings? Yes." She scrunched her nose, smiling at me with so much warmth that my chest got tight.

I focused on the books and her loopy writing. "How does this work?"

"Which one sounds good to you?"

Scientist abandoned on a planet and becomes a pirate to survive

Grumpy writer lives next to sad writer and form a slow burn relationship

Friends go skiing but one dies, and then another.

Five teenagers go into a room. One dies. But who did it?

I picked up the four options, enjoying the feel of the first choice. It was floppy. Plus... Pirate? Space? Abandoned? Those sounded more up my alley, and a flicker of excitement weaved its way in my soul. Elle glanced over at me, her teeth coming down on her bottom lip as her eyes lit up with anticipation. This mattered to her.

"This one." I set the other three off to the side and unwrapped the floppy pirate book. Elle pushed up onto her elbows, leaning closer to me as I opened it. Her excitement hung in the air, and if me reading made her this happy, I'd buy every book in the world for her. Once the paper came off, Elle took it and folded it into nice squares.

"*The Martian.*" I eyed the orange cover and read the back. "Saw the movie a while back but never knew it was a book."

"It's an interesting writing style. Please, read it, and next week you can tell me about it. I loved his storytelling." She tapped her fingers on the table, her nails yellow and orange, and she took the stack back. There was another one, a fictionized true crime one that also caught my interest, but space was cooler, and you couldn't tell me otherwise.

I could schedule a few hours a day to read it in between the gym and my plants. Honestly, hours went by without me doing a single thing some days, so it was better if I had a plan. Gave me purpose. Hanging with the guys after Ty's invitation was different. Not bad, not amazing, but all right. My skin felt too tight, and I had to force myself to laugh instead of fully relax *off* the ice, but they didn't look at me like they wanted to hit me the entire time. There were even insides jokes I was a part of now instead of looking outside in.

Even if I hated the book, I wanted to read it so I could have something else to talk to her about. "I can't wait." I held the book up and smiled.

Elle's entire face lit up, and her cheeks pinkened. "You need to smile more, Cal. You have a great one."

"Uh, thanks." I pulled on the collar of my shirt, the café seeming a little bit too warm. I set the book on my lap and retrieved my laptop from the other chair. "You ready for day one of boot camp?"

"Yes." She yawned, covering her mouth and apologizing. "Sorry, I'm exhausted."

"Late night? You should've rested since you weren't at the bar." I didn't like knowing she was tired. She worked her ass off almost every night, so I hoped she'd rested and watched TV.

"The writing group met for three hours and continued at a coffee shop and an acoustic show. I don't think Ty and I left until eleven. That was like ten hours of talking, and you know I'm a chatterbox." She shrugged, her self-deprecating joke not hitting.

All I heard was *Ty and I.* "Ty?"

Something dark and dangerous flared in my gut. It was different than my usual anger I carried like a personality trait. It was green and large and made my hands into fists.

"Yeah." She smiled, narrowing one eye like she was unsure to continue. "He asked me on a date to a baseball game first, then we met with the writing group the rest of the time."

"A date?" My mouth tasted like expired milk and I wasn't hungry anymore. Acid pooled low in my stomach, which twisted as images of the two of them flooded my head. Ty and her kissing, him touching her skin, him helping her with her plants and reading and going on trips to nurseries. I gripped the side of my chair and swallowed. I had no reason to be upset besides my own envy and fantasies. I'd practically yelled at her at the mention of a blind date, so I had no business entertaining my secret wishes.

She nodded, a wrinkle forming between her eyebrows.

Damnit. I didn't want to make her feel bad. She could date every guy on the team, and I had to be okay with it. We'd both made it clear we'd only ever be friends. I forced myself to fill the silence and remove that worry wrinkle. "Uh, how did it go?"

She rubbed her lips together, playing with the end of her hair before she shrugged. "Meh, honestly. He's great. It's not him."

"The 'it's not you, it's me' speech?" I couldn't stop my smile. *Meh* was great—for me—for purely selfish-asshole reasons. I used a hand to cover my grin so she wouldn't get suspicious, even though she dropped her gaze to my lips for a second.

"Honestly? Yeah." She made a goofy face, twisting her lips to the side and bugging out her eyes. "Shocking *no one,* but I'm a bit of a hopeless romantic. I want the swoons."

"Swoons?" That couldn't be a legit word.

She chuckled. "You know, the romantic gestures, the buzzing chemistry, the swept off my feet thing. Ty's nice, and I should be into him. On paper, he's perfect."

"Perfect?" I tilted my head to the side. He was fine, I guess. *Perfect* was a bit too far. "I wouldn't say that. I've known the guy almost three years now."

She scrunched her nose. "Perfect *for me,* I should've clarified. He's kind, patient, and loves and respects writing. That's what I meant."

Ah, right. Someone like me wasn't kind nor patient nor loved writing. I was a jerk, angry every single day, and would rather cut grass with scissors than try *writing.* She wanted everything I wasn't, and my jaw tensed. Hearing her list reasons why I wasn't the guy for her sucked, but I nodded. "Got ya. So, no swoons."

"Nope." She traced a finger—her nail orange—over a crack on the table, and a dreamy looked crossed her face. "Mr. Three Nights Only, I take it romance isn't on your top priority list?"

"No." I scoffed. "I'm one call away to leaving this place and going to the NHL and never looking back." I wasn't sure why I said it with an aggressive tone or why I didn't tell her I had no plans to do that. My degree was in honor of my parents. I wouldn't back out of that, but it seemed like I wanted to drive an even bigger wedge between me and Elle. I found myself wanting more with her without having anything to offer her. Pushing her away was for fear of me getting too attached and to not hurt her. Safer for her. I'd hate myself if she looked at me the way Sherry did. Elle was the last person I wanted to upset, and that meant protecting her from *me.*

But, even with that goal, I didn't want her with fucking Ty. A sick twisted circle. I rubbed my chest as her eyes darkened, like she was sad at the fact.

"Could that really happen?"

"Yes. I could call my agent, and he'd confirm with the team and then bam, I'd go to their minor teams in Philly." I'd thought about making that decision a million times. It'd be easier than doing college life, but lately, I'd been having a better time. The bar helped. *Elle* helped. The change on the team certainly made it more fun. The guys included me more, which... getting *attached* was too strong of a word, but I didn't feel like everyone hated me as much.

"Promise me you'll tell me if you do that." She frowned, and her shoulders bunched up by her ears. "If you leave, I want to know."

"Sure, but why?" *So she can get more support at the bar. That's why.* I tensed, needing her to confirm it was about the bar and not about me. It stung, but reality was better than living off hope or unfulfilled wishes.

She smiled. "Cause we're friends, and friends support each other. Maybe I'll get a Grizzlies shirt with Holt on the back."

God, that'd be hot. Warmth spread from my face to my thighs, a pleasant buzz of truth making me smile. She had to care about me a little bit to wear a shirt with my name on it. Knowing that there was one person besides Charlie or Reiner who gave a shit about me filled me with a weird sense of joy. I knew it'd be fleeting, but Elle cared about me. I wanted to bottle this feeling up forever. Her smiles and joy made me breathe easier.

"I'll send you one for sure," I said. "I promise."

Our gaze held, and I swore there was a moment. It was weird, like time stopped, and I could see her coming to my games and wearing my jersey and the two of us getting dessert after. She could watch my plants on road trips, and I'd make sure she didn't kill hers. I'd read every book she'd recommend, and I'd help her with money. Hell, I had enough of it that she never had to worry even though I knew she'd never let me give her any. We could argue over what was more entertaining, hockey or reading, and I could kiss her any time I wanted.

But then she blinked and sat back in her chair. The moment came and went, and I wondered if *this* was how she felt about getting lost in her mind in a good way. I didn't hate it.

"Bootcamp day one." I shook my head a little, resetting it to normal status, one where I wasn't daydreaming about being with Elle. This headspace was significantly less happy than the one I'd been in, imagining her in my life. I opened the PowerPoint and hit present. "More money, more problems."

"Oh my god." She laughed. "You didn't."

"Oh, I did."

Her answering smile made it all worth it. I clicked through the lessons, asking her to go back three months and categorize everything she'd spent money on. Then to document everything for the next few weeks. We'd look at it next time and figure out a pattern. Then we'd sort it by essential, important, and fun. She wrote down my instructions in a little journey and had a determined look on her face: all set brows and tense jaw.

"I'm impressed at your use of GIFS. You don't strike me as a GIFs kinda guy."

"Who would be?"

"I don't know, him?" She pointed to a guy in our vicinity wearing a shirt with a famous meme on it. "He totally uses GIFs."

"Fair."

We shared another smile, and I felt it low in my belly. Yeah, things had been better with her around. "Have you talked to Charlie? I wonder how he's doing."

"Just a couple of texts. He, uh, sent a bunch of stuff again to my place for Lizzie. Probably going to take it to his after this."

"Oh! Let me help! I love organizing!" She about bolted up from her chair, eyes wide with excitement. She picked up one of the croissants, shoved it in her mouth, and snapped. "See? All done."

Amused didn't begin to cover it. Charmed. Obsessed. Those were more the truth. Her expressions and way she tossed around joy were almost contagious. Three months ago, the thought of opening boxes and setting up a girl's room would've been preferred only to a root canal. But now? It'd be fun, probably.

I scratched the back of my neck, squeezing for a second. *Of course* I wanted her there, but she might be tired. "You sure? You work tonight."

"Is the sky blue? Yes, I'm sure. I drew floor plans of having my own space for three years. Room organization is my fav. Have you heard of *Get Organized?* The Netflix show?"

"No, that sounds like homework."

"Calzone, you don't even know." She gave me a goofy, almost ridiculous grin. Hearing her say a silly nickname for me made me feel lighter than I had in *years*.

"We're gonna rainbow the shit out of this. You wait and see."

CHAPTER
THIRTEEN

Elle

My forearms ached as we loaded the ten boxes for Lizzie into the back of the GLO Mobile. Charlie had really gone all out. I loved the fact everything was yellow and pink. Gendered colors were a thing of the past, but pink and yellow were my favorite combo. They were just happy colors, meaning springtime and fresh blooms and summer was near. I'd do my damndest to make sure Lizzie's room was warm and welcoming when she came back to live with Charlie.

"Regret helping?" Cal asked. I stopped rolling my wrists and doing weird stretches.

"Not even a little. Do I regret not getting into sports? A bit. My muscles are weak. I'm basically cooked pasta. Noodle arms."

"If you ever need a workout buddy, you know where to find me."

"Look at us pals," I said, needing the reminder in the universe to put me in check. We were definitely friends. We balanced each other out, but I wanted romance, and he wanted three nights.

He was emotionally stunted, like plain vanilla ice cream, and I was an extra-large milkshake with whipped cream of feelings.

Reminding myself was smart. I should set an alert on my phone to remind me every other day—JUST FRIENDS!

He shut the trunk, and we headed toward Charlie's house. Having only known the man three minutes, I had no idea where he lived, and I was pleasantly surprised to find a beautiful brick house just off of campus. The yard was perfect, grass cut. "Damn, does he have a landscaper?"

"No, I came by and mowed it."

"Don't let the hockey guys know how nice you can be. It'll ruin your terrible rep."

"I like my rep. People leave me alone," he grumbled.

"Healthy."

"Shut up."

I smiled, biting my knuckle as I admired Charlie's house. It'd be perfect for a four-year-old. Children's toys lined the street in the yards, and it really reminded me of our home back up north. Families living on the block and letting the kids play together. My heart burst for Lizzie, hoping she'd find a good life here.

I couldn't do much to help, but I'd get this room to be the best damn thing ever. "I'm going to need more than one afternoon here. I'm telling you right now." I undid my seatbelt and hopped out of the SUV. Adrenaline for a new task left me feeling high, almost like a buzz. The wire shelving, a new recipe, the bar. I loved a different focus and to go *all in*.

"You're radiating frantic energy right now."

"You have your championship, and I have my projects."

"Home renovation your thing?" He popped the trunk, and we each grabbed a box. He put the code in the garage pad, and the door opened. The smell of gasoline and grass filled the air.

"No, but I get excited about ideas and things. Daniella always said I was like a puppy with new assignments. They distract me for a white-hot minute, then I move onto something else."

He paused, a deep wrinkle in his forehead. Then he shook his head and jutted his chin toward the door. "After you."

Charlie's house smelled like a home. Evergreen candles and

coffee. I would never stereotype anyone, but I'd pictured his place as a bachelor pad. Cigarette trays. A beer sign. This was homey and nice and oh shit.

So many wooden corners. The table, the TV stand, the counter. Were four-year-olds able to navigate that? I wasn't sure. The wooden figures that looked carved would be a problem though. She'd dive right for those. Unless she had her own space.

"We need a Lizzie area, or she'll go into his stuff." I nodded, already forming what it'd look like. An arts and crafts table, a little cabinet of fun supplies. A box of toys. "Right there."

There was a spot between the TV and the front wall where we could easily move a fake tree and make it her space. Again, would never have guessed Charlie had a fake tree in his place. I loved it.

"I'll trust your judgement."

"As you should." I winked at him, quickly looking away so I didn't admire how his eyes lit up. I was a great winker. Did it all the time to people. But with him, it felt flirty. Dirty, even. It made me feel adventurous, like I was living my own romance heroine life. If I wasn't careful, I'd start daydreaming again, and my thoughts would definitely take a filthy spin. I cleared my throat. "Okay, where's her room? Do you know?"

"Upstairs, guest room. We might have to move stuff out."

"Glad I brought these guns." I flexed, earning a wicked Cal smile. Ugh, I loved it. It was probably for the best he didn't grin all the time or I'd get nothing done and stare at him. The beautiful bastard. It made no sense to be drawn to him because he was so damn grumpy, but somehow, that turned his smiles into gifts. Precious ones that very few people saw and *ugh*. My heart did a weird pang again. I rubbed my chest, willing it to go away, and it listened to me *this* time.

We treaded upstairs, and he headed to the first door on the right. It creaked when I nudged it with my foot, and a twin bed with boxes upon boxes greeted us. A lonely lamp on a black table. A stack of suitcases. Oh no, this wouldn't do.

Channeling the ladies of *The Home Edit,* I set my box down. "We need to edit and by that, get rid of."

"Charlie might not want the lamp thrown out."

"Fine, then the garage. This isn't staying in a little girl's room. That's for sure." I eyed the boxes on the bed and sighed. Definitely wouldn't be doing this in a day. I was due at the bar in two hours, and I knew my mind would be here the whole time. "Before we bring anything more in the room, let's figure out where to put this stuff."

"Okay."

There were books and magazines and glasses in the boxes. Fishing gear. Old sweatshirts? "Charlie can go through all of this, but let's move it to the garage for now, and we can sort later. What time can you meet up tomorrow? Like six?"

"Am?"

"I want to dive into this and get dirty. Yes, six am."

"Ah, well, I can miss a workout I guess."

"Or, drop me off here and go do your hockey thing. Mama will be just fine alone."

"You're a little frightening right now."

I flashed him a grin. "Thank you, Callie-Boy. Now get to work. I want to play tomorrow."

We worked for an hour straight, moving all the stuff from here to the garage. We could buy containers to sort through it later. We left the twin bed, and that was it. No sheets. We needed fun ones for her. "Could you text Charlie to ask what she likes? Shows or books or characters? We could get a comforter set for her."

"Sure." He got his phone out and texted. "Will let you know when he responds. Hey, let me carry everything else up. I can handle it. You…plot. Get lost in your head for a bit."

The soft tone and gentle look in his eyes told me he wasn't poking fun at me. He meant it, and for some reason, that got me all warm inside. "Could be awhile for me."

He reached his hand out and squeezed my wrist for two seconds. "Take your time."

Damn. He left me alone in the guest room, sweating from a little touch. His rough thumb pad trailing over the sensitive area was like a taser of attraction. I took a calming breath and sat on the end of the bed. He told me the plot. So, I did.

I knew where we'd put the toy chest, the play area, and the little vanity. We could buy picture frames and bedsheets and get a large dollhouse. I closed my eyes and pictured purple tube lights and hanging pink ones. Depending on what she was into, we could play into that too. I smiled, really hopeful that a nice room would make the journey better for her. This couldn't be easy, but kids were resilient.

Heavy footsteps thudded up the stairs, and Cal came in carrying three of the boxes. He set them down, gave me a quick smile, and headed down again. He was getting a little too loose with those grins and needed to knock it off. They messed with my plotting, that was for sure. Because I wasn't thinking about the room anymore but his mouth. He was angry at life, but would he kiss that way? Aggressive, like how he played. Dominating like the captain. Or would he kiss slow and drawn out, using his hands to explore my body before finally taking me harder?

Shit. My pulse raced, and I ducked my head the next time he came up. He had the rest of the stuff, and I pretended to look under the bed. "Nothing here."

"I'm gonna give her a hockey stick and a jersey."

I faced him, sucking in a breath at the range of emotions on his face. Open, worried, scared. He shoved his hands in his pockets and looked at me with hope.

"Yeah?"

"So she knows I'm looking out for her. Unless, that's stupid?"

"No, I love it. She has this awesome cousin on her side now. Of course it's a great idea. We could get a poster of you too and some pucks?"

"Yeah?" He lifted half his mouth up, the lack of confidence endearing me to him. "It'll go with your vision?"

"Even if it doesn't, that matters more." It was my turn to

squeeze his wrist. His was strong and warm. "It shows you care about her."

"I've never even met her and I do. It's tough."

"That's okay if it's hard, but think about this—the two of you are in the same position. Charlie is your only family, and you've both lost so much, but you gained each other."

Cal's mouth lifted up on one side for a brief second, and the same buzzing connection filled the room. I stared at his mouth, his perfect lips, as the pull to get closer to him dominated my mind. Our breathing synced, his skin warmed, and I immediately let go.

He stepped away from me. "Come on, let me take you back. We have time to get this ready." His voice was all gravely and rough.

"But tomorrow morning, we'll return?"

"Yes."

Spending an entire Tuesday morning with Cal was better than I thought. Daniella was at camp all day, and I was working during the night and was often alone, so this was a nice change. After finally exchanging numbers, Cal texted he was ready at five minutes until six. I wore an old high school shirt and shorts with paint stains on them from the one time I'd volunteered to touch up fire hydrants.

He though... mm. He wore a backwards hat, a white shirt with a hockey logo on it, and sport shorts. There was something about the athletic shorts that made his thighs seem thicker. Stronger. I buckled into the passenger seat and tried not to ogle him. It wasn't even six am yet!

"I brought you coffee and croissants *and* made some trail mix so you eat." He picked up a brown sack and handed it to me. "There is cream and sugar and almond milk in a tiny cup in there too. Wasn't certain how you preferred your coffee but wanted to make sure it had all the stuff."

I swooned at his attempt to take care of me. It was very romance hero-ish of him, even though I knew he wasn't a long-term kind of guy. Had anyone else in my life ever done anything like this before? No. It was simple and intentional.

"Very thoughtful, Cal, thank you." I sniffed the hot cup of coffee. *Vanilla.* "I'm not picky about caffeine, which you wouldn't assume about me because I'm opinionated. I like it black some days, then others with almond milk. But sometimes I just want it sweet."

"That fits you."

"Thanks? I think." I laughed and took a small sip. Still freaking hot. "You excited for our project today?"

"I'm tired, honestly. I'll wake up in a bit."

"You didn't need to walk me home last night. Alex could've." It still charmed me that on his nights off, he showed up at close and waited for me. There was no way that could continue past a week or so. He needed time to rest and relax and not worry about me. It was endearing and just another moment where Cal proved he was more than he thought. "I'll carry a knife or a bat."

"Not why I'm tired and that's not up for debate. I started reading *The Martian*."

"Oh!" I got so excited that I swatted his shoulder. He gave me a "what the fuck" look. "Sorry, I hit people when I get overjoyed. Probably not a redeeming quality. My brother hates going to movies with me because I smack him too much. Anyway, I'm a chatterbox. Tell me what you think!"

"I'm not a fast reader, but I'm enjoying it so far. Made me think about what I'd do if I was completely alone for months at a time… but then realized I kinda already have been."

It knocked the breath out of me. His admission. His self-awareness of his grief and attitude. Moments like this were tough because I wanted to have the correct response, but what was the *right* thing? Thankfully, he turned onto the side street near Charlie's house, and he continued speaking.

"His will to survive and live and try everything possible spoke to me. I haven't been that way. I chose to suffer in my solitude, and maybe I'm ready to do more now. Celebrate the good and move on."

"That's amazing, truly." The urge to hug him again overtook me, and it was a damn good thing we were in the GLO Mobile. "Nothing makes me happier when a book can really change your mindset."

"The book, yeah." He slid me a heavy glance, his eyes swirling with unsaid words. That look… shit. My breathing got heavier, almost like pants. His insinuation was clear—*I'd* helped him change his mindset, and that alone made me struggle to keep distance between us. I *loved* being his person, and it made me think about a future that wouldn't happen. Even though I realized I had feelings for him, big fat messy ones. Feelings that would eat me up and spit me out because while I knew Cal *cared* for me, that's all it would be. More than indifference. He'd never give me the happy ending and swoons and the love I'd dreamed about my whole life.

"I'm not done yet, but thanks for recommending it."

I clicked my tongue and pointed to my head, dead set on lightening the mood. "I got all sorts of ideas and recommendations in here, buddy boy. Ask and I'll deliver."

"I'm counting on it."

He pulled into Charlie's driveway, and I was anxious to get started, but the weight and warmth of his words took root in my soul and grew. I was dangerously close to getting feelings for him beyond wanting to kiss him silly. I had to come up with a way to prevent it and fast, because watching him stare at the hockey stick and jersey he brought for his little cousin? The care he put into helping Charlie? Yeah, it wouldn't be long before I dove headfirst into heartbreak.

CHAPTER
FOURTEEN

Cal

Spending the entire day with Elle made everything go by so much faster. I blinked and it was noon. Blinked again and we had to head back to get ready for the bar. I'd rather bite my tongue than admit it, but Wednesdays were my favorite because it was just us there. Her behind the bar making drinks, and me doing everything else. No Alex to catch me staring at her. That little shit made it clear they wanted me to fall on my ass.

Even after being around Elle for twelve hours straight, I craved more. I couldn't recall a single human being who I could tolerate for this long. Anyone else, I'd need at least a three-day break in between seeing their face, but with her? I didn't even want to go shower upstairs. She was infectious and wonderful. I didn't have to hide my grief or inner thoughts with her. Fuck, she'd already seen the worst parts of me and still was my friend.

That fucking F word again.

I stretched my arms over my head, working out the tension in my chest as I stood near the door. The weather was weird for a summer June day. The humidity was horrible, and the temperature had dropped majorly by the time we got here. It wasn't uncommon to have a summer storm, and I checked my phone: *tornado watch.*

Figures.

It was six, and we only had about ten people at the bar. No major sports games were on, and I grabbed the remote from the bar top. I turned on the news as Elle caught my eye.

"Tornado watch," I said.

"Oh." Her eyes lit up. "Mind if I step outside for a second?"

That was a weird ass response to learning we might have a tornado, but Elle was weird. In the best way possible. I snorted. Her brain had to be wild to visit. "Sure?"

"Thanks."

She almost jogged toward the end of the bar and out the front door. Her black ripped jeans and white shirt were torture. So simple, yet they hugged every part of her I wanted to explore. She was effortlessly beautiful, and I wished I could go back in time to that day when I'd said the terrible comment about her major. The one where she thought I'd made fun of her intelligence. Then, if I erased it, we could be something more. Maybe. If I was capable of a real relationship.

It had been more than a few minutes, and I wanted to know what she was doing. I gave the patrons a quick scan, and it was clear no one needed anything. So, I opened the door and found her standing in the middle of the road glancing up. "Elle?"

"The clouds, Cal. Look at them!"

I did, and my gut churned. They were wicked green and the sky so dark it looked like nighttime. Lightning flashed in the distance, and the air felt heavy. Really heavy. "Get inside."

"I will, but I love when the wall cloud comes in. It's romantic."

"A storm with a tornado is not fucking romantic, Elle. Get your ass inside."

She narrowed her eyes a me before tilting her head up and grinning wide. "I read once that when the rain stops, that's a bad sign. It's only sprinkling."

"Yeah, forgive me for not caring that you read something

about a storm once. They are dangerous." My impatience flared. I wasn't afraid of storms like she was of bees, but I had a good, healthy fear of them. Like a normal human being. There were a few things I didn't fuck with, and Mother Nature was one of them.

She got out her phone and took a couple of pictures, and I about had it. My skin itched with irritation at her lack of safety. The sky was so black it was like midnight, and nothing good would come of this. The bar was on the ground floor, and we had a little cellar downstairs, and I was half-tempted to carry her ass there. "Thirty seconds and I'm removing you from the road."

She shook her head and waved her hand, like I was a pesky little gnat. "Settle down, just a few more pictures."

The sirens went off, the eerie sound that reminded me of Tuesday morning drills in school. My heart skipped a beat as the dread sank its way down my body, freezing me to the spot. "That means it's a warning, not a watch, Elle!"

She finally fucking walked toward me, her face all smiles. "We rarely get tornados here."

"Don't care. Get the fuck inside." It took all my power to not yank her in the door. This damn woman was wild and got under my skin.

"Bossy." She winked at me, the little tease, and I balled my fists.

Her attitude and complete disregard for my anger only made me crave her *more*. The sirens continued, and the news said there was a tornado heading toward our city from the southwest, moving in direct path of our college town. Sweat formed on my neck, and I didn't understand why no one was freaking out.

Weather wasn't to be messed with. Mother Earth was a boss and didn't stop for anyone. Using my captain voice, I clapped my hands. "If anyone wants to make their way to the cellar for a bit, we're under a tornado warning. I'm heading down as a precaution, and you all are welcome."

Elle stared at me with a half-smile, her cheeks all rosy, but made no moves to head down where it was safe. Sure, there weren't any windows in the bar, but they said to take shelter in a basement if you had one. We did. Despite being inside, I swore the sirens got louder and then *bam*.

The entire place shook from the strength of the thunder.

The few patrons we had glanced up, and a man rose, holding his beer. "I can drink this down there, right?"

"Not a bad idea, champ." Elle cupped her hands around her mouth. "Anyone who heads downstairs gets a drink on the house. Come on, people."

That got everyone moving as another clap of thunder caused the walls to tremble. Fear was healthy. Kept people from doing stupid things—like standing outside and taking pictures of clouds, but my heart raced.

My parents had died from a rainstorm. They said the road was wet, and they must've swerved into a median, causing the car to flip over. I didn't have any trauma about rain from it because it was a freak accident, but this storm?

Any number of things could happen. Ripping the bar up from the ground, a tree coming in the door and hitting Elle. The entire foundation moving into the air. *Fuck*. I marched toward her. "Get down there."

"I'm making sure they all have drinks."

"No. I'll do it." My words came out in a pant. "Please, just go."

The TV said the tornado was miles out from our city. Miles. Tornados moved a crazy amount of miles an hour, so that meant we had minutes. "Elle, *please*."

She searched my face, the walls shaking again, and she took my hand. "Fuck the drinks."

I nodded, and I gripped her fingers hard, like she was the only thing holding me from losing my mind. She guided us down the rocky stairs as the other patrons sat on boxes or the ground. No one seemed to complain about the lack of drinks. If anything, they all looked worried.

Thunder and wind howled from outside the bar. Someone

played the radio from their phone, which announced people to take cover. If you were driving, get out of your car and find a ditch.

I swallowed and focused on Elle's fingers. They were small, and the silver ring dug into my own hand, but I didn't care. It grounded me. The dim lighting of the cellar did nothing to dampen her beauty or the worried look in her eyes. She stared at me, frowning, and then moved closer to me. She let go of my hand and put it around my waist. Like she *comforted* me. "It'll be okay, Cal. I promise."

Then the power went out.

"Oh *shit*." Elle tensed, and her grip tightened. I, too, put my arm around her shoulders, needing her closer. She smelled like strawberries and sweat, a perfect combination to settle me down.

"You got a generator?" one guy asked.

"Not sure. Let's just hang out here for ten minutes, then we can go look." My voice had an authoritative tone even though my insides were going bananas. I could throw up or scream. It was a real toss-up. It was pitch black besides the light from people's phones, and despite the fear, the darkness enhanced my other senses.

The softness of Elle's shirt and hair as it tickled my chin. The fruity way she smelled. The worry in her voice and her shallow breaths. The way her fingers dug into my side, like she was as nervous as I was while she tried to help me. The taste of the damp cellar air, a little bitter from all the cement and stored bottles.

Another thunderbolt hit, and she jumped. While I focused on her, my own fear trickled away. I ran my hand up and down her spine, closing my eyes and enjoying the slow way she relaxed into me. She set her head on my shoulder first. Then, she let out a little hum of pleasure when I got to her neck. I massaged it, then traced the outline of her ear. She'd worn hoop earrings again. I had to tell her I liked them a lot. They were playful.

In a different life, I'd be with her. I knew it in my gut. I could've made her really happy and given her what she deserved.

But it didn't do well to think about *that* version, where my parents hadn't died and left me alone.

"Think we're good now?" a patron asked, pulling me from the melancholic thoughts overtaking my brain.

It had been a bit, time losing meaning for me. Maybe ten minutes had passed? The power was still out, but Elle nodded even though no one could see her. "Yeah, I do."

"I'm gonna check it out. My wife's at home with our kids, and I want to get back."

"Be safe," she said.

The guy went up the stairs, and his footsteps pounded until the door opened. He didn't come back in, nor did Elle move from my embrace. The walls had stopped shaking at this point, so maybe the worst had already passed?

"What's the radio saying?" Elle asked.

"Moved on toward the next town. We're good." The guy pocketed his phone. "Might hang back for a few minutes then leave."

"Me too," another man said.

Without discussing it, we all headed back upstairs where it was still dark. Charlie had never installed emergency lights which made sense, but it would've been nice to not have to use our phones to avoid tripping. Elle and I still held hands, which I wasn't going to mention. I liked the connection. I guided us toward the bar where we left everything as it was.

"Don't bother with the tabs tonight." Elle took a shaky breath. "Our system is down."

"Hell, just keep the change. It's on me." The mustached man with long gray hair slapped a hundred on the bar. "This should cover everyone's, right? Plus tip?"

"Thank you, but it's not necessary."

"Tough, Sunshine. Take it."

She smiled at him, the flashlight hitting her eyes so that they seemed even more brown. Speckled with gold and green on the edges, they almost looked hazel, and *fuck* I was thinking about her eye color and how it reminded me of plants and moss. I broke apart our hands and ran my fingers through my hair. I didn't even know who I was anymore.

"Be safe out there, y'all." Elle pushed herself to sit on the bar, her bare legs dangling over the edge. She crossed them at the ankles. "Cleaning up and shutting down should be fun, huh, Calzone?"

"Let's do the bare minimum and come back tomorrow." I squinted in the dark toward the trash and the few glasses we had to clean. Thankfully, since it had been slow, we'd both kept up on side work, so the final touches wouldn't be major ones. I got out my phone and searched for power outages, and there was a social media post about multiple powerlines being hit. *Hours.* It could be hours until there was power. "Probably won't come back on tonight."

"The freezer." She frowned, and I traced the curve up her lips with my eyes, damn near able to picture every feature of hers from memory. "I don't wanna throw all the food and storage away."

"Charlie doesn't have too much back there." The walk-in cooler though…that would be a lot of spoiled items. "We could go buy a generator and use it for that?"

"I think we have to. That's thousands of dollars." She chewed on her lip as the last customer left. They'd all slapped a few bills on the bar, leaving Elle and I each a hundred bucks in tips. It felt weird to do nothing to earn it, but if I put it toward the generator, it'd make me feel better.

"Let's pick up the glasses and go. I'll drive."

An hour later, we returned from the hardware store with a generator. The stormfront looked super cool when we were on the back end of it, and Elle even got me to stop and take two photos. The wall cloud was artistic in a way, just terrifying.

After a lengthy call with Charlie on how to set up the generator to the walk-in cooler, we had it up and running so the perishables wouldn't need to be thrown out. It felt good to save them.

Without the air conditioning though, the bar was hot as hell, and Elle was feeling it too. Sweat beaded on her forehead and upper lip, and her white shirt kept sticking to her. She wore a lacy bra thing underneath, and every time the fabric clung to her, my stomach swooped.

"My brother just texted me. Want to head over there for a bit? He has power and air. God, I'm a hot potato." She fanned herself with her shirt, lifting up the end to wipe her face

Jesus. Her stomach and her skin and the bottom of her bra showed as she wiped sweat from her brow. Nothing about the situation was sexy, but my skin prickled with need. I wanted to lick the sweat off her. *Too far.*

"Um, Van Helsing's?" Did I want to hang out at his place? Not at all. But Elle should, and I knew, somehow, she'd refuse to go if I stayed back. My former teammate and I had come a long way to be friendly, but he'd warned me off his sister countless times, and he'd see right through my restraint. I ran a hand over my face, sweat dripping down my temples. "He has air, you say?"

"Sure does. Lots of it." She wiggled her eyebrows before her gaze dropped to my chest. "You're so sweaty, Cal."

"So are you." I eyed her right back, trying not to stare at the faint outline of her breasts. They were *right* there, and with the damp shirt..." We should change before we leave."

She rubbed her lips together, an odd look crossing her face. "So, you're coming?"

My stomach sank. "Unless you'd rather I don't. I can hang here. Actually, it's best if I do. You go. I'll drop you off."

"What? No! If you're not going, I'll stay with you." She shook her head and walked toward me. Her loyalty and care knocked the breath out of me. It made me feel *too damn much.*

I held up a hand. "No."

"Cal Holt. We've been buddies all day, and we're not stopping now. Your nose is sweating, and our apartments will be even hotter. Let's shower and head to Gabe's for a few hours."

Buddies. Pals. Besties. It was a gift and a punishment for her to call me *buddies*. I wanted so much more but knew I couldn't offer it. I pinched my nose, feeling the moisture, and sighed. She was right. The rain had brought more humidity, and I'd admit I smelled. "Fine. Shower, then we leave."

"Yes, sir." She saluted me before we left the bar and made our way to our building. It was wild to me how these walks and bar-shifts were becoming my favorite part of the day. It had only been two weeks of us doing this, but it seemed like so much longer. I didn't even want to think about what happened when Charlie returned. Did I stop working? Did I want to?

No. I planned to hang out with Elle in any capacity she'd have me. Even though I couldn't offer her more than friendship or three nights, it made me wish I could. However, I couldn't go through the pain again. That part of my heart had already been destroyed.

CHAPTER
FIFTEEN

Elle

Gabe was one of those sneaky hosts. I thought I'd be nice and responsible and have one glass of wine. One. Uno. But Gabe would refill it every so often, and I'd lost count. It had to be more than one. My tongue felt lazy, and I really wanted to lay down on the fluffy pillow on his couch. Who bought him that fluffy pillow? Dani? Didn't seem likely.

Wine and a cards game. How Midwestern of us. Well, Dani wasn't drinking wine. She went for beer. Gabe went for whiskey. Cal… hm. I studied him and his pinched lips and wide-eyed expression. He reminded me of those deer you saw driving late at night in the cornfields. The *how the hell did I get here* face.

"I invited you," I said, nudging his shoulder. He raised his eyebrows and tilted his head to the side like a cute lost puppy. "You had a face. Like a deer. Like, *why* am I here and how did I get here and what's life's purpose?"

"That's a lot of questions for one look."

"You're the one doing it." I reached my finger toward his forehead and smoothed one of the wrinkles there. His skin was warm to touch, and I swore he leaned into me for a bit.

"Do you usually touch people's faces?" my brother asked. His tone was off, a little edge to it. "Or just *Cal's?*"

"She does it to everyone," Cal said rather quickly. Too quickly in fact.

"No, I don't."

"You touch people at the bar all the time."

"Not their foreheads. That'd be weird. A stranger touching your face?" I frowned, confused as to why Gabe glared at Cal and Cal narrowed his eyes at me. I was not a forehead toucher? "It's your wrinkle. It's like, permanent on your face from the frowns."

"Elle." Gabe pointed his thumb in the kitchen. "Can I talk to you?"

"Um, okay?" I shared a look with Daniella, and amusement danced all over her face. "Why do I feel like I'm going to end up grounded?"

She snickered. "You might be."

I pushed up from the couch and took my time dragging my feet to talk to my brother. This felt dramatic. Like our family had secrets or something. He stood with his hands on his hips, and when I hopped in the room, he glared at me. "You and Cal."

"What? You and Cal, what? That wasn't a question or even a statement. It was naming two nouns in the room."

"Jesus, Elle." He ran a hand through his hair. It had gotten longer. He could almost do a bun at the very top if he wanted. I could get Dani to try it and send photos. Yes, that idea was great.

"Why the hell are you smiling? This is serious."

"I was thinking about your manbun situation."

"I don't—" He played with his hair and frowned. "Wow, it is long."

"Yup."

"Anyway, you and Cal. What is going on?"

"Nothing? We're friends? Which, I don't appreciate this tone of conversation. It shouldn't matter if him and I were doing it every hour of every day. Don't pull the big brother bullshit with me."

"Ah." He covered his ears with his hands, real maturely. "None of that."

I rolled my eyes. "You're banging my best friend, so shut your mouth."

Gabe groaned and shook his head fast before refocusing on me. "He's been through a lot, and I don't think he's in the right headspace to be good for you."

Irritation danced down my spine. "Thank you for your opinion. I will file it away with the others you've given without asking."

His lip almost quirked. "God, you're annoying."

We shared a smile.

"I appreciate you trying to look out for me, I do, but Cal and I really…we're friends. We agreed that's best, but even if we weren't, I'd expect you to be nothing but nice and *normal*. So, I'm going to say you asked me about a gift for Daniella when I go back out there, and you will behave."

"Were you always this bossy?"

"Eh, I'm growing into it. Feels good. Fits me."

"Be careful, alright? I know you. He's not the guy for you, and the last thing I want is for you to be hurt. Because he will hurt you. He can change, but at the first snag, he'll go back to that asshole who almost broke our team."

I refused to judge someone on past behavior when they'd grown. Sure, Gabe meant well, and his words weren't entirely wrong. I *knew* Cal would crush me if I let myself continue down this path of feelings. He wasn't my romance hero, but I still wanted him. Even if it was just as friends. "Thanks for the warning, I'm well aware of who he is."

"Good."

"Now is that all?"

"More wine?"

"No, you little dog. I was planning on having one glass. One! And it's been more than that because my tongue feels weird and fuzzy. That only happens when I'm almost drunk."

He shrugged, not looking one bit sorry, and marched right on back to the living room with Dani and Cal. His warning couldn't have been more obvious. *Can we talk in the kitchen?* Ugh. I had to come up with something plausible if Cal asked about it later.

A part of me didn't want him to hear Gabe's warning. It felt like betraying him, to hear someone else say the words I already knew. I blamed the wine fog for the heavy weight in my body, and I forced it away when I went back to join the group. We were having an aggressive game of *Life,* as one does when the power is out. I didn't want to get too cocky, but I was winning. Sure enough, I had enough *Life* tiles to make me a billionaire, and I was not only tipsy but also smug when I won.

Life turned into *Cards Against Humanity*, then card games. Cal laughed three times, and I knew because I watched him like a hawk. He obviously gave nothing away, but the laughs made me hope he enjoyed himself. By the time I looked at my watch, it was almost midnight. On instinct, I yawned. "How is it already this late? Ooh boy."

"I'll get you water." Cal got up and returned a minute later with a water bottle from the fridge. "You should hydrate."

"You too!" I thanked him and took the cap off. He chugged his own, the tops of his cheeks a little pink. It charmed me. Was Cal Holt tipsy?

Gabe put the final game away in a closet before coming back out, arm around Dani. "You both drank too much to drive back. Stay here where there's air."

"I can call a rideshare if you'd rather I leave." Cal's voice wasn't rude, but it was firm. "I had too many to drive. Usually I'm more controlled."

"You were getting into the games, bro."

"I know." Half of Cal's mouth curved up, Gabe smiling back at him, and I was all heart-eyed emojis. They'd bonded. How adorable.

"Don't call a car. I have an air mattress, and the couch is great. Slept on there a few times." Gabe tossed a green bag on the ground. "I have to work in the morning, but I can make breakfast before I go."

Cal looked at me, uncertainty in his eyes, like he wasn't sure what to do. I nodded, almost as if he wanted my permission, and his shoulders relaxed. "Thanks."

"Sure thing. I gotta sleep though, or I'll be shit tomorrow. This job thing is no joke." He said good night, Daniella following him but not before making wide eyes at me and Cal.

I flipped her off.

But then it was me and Cal alone in their living room with a couch and an air mattress between us. A million and one questions raced in my head. He'd slept on my couch before, but things were different now. Somehow. I chewed on my lip as he handed me the water I'd set on the table. "Finish this, Elle."

"Always taking care of me." I smiled up at him, my heart beating fast despite the alcohol. "Walking me home, bringing me snacks, the storm, now."

I wasn't certain because he ducked his head, but I swore the tips of his ears turned red. A blushing Cal would kill me. Murder my feelings completely. My insides got warm and gooey, and I wanted to stare at him the whole night. Maybe say more things to make him get red. The infamous *punk* hockey guy blushed because of me. I was drunk on the power. He took the mattress out and plugged it in. He didn't look at me, and I knew he'd heard the compliment.

I poked his shin with my toe. "You ignoring me?"

"Hardly," he said, all gravelly and grumpy. "Would you prefer the couch or mattress?"

"The couch is longer, so would that be better for you since you're taller?"

His shirt stretched across his back, his muscles pulling firm, and my mouth dried up. *Damn wine.* I took another sip of water, to be healthy of course, and let my gaze move toward his ass. The fabric hugged his glutes tight as he bent over and made sure the air mattress was set up.

He really was delicious.

"What?" He turned, eyes wide and focused on my mouth. "What did you say?"

"I think I asked about the couch."

"No, the *other* thing you said." He seemed tight enough to break. His shoulders tense, his chest all thick, and his arms. *Mm.* His hands were fisted, and the movement caused his forearms to bulge.

"Uh," I said, licking my lips to get moisture on them. "You're tall?"

"Elle." He stepped toward me, his nostrils flaring.

"I didn't know I said anything else. To be fair, I'm tired and tipsy and you're really hot. Oh! Did I say you were delicious out loud? Shit. I thought I'd thought it in my mind. Oops." I giggled, the wine preventing any shame or embarrassment. That would surely come later. Cal looked in pain. I took pity on him. "Don't worry, Mr. Three-Night Stand, I'm not hitting on you. Just admiring your body." I gripped his forearm and squeezed. "These bad boys are dangerous. All these cords and muscles?" I traced one with my pointer finger, and he shivered.

Interesting.

He sucked in a breath. His skin was so warm to touch. "Elle, please."

I wasn't sure if it was a plead to continue to or to stop. There was fire dancing in his eyes, and I really wanted to explore that. But he stilled my hand with his and dropped it to my side. The fire disappeared from his gaze, and his mouth was set in a firm line, like he was pissed.

My stomach sank, and the *oh shits* blasted through the wine filter. I felt stupid. My throat got tight, and my eyes almost prickled. The removal of my hand was pure rejection. I wasn't even sure what I was offering, but it was a hell no from him, and I didn't know how to handle that. With a shaky breath, I focused on getting pillows. "Uh, I'll search the closet."

"Elle, look—"

"No, it's okay. It's great. Please don't." I didn't want to hear his thoughts. Not right now when I still felt the tingling from his touch only to be cooled down by the look in his eyes. The closet faced away from where he stood, thankfully, and I used the second to settle. Gabe legit had just warned me that Cal would hurt me.

I *knew* better, but the pained expression on his face did me in. Did I think maybe, secretly, that I was different? Ugh, how fucking cliché. I wasn't. It was the same with my family... I wasn't extraordinary. I wasn't one to break the mold or be an outlier when it came to a writing career.

Damn wine made me spiral in self-doubt. That was what this was. I sighed, took a few deep breaths in the safety of the closet, and grabbed two pillows and cases. There was an old gray sheet that would fit the air mattress, and I got that too. "Decide on where you want to sleep?"

"You take the air mattress." He neared me and took the sheets out of my hand. "I'll make it for you."

If he looked at me, I wasn't sure because I focused on the pattern of the pillow. It wasn't fancy at all. God, I was tired. The constant working at the bar, then getting Lizzie's room ready, then the wine...and the emotions I got around Cal. It was a lot. Gabe had two fuzzy blankets that he'd totally stolen from our parents' house, and I grabbed the dark green one. I wanted to burrito myself and pass out.

"Here. Your bed is ready."

"Thanks." I ducked my head and fell onto the mattress, letting out a little oomph from the pressure on my chest. It wasn't the coziest place to sleep, but it would work for a night. I fluffed my pillow and got comfortable. I was a stomach sleeper most of the time, and I made sure to face away from the couch.

Cal shuffled around for a bit before I heard him sink onto the couch. He was heavy so the springs creaked, and he exhaled, loudly, like something was on his mind. I sure as hell wasn't gonna ask. Nope. I couldn't handle being rejected twice in ten minutes. A girl only had so much confidence.

"We're at your brother's place, Elle," he said, a few minutes later.

My eyes were closed and my breathing relaxed, but my mind wasn't near ready to fall asleep. And then he'd said the most obvious statement ever.

"Yes, great observation."

He laughed. "Wow, the attitude. I kinda like it. I meant," he paused. "You touched me, and I fucking loved it. But we're here, and your brother...doesn't approve."

Split right in the middle. I was thrilled to know he loved my touch, but I was annoyed at the excuse of my brother. "I wasn't gonna strip down and fuck you, Cal. And, if I *did* want to do that, it should be up to me. Not my brother."

Damn. That was bold. I smiled into my pillow where Cal couldn't see. Maybe the lack of filter had a time and place. Normal me would've come up with that line hours or even days later. Plus, I was pretty sure I'd stunned him into silence. Five minutes had gone by without a response. The silence grew, and the hum of the fridge and the weight of the day got me sleepy. I could figure out the emotions I had, or didn't have, for Cal tomorrow.

For now, I needed sleep.

CHAPTER **SIXTEEN**

Cal

This was a form of hell. Elle's soft breaths might as well have been freight trains with how they stole my attention. At some point in the night, she'd rolled over and faced me. The blanket had been tossed to the side, and her shirt rode up her stomach.

She was a dream. Off-limits because I wasn't good enough for her, but a dream.

The hurt in her eyes earlier upset me more than she realized, but it further reinstated the ultimate truth—one her brother had made very clear. They didn't realize their voices carried into the bathroom. *I'm well aware of who he is.*

The few beers I had caused the guilt and regret double with their impact. I put my arm over my eyes, slowing my breath because Elle was right. She did know who I was. The guy who was a total dick to her all those months ago. The guy who did three nights, who was allergic to feelings, and was obsessed with rehabilitating plants. The guy who at first had said they weren't excited about getting a cousin.

And more importantly, I was the one her brother would never approve of. God, Gabe had seen some shit. My stage of hooking up with a different girl every night. The fighting. Fuck, that was a rough freshmen year. The partying. The asshole behavior. Even if things had changed…I couldn't be the guy Elle deserved. So, when her fingers had caressed my skin, heat flaring in her eyes, I had to stop it.

She would end up hurt, and I refused to be that person.

I had to make that clear in the morning because she'd assumed I was turning her down. I saw her disappointment and the way she'd avoided my gaze the rest of the night. Her flushed cheeks, the slump of her shoulders. I rubbed my eyes hard to the point white lights danced around them, and I tried to relax. It was four am. Way too early to get up. But my mind raced with impatience.

I thought about the bar, what we needed to do. Then Charlie's house and Lizzie's room. Didn't Elle realize that we would be spending hours together? There'd be no escape until Charlie got back and hired someone else to take more shifts. That was weeks, maybe months. When, not if, I hurt her, she'd have to be around me, and I'd make it worse.

She groaned in her sleep, and I froze, like she could read my mind. But she readjusted her position and faced the other way. It wasn't entirely better because her shorts hugged her ass, and her lower back teased some ink. *Fuck.* Was there a tattoo on her spine? A hint of letters peeked out from her shirt, but I couldn't figure out what it was. I wanted to know. Desperately.

Instead of falling back asleep, I thought about Elle's tattoo until the sun rose and Gabe came into the kitchen in black pants and a nice shirt. Coach made us dress up for games, but seeing him in a suit for *work* was weird. Glad to have someone up so I could get off the damn couch and away from Elle, I padded into the kitchen to join him. "Thanks for letting us stay."

"Like I'd kick my sister out." He made a pot of coffee, his gaze assessing me.

"Okay, thanks for letting me stay."

"Sure."

There was something about his tone that had me on edge. He sounded defensive, and I thought about their conversation I overheard. I scratched my chest and waited for him to face me. "I'm not going to hurt her."

He snapped his gaze to my face, and his eyes narrowed. "Cal…"

"No, I heard you last night. For what it's worth, your voices carry into the bathroom if you want to warn someone about another guest."

"I'm not apologizing." He smirked. "You've made great progress on the ice. You've stepped up as a leader for the team, and I know Coach is pleased. I'm happy for you and the team. But the same sentiment doesn't apply to Elle. She's… hopeful. Romantic. Her head is always in a book. She deserves the absolute best."

And I'm the worst. I heard his unsaid words, my gut aching even more. None of these things were untrue, but a part of me had held some flicker of hope that I was enough. That I could *maybe* one day find what my parents had together, that I could get over my fear of getting hurt and open up to someone if they gave me a real chance. His insistence that I wasn't chipped away at that hope, little by little.

"Agreed." My voice was lower than before. I refused to show him that he'd hurt my feelings because I didn't have those. Feelings were what caused my issues from the start and the less I had, the happier… well, the *less-angry* I'd be.

Van glared at me. "I see how you watch her."

"Glad your eyesight is going with your age."

"Oh, it's like that?" He laughed, the warning leaving his tone.

"I care for her, alright? Not in the way you're threatening me, but I worry about her. I walk her home from the bar every night, bring her food. I'm going to be there for her as a friend as long as she wants me to be. You can't stop that."

He frowned, rubbing his lips together. "Thank you for making sure she's safe. I figured something happened, but she won't tell me about it."

I shrugged. She could share what she wanted.

Gabe shook his head. "Protecting her secrets?"

"Is that coffee ready?"

Gabe laughed and got two mugs, a lightness to his tone that hadn't been there at the start. I hoped I'd reassured him that a) I knew I wasn't good for her and b) I would never hurt her (again). It was clear Elle hadn't told him about our conversation with his parents, which I was glad of. He would've punched me in the jaw.

"Now that I'm convinced you'll stay in the friend zone, I actually think you two are perfect as friends."

"Why?"

"Both can get into trouble. Smart asses. Talented in your own way. Total opposites though. You can learn from each other, ya know?" He poured his coffee into a to-go mug, mine in an old black one, and then he got two more out. Sugar and cream in one and sugar in the other. That one was Elle.

"We already are. We have this deal—"

"Morning, gentlemen." Elle yawned as she walked in and sat on the stool next to me. "Heard your dumb voice going through all the reasons why Cal and I are friends. Did you also do this with me and Daniella? Who was mine first by the way."

"Aware of that, Eleanor."

"*Eleanor?*" I repeated, my lips curving up, because what a name. "That's your name?"

"My parents love Eleanor Roosevelt. I can't help their choice twenty-one years ago, Calzone. Elle is just fine."

I snorted and hit my shoulder into hers. "Eleanor. I see it."

"Whatever." She rolled her eyes and yawned again. "I need caffeine and aspirin."

"On it." Gabe handed her the mug with sugar and a bottle of aspirin. "So, what deal do you and Holt have?"

"A sex deal."

Gabe choked as I lost my balance. "Elle, what the fuck?" Gabe yelled.

She laughed hard, throwing her head back and sounding wonderfully insane. "Oh, the two of you. Chill out. He's helping me with finances, and I'm getting him to read."

"Do you need money?" Gabe asked, glaring at me like I was the reason she made the joke. My own face burned, but her witty reply amused me.

"No. I told you already."

"They why ask him?"

"This is fun to listen to," I said, earning a cheeky smile from Elle.

Gabe scoffed at me. "I could've helped you."

"Sure, but then I get to make Cal read which is way more fun." Elle leaned into me, her head on my shoulder, and I froze. What the hell was she doing? Taunting her brother like this?

The floral scent of her shampoo hit me, and I had to slowly breathe it in because Gabe looked furious. His gaze zeroed in on where she touched me, and I took a step the other way. Clearing my throat, I asked, "You ready to leave, Elle? I want to check on the bar."

"Probably a good idea. Plus, I want to get back to Lizzie's room?"

"Who is Lizzie?"

"We're preparing Cal's new cousin's room ready at Charlie's house. Charlie, the owner of the bar and Cal's uncle, just found out he has a daughter. He's visiting her for a few weeks, and we're preparing for a little girl. It's so much fun."

Gabe blinked and looked between the two of us. "So, you work at the bar together and are getting the house ready?"

"Yup." Elle popped the P, downed the hot coffee, and set the mug on the counter. "Thanks for the wine, games, and air. Appreciate you."

"Cal, why don't you start the car?" Gabe said, not leaving

room for argument. I took the cue and got out of there. It had been stupid to stay the night. Nothing good had come from it. I headed out the door but not before I heard Elle's voice.

"Before you say a word, Gabe, please understand I warned Daniella about you multiple times. If you want a mirror to talk about your past, let me know, and I'll gladly remind you. Now, I'm leaving."

She walked out, paused when she saw me listening, and a wry smile filled her face. "I'm impressed you were eavesdropping. Thought you'd be too scared of Gabe."

"No." I shook my head and hated how I flushed. "You're loud. Your voice carries."

"Sure, sure." She hit my arm and bounced toward the car. I had a small headache, and it wasn't even fair she wasn't a little hungover. If she was, she hid it well.

We hopped into my car, and my comfort went right back to normal. She never mentioned her joke about the sex deal or the fact she'd thought I turned her down last night. If anything, she was in a better mood?

"What's the smile for, Eleanor?"

"Ugh, that was a terrible rhyme, and I hate it." She slid me a glance. "But I'm just happy. I've been looking forward to leaving my hometown and attending Central State ever since Gabe signed here, and I'm doing it. Found a job I enjoy, am living with my best friend, and had a game night. Game nights back home included my parents, who I love. But I crashed on an air mattress? Like, this is the life!"

What an odd thing to be excited about, but I didn't say that. I just admired her joy and outlook. She was so thrilled about simple moments. When had something like a game night made me happy? Years?

"How did you envision your future here?" I asked, wanting to know more about what went on in her head. Her mind and daydreams fascinated me. *Does she daydream about me?*

She rolled her teeth over her lip a few times before messing with her hair. "Don't laugh or snort or make fun of me, but *romantic* is the word I'd use. Late library nights where I'm meeting a writing deadline. Coffee shops. The smell of leaves in the fall. College gear. Oh my god, I love wearing clothes with the Central State Logo. It's a problem."

"That sounds nice." It did through her lens. Not mine.

"That's not all though, I want the stories I talk about for twenty years. The staying up too late nights. The secret places not every student knows about on campus. The internships or group projects that give you friends for life as you suffer through the pain. The bookstores with funny drink names. I want the romance, finding love that consumes me. Even if it breaks my heart, I want to feel like I'm one thousand percent someone's *yes*. Like, *yes*, I make their soul dance." She sighed and had the biggest smile on her face, I wanted to scream *let me be that person*.

I'd been doing college wrong. I had none of that, none of her vision and hope and dreams. I had a team who only started maybe not hating me the past year. I had Reiner, my uncle, and...*her*. The picture she painted left no room for my dark soul, and it physically hurt my chest to accept I could never be hers.

I knew it'd end in heartbreak for her, and she deserved the best.

With a defeated sigh, I focused on the road. Leaves and debris littered the streets from the wind, but there wasn't any real damage from the storm, thank goodness.

"Okay, what are you thinking, Mr. *Sighs Like That* and doesn't respond?"

"I hope you find that. That's all."

"You and me both, buddy. Now, should we make sure the bar is alright now or show up early before tonight's shift?"

"You go home. I'll double check everything and call Charlie."

"I can help!"

"I need to be alone for a bit." My stomach sank as soon as the words came out, and I prepared myself to take even more steps back with Elle. My face burned hot, and I gripped the wheel tighter, trying to do mental gymnastics on how to retract that statement. "It's not... you're not—"

"Hey, no reason to explain. I get it." She squeezed my forearm but immediately let go. "Thank you for being honest."

"You're not mad?"

"No. You're stating what you need, and I'd be a dick to disrespect that. We all require some solo time every once in a while. Plus, my brother is extra as fuck. Throw in you have a complicated relationship with him? Yeah. I could use a few hours of silence too."

I swallowed hard, unable to express my gratitude. She got it. One thousand percent understood my need, and it was the first time ever someone didn't call me an ass or make a jab about being a dick. Even my teammates were jerks when I went off on my own after a road trip. When you spent the last four years alone, you got used to it and missed the silence.

We arrived at our apartment a few minutes later, neither one of us saying anything as I locked the car and walked her to the front of the building. She flashed me one of her sunshine smiles, all teeth and wrinkles around her eyes. "Text me if you need help, okay?"

I nodded. I had to express what this meant to me, but no words came except "Thank you, Elle."

Her eyes warmed before she headed inside, and I stood there, hands in my pockets, looking up at the sky. *Why* couldn't I be different? Why couldn't I have another life, one where I could enjoy her daydream about college?

I rubbed my chest at the rush of unfamiliar pain. It made it hard to breathe for a second, not unlike the panic attack but nowhere near the racing pulse. It was more of a pang, like I was so close to getting something I wanted, but it was just out of reach.

Ignoring it, I went to the bar and counted down the minutes

until I could see Elle again. She was the best part of my day, and I wanted to enjoy her as long as I could. I certainly didn't deserve someone like her in my life and it was only a matter of time before I pushed her away.

It was what I did best.

CHAPTER
SEVENTEEN

Elle

For two weeks after the *forearm* incident at my brother's, I kept my attraction to Cal at bay. It was there, hidden, deep down that came out at night when I might've thought about his arms while I used my vibrator. Okay, I did. All the time. In fact, I was getting sick of using a toy every single night when the man in question was *right* there.

But. He'd made it clear we were friends, and I was cool with it. For the most part. I definitely vetoed any ideas about dating other people though. It wasn't fair to go out with someone else when my mind was surrounded by Cal.

His cologne, his disgruntled laugh that sounded like he faked it. His throat when he drank water. Yeah, I was so horny for him that watching him sip water out of a glass at the bar was like porn. The drop of moisture fell down his wicked jawline and over his throat. My tongue swelled, desperate to suck the water drop off his skin.

I'd gotten off in the shower before tonight's shift to get a handle on it, but it did nothing to stifle my feelings. Those bad boys were dangerously tipping close to *more* than friends.

Especially watching him right now as he paced the bar. I was close to asking to be his *three-night stand* just to get rid of my desire for him.

"She's gonna be here in ten minutes." He clasped his hands behind his back and stared at the door. "My cousin."

"It's going to be great, Cal, don't worry." I smiled at him, but he didn't see. Alex and I shared a look, their eyes softening. Charlie was bringing Lizzie to the bar today to show her where he worked. We all wanted to meet her, and we'd even gotten pink and yellow balloons, her favorite colors. Cal and I had worked like mad to get her bedroom ready, and it had a yellow and pink unicorn theme.

"What if she hates me?" he asked, a rare vulnerability entering his dark eyes. He met mine for the first time since he arrived, and I wanted to hug him so badly.

"She's a child who lost her mom. She's not going to hate you. I bet she's excited to have a new family member. I promise."

"Everyone I've met has hated me at some point. Alex, you, even Charlie thought I was a little shit. I can't fuck this up." He ran a hand through his hair once, then twice, pulling on the ends so it looked a little wild.

"Then don't." Alex walked up to him and put their hand on his shoulder. "You might be rough around the edges, but you have a good heart buried deep under that muscle."

Cal held my gaze before exhaling long and slow. "My gift is stupid."

"What did you buy her?" We all bought little presents to welcome her to the bar. Alex got her a black pair of boots—surprising no one. I found a cute unicorn stuffed animal and backpack, but Cal hadn't shared.

Until now.

"A shirt with my name on the back. A pink hockey puck. A unicorn lunch box." He gulped and tensed. "I hear them."

"Hey," I said, walking up toward him so I stood on one side

and Alex the other. I slipped my fingers into his and squeezed. "Love her. That's all she needs."

"What if I've forgotten how to love?" he whispered.

My heart shattered into little Cal pieces, and I wanted to answer that question with a megaphone. He hadn't forgotten how to love, but he just showed it differently. He wasn't kind words and big proclamations. He was gestures and caring from behind the scenes. My chest ached as my own feelings for him doubled in size. I tabled my thoughts until Charlie and Lizzie walked in.

She was *adorable*. She wore white jeans with navy chucks. An orange hat, big sunglasses, and her hair was in a messy ponytail to the side. Her dark brown hair and little hand in Charlie's was too much.

"Hey team, this is my daughter, Lizzie."

"Hi!" I bent down, letting go of Cal's hand. "It's so nice to meet you. I love your glasses. You look fabulous."

"They were my mom's."

"She had great taste then because you look like a princess." I smiled as she pushed them up and put them in her tiny pink purse. "Are you ten? You look ten years old."

"No, I'm four." She moved closer to Charlie, her eyes moving over me and Alex to Cal. "Is that him?"

Ugh, my heart. She stared at her cousin, eyes wide and filled with hope. I watched as Cal mimicked my stance and got onto his knees. "Hi, Lizzie."

They stared at each other for a second before Lizzie *dove* into his arms. She was so tiny compared to Cal, and I tried not to cry as Cal hugged her back. She rested her head on his shoulder, and he lifted her, blinking a lot.

"She was so excited to meet her cousin." Charlie beamed. "Talked about you the whole way here. Her school had a family day, and she learned about cousins but was upset she never had any. Until now."

Cal still held onto her as he leaned her back to look at her.

Lizzie smiled up like he hung the moon. "I've always wanted a cousin."

"Me too."

"Then I'm glad we have each other." Cal swallowed hard, flicking his gaze to me for a beat. I nodded, overcome with emotion at seeing him and her together. The bastard might think he'd forgotten how to love, but how could he know that for sure? He looked at Lizzie with so much warmth and adoration that tears were absolutely gonna fall down my face.

I sniffed and turned away, Alex coughing into their fist. What an emotional moment.

"Everyone brought you gifts, Lizzie." Charlie ran a hand down her back. "Want to open them?"

"More presents?" She hopped down from Cal and stared at her dad. "For me?"

"It's a 'welcome to our town' gift, yeah." Charlie pulled out a chair, and she plopped on it. "We can take all of them back to our house."

"Right. I live with you now. Because mommy is gone."

"We're a new family, but we can hang up the pictures of your mommy in your room."

"I miss her." Lizzie's voice cracked, and soon tears came. I wanted to pick up this brave girl and hug her hard. I couldn't imagine her emotions right now. If I tried, I'd break down. Charlie looked tormented, but before he did anything, Cal got back onto his knees and held Lizzie's hand.

"I miss my mom. Every day."

"Yours is gone too?"

He nodded. "It's hard. It's okay to cry and miss her."

She sniffed. "Do you?"

"Yes."

Watching Cal comfort her made me fall for him even more. He was so damn kind and gentle, and my throat ached from holding back all the things I wanted to say. That he was amazing and strong and wonderful in his own grumpy way.

She wiped her nose on the back of her arm as Cal grabbed one of the presents. "Want to see if you like it?"

"Yeah."

We sat around watching the cutest little girl in the world open our gifts. She squealed over each one, even Alex's. She wanted to put on the black boots, making us all laugh. Charlie and Lizzie didn't stay long before Charlie insisted they get back to their house. She hugged Cal hard before leaving, and when the door shut, there was a comfortable, emotional silence.

"Fuck, I love her." Alex broke it, laughing and hitting their hand on the table. "She's a diva, but god, she's strong."

"Yup. She'll be alright. Charlie was just bursting with love. How amazing?" I said, both of us looking at Cal.

He seemed stunned, staring at his hands before saying, "I can't describe this protective urge right now. There's nothing I wouldn't do for her."

"That's love, Calzone."

"Yup. A big heaping pile of emotions." Alex grinned. "That kid is lucky. Even with losing her mom, she's gaining a great guy of a dad and you. Did you see how excited she got about the black boots though?"

"Oh my god, yes. And how she threw the puck thinking it was a ball? You have so much to teach her Cal."

He ran his hands over his face before unleashing the biggest, best, sexiest smile I had ever seen on him. It was pure joy and excitement, and I felt it all the way to my toes. *Oh my.*

"I didn't fuck this up!" He clapped his hands. "Damn. I have an adrenaline rush. I was so fucking nervous. Woo, it was like a pre-game warm-up on steroids."

"You did great." Damn, emotion flowed through my voice. There was no way he'd missed that tone and didn't know the depth of what I felt for him. It gushed out of me. I cleared my throat and busied myself by pushing in chairs. They were already straight, but realigning them gave me something to do.

Alex stared at me too hard, so I turned my back to them and redid the napkins at a table. Just the resident cleaner here.

"I know it won't be easy, and she'll get to know me more, but I can already see taking her to hockey games or for ice cream or to the doll store. Does she like dolls? I don't know, but if she does, we're going there."

He had to stop with all the cuteness, or I was gonna burst. Thank god it was a Thursday without a playoff game. Cal would surely leave soon. We weren't set to open for another hour, but being attracted to him was one thing. Being drawn to him and his way of showing love was another. That was harder to resist.

"You heading out, Calzone?" I asked, keeping my voice even. My teeth dug into my lip so hard it hurt. Better biting my own lip than Cal's because that's all I wanted to do. Lick him. Kiss him. Bite him.

"I have too much energy. I might stay." He bounced on his feet.

"Nah, we got it tonight. Go hang out with Charlie and Lizzie." Three tables had their napkins resorted. Great.

"They're doing their own things, but I kinda like the bar."

I was about to growl. I couldn't yell at him or it'd be obvious. I tried the Alex route. They'd help. I was sure. They'd see my manic smile and help me out. "He in the way for you if he stays?"

They pursed their lips, their eyes sparkling. "Not even a little bit. Is he in *your* way, Barbie?"

"Nope." I faced Cal, plastering on my best fake smile. The muscle in my jaw twitched, and my pulse raced, and my fingers tapped against my side. I couldn't get it together. The damn guy would be the death of me with his protectiveness and love for Lizzie. "Guess you're staying!" I shouted, the words coming out too fast.

He frowned at me, his lips that were once lifted in the best smile ever turning down hard. He looked like he wanted to say something, but I refused to go down that route. I had to get my own head on straight before engaging in any conversation with him.

A talk right now would end in a kiss. Or with me jumping on him. Or me confessing my huge, loud messy feelings for him that would complicate everything. I knew better than to think I was different than everyone else, and plus, he only did three-night stands, and I wanted forevers. We didn't match, even though my heart and soul and body wanted him more than air. Fuck. I put a hand on my chest, forcing myself to calm down. Never in my life had I experienced *this* aggressive pull toward someone. It was terrifying.

Thankfully, there was a busier rush than we planned for, so we kept busy for three hours straight. I did my best to avoid Cal, but everywhere I went, he was there with his signature frown. Guilt ate at me because I'd put that expression on his face with my weirdness. He hadn't done anything wrong, but I was already crashing headfirst into falling in love with him if he didn't stop being… him. When I brought drinks to the tables, he was there picking up wrappers. On the way to the walk-in, he held the door for me.

It was too much!

By the time everything settled down, we cleaned up the bar and closed fast. The three of us had a good system at this point, everyone falling to their own roles to make the process faster. Charlie would have a hell of a time finding a better three people to run this place, that was for sure.

"Y'all good? I'm meeting up with some friends," Alex said.

"You have them?" Cal quipped, earning a middle finger from Alex.

"Night, Barbie, have *fun.*"

They winked at me when they walked out, and my face heated. How dare they? Was I that obvious?

"Hey," Cal said.

I grabbed my small bag and double-checked my phone was in my pocket. Nothing else to do besides talk to him for our one-minute walk. I was about to open my mouth when his soft fingers landed on my elbow. He gently spun me around, his eyes lowered in worry.

"Elle, please, you're killing me. What's wrong? Did I upset you?"

"What? No!" I swallowed, every particle in my body tuned into his damn fingers on my elbow. They were warm and rough and wonderful. Flames danced along my neck and face as he stared at me harder, clearly wanting an explanation to me being off.

"Did I say something wrong to Lizzie? I've replayed everything, and I don't know how else I could've supported her. The shirt with my name might've been too much, but I wanted her to understand I had her back. I just—"

I couldn't take it. Fuck all the reasons this was stupid. If I didn't kiss him on the mouth, I would die. I was certain.

I cupped his face with my hands and stood on my tiptoes, and I finally *fucking* kissed him.

His lips were soft and cold, and he tasted like mint. He stood, frozen, and shame consumed me. How could I just do this without permission? He might not want to kiss me! I jumped back, horrified at my action. "Cal, I'm—"

He gripped the edge of my shirt and yanked me to him. Our chests slammed together, his one hand cupping the back of my head as the other came to my hips. He dug his nails into my scalp and skin, a deep loud growl coming from his chest. He tilted my head as he kissed me back, only he went harder. He slid his tongue into my mouth, picking me up and setting me on top of one of the tables. My skin was on fire.

Hot, passionate, sexy fire.

"Cal," I moaned, gripping his broad shoulders as he sucked my tongue. Every sound he made was deep and erotic, and I was gonna die of horniness. He moved one hand to cover my throat, his thumb dipping into the base of it as he stared at me. His eyes were intense, burning with fire.

This was heaven. Him touching me and looking at me like that, like I mattered to him. His jaw tensed, and his chest heaved.

"Give me that mouth."

Oh damn.

I leaned forward, kissing him again and sinking into him. He stood between my thighs, our bodies pressed together so there wasn't an inch between us. He smelled like laundry and sweat, and I wanted to rub myself on him. I couldn't get enough of his mouth, his large fingers exploring my neck and back, the heavy movement of his chest under my hand. He kissed like he played hockey, like his sole survival was determined from our kiss, and the intensity made me shiver.

I felt each stroke of his tongue down my body, my thighs clenching together at how much I wanted him. This was more than lust and longing—this was my soul aching to be his.

"Cal," I said, panting between kisses. I gripped his pecs, the muscles connecting his shoulders to his neck. I didn't even know what they were called, but his were big and thick enough to hold onto.

"I know," he growled, moving his mouth along my jawline with light kisses. The opposite of his featherlight touch of his mouth to the aggressive grip of his fingers did me in. Then he nipped my neck and inhaled. "I could eat you up."

"I'd let you." My body trembled with need. I wrapped my legs around his waist, rocking into him, and he bit down on my collarbone. *"Cal."*

He slid one hand inside my shirt on my lower back, gliding it up toward where my bra was, and he traced the lining. His body shook too, I was pretty sure, but it could've been my own shaking distracting me. His eyes never left mine as he moved his fingers around to dance along my ribcage. I sucked in a breath, my lower gut throbbing. His lips were wet, from me, and his nostrils flared as he traced the outline of one nipple.

Explosions went off inside me. Like a trapped firework. The

sensation was divine, and he smiled at me. "I need to hear you scream for me."

I shivered at his words. I'd do whatever he wanted if he kept his hands on me. I nodded, desperate and on fire as he bent his head and sucked my nipple through my shirt and bra. I jerked my hips forward, feeling how hard he was, and groaned. "*Yes.*"

Something clicked in the background, but all I cared about were his fingers moving down my stomach and over my thighs. It smelled like cleaner and beer, and I didn't even care we were on a table. He needed to touch me, now.

"Shit, sorry!" someone said, someone who wasn't Cal.

I opened my eyes as the front door swung shut. I met Cal's gaze for a second, the same lingering heat in his before I said, "Oh my god."

An icy splash to my libido.

A patron saw us do that. Fuck.

Mortification grew through my body, and I had to get off the table, now. "Did you see who that was? Oh my god. A customer could've seen that! I thought the door was locked."

He worked a hand over his jaw a few times. "I did too." His voice was gravelly and deeper in timbre. He breathed hard and didn't look the least bit worried.

"Charlie would kill us. Shit." I adjusted my own hair and shirt. There was a wet spot where Cal's mouth had been, and heat and embarrassment flooded into one horrible combination. *Regret.* I'd kissed him without permission and then we did… whatever that was.

With the realization someone saw us, my mood dampened, and the letdown without release made me want to cry. I couldn't lose this job—I loved it too much. "We should go."

"Right."

It was painfully awkward as I quickly wiped down the table and made my way to the door. We'd crossed the line, more than crossed it with that kiss. We stumbled into the phase after friends but not quite *together*. Was he thinking about every touch like I was? Or the fact I would've done anything he asked? Or how fucking good it felt to finally give in to the attraction? His skin on mine, his mouth against me... my body heated. I'd *never* had chemistry like that before with anyone. But we weren't talking now. We walked in silence. I snuck a glance at him, and his face was unreadable.

The harder question swirling around my head... was he regretting it?

I swallowed down the ball of emotions in my throat as we got to our building door. My shirt stuck to my neck, and I hated the tension in the air. "I think—"

"Goodnight, Elle." He didn't wait for me to get into my unit before foregoing the elevator and shoving the door to the stairs open. It was somehow worse than a rejection.

My stomach dropped in a painful, awful sort of way where I hunched over. His cologne hung in the humid air, and my lips still tingled from our kiss, but everything unsaid between us felt like a knife to the gut. My eyes prickled with tears, and my hands shook as I opened the door to my place. I leaned against it, slid down, and hung my head. I'd given in to my desire for him, and he'd run away from me at the first chance.

What have I done?

CHAPTER
EIGHTEEN

Cal

I couldn't sleep for shit. My mind was split right down the middle, two very different and conflicting events keeping me up. Meeting Lizzie and the impact she had on my emotions. It was a lot to digest and terrifying because hope was a bitch. I'd *hoped* for so much before my parents died and lost all of it. But with Lizzie? It had returned, and it made me want to throw up.

Hope for the chance to watch her grow.

Hope for holidays to be filled with her laughing.

Hope for a family to share things with.

As soon as I stopped thinking about that, my mind went to Elle. *Fucking Elle.* Her kiss destroyed the tiniest string of self-control I had left. I wanted all of her, all the time. Despite the reasons it would never work, I needed another taste of her. But now, without getting my head on right. I'd lost control and would've fucked her on a table in my uncle's bar.

How shitty of me. She deserved more than that, but *fuck*. The sounds she'd made, the way her body trembled against mine. Her tiny perky nipples straining against her shirt. The heat of her skin under my hand. Her mouth... god, she tasted like how she made me feel—alive, warm, happy.

My cock stiffened even after I'd already taken care of myself in a long shower. I'd barely gotten started with her, and she'd come alive with me. Hearing her come, making her feel good... I wanted it more than playing in the NHL right now.

But fuck, the person who opened the door. I knew it had rattled her, and yeah, Charlie would be pissed as hell, but that was on me. I'd taken it a step further. She'd kissed me, but I was the one who attacked her face.

It was just after one am, and I hated how I'd taken off like a hormonal teenager. I turned over to my side and debated texting her. She could be asleep already.

Fuck it.

Cal: are we good?
Elle: go to sleep
Cal: that wasn't an answer
Elle: I don't know

Fuck. My body sank into the bed with a heavy sadness. Had I ruined everything? She'd kissed me, so she was attracted to me at least, but I didn't have to go so hard right after.

Cal: I'm sorry
Elle: I can't handle another rejection from you. Don't say you regret it, please
Cal: Are you fucking kidding me?

My pulse sped up at her insinuation. What was the opposite of regret? Replaying the kiss in my head a million times? Of course I didn't regret it. I regretted the timing of the door opening and the location of the bar but not once touching her.

A few minutes went by without an answer. Worry wedged its way into my shoulder blades, and I hopped out of bed. I wore shorts, which was enough, and I marched downstairs and knocked on her door, hard. There wasn't a world in which I could relax until I got the truth out of her.

"*What* are you doing?" she asked, opening the door and glaring at me. "It's the middle of the night."

She wore a tight black tank top and equally tight black shorts. Her hair was down, her mouth parted. Her flushed cheeks and collarbone and long lashes and perfect pink lips...My god, I almost fell forward from how she knocked me off-balance. My hands fucking shook with anticipation, nerves, and desperation.

"You think I *regret* kissing you?" My voice took on a dangerous tone.

She gulped. "I don't know. You stormed upstairs."

"Because I want to devour you." I barked out a laugh. "You think I regret it? God, I've done nothing but dream about you, your mouth, how you taste. I had to take a breather, Elle."

Her chest heaved, and her eyes got heavy. "Why didn't you say that?"

"Because this feeling was new for me, and I didn't know how to handle it."

"Then what did you do?"

"You really want the answer to that question?"

She panted at this point, her face flushed and her lips wet from her tongue. The same heat I felt in my core reflected in her eyes, and I leaned on the doorframe, crossing my arms and waiting for her to make the decision we both wanted. She struggled, but only for a few seconds.

She tucked her pointer finger under the edge of my shirt and pulled me into her place. I opened my mouth, but she moved that same finger, putting it over my mouth. "No talking."

God, her bossing me around was fucking hot. "Yes, ma'am."

She turned, fast, and walked away. I followed like the dog I was. Her shorts *killed* me. They were so tight and showed each globe of her ass perfectly. I wanted to bury my face in there with her legs wrapped around me. God, she was perfect.

I trailed her into her room, fighting the urge to study everything on her walls. That could come later. Right now, I needed to learn every part of her body. She shut the door, locked it, and stared at me. She looked wild, feral even with her wide eyes and the pulse racing at the base of her neck.

"I want to do everything all at once with you. It's… overwhelming."

"I know the feeling." I did, I really fucking did. I closed the distance between us and picked her up to toss her onto her queen-sized bed. She had yellow flowered sheets—of course she did. She let out a soft oomph before I pulled her ankles so her feet hung over the edge. "These legs."

She took a shaky breath as I ran my fingers up and down her soft skin, tugging the end of her shorts until they slid off her thighs. *Good god.* She was bare underneath. I inhaled and ran my nose from her knee all the way up. Her fingers wrapped around my hair as I teased her pussy with my tongue. I wanted between her thighs, but before I dove in, I needed to know we were on the same page.

I kissed below her belly button, lifting up the tank top and breathing her in. Her skin smelled like vanilla lotion, and I starved for her. "God, Elle." I slid my hands under the tank, grazing her raised nipples as she squirmed beneath me. Her nipples were tight and pert, and I took the shirt off. Her hair got stuck in it, but I didn't care. She helped me with the last part as her fingers came to my waistband.

"Are you sure?"

"Off," she demanded.

"In a minute." I closed my mouth around a nipple, sucking and teasing it with my teeth. She arched, bringing her even closer to me, and I gripped her back with both hands as I buried my face between her tits. I licked the valley between them, the salty taste of sweat driving me even wilder. I wanted all of her. How she sweated, laughed, and orgasmed. I pushed her breasts together, licking from one nipple to the other as her hands greedily pulled at my shorts. Her urgency made me laugh. Made me feel like I wasn't alone in this frenzy.

"Cal, please."

She'd said that a lot at the bar, and I'd never gotten to answer those pleas. I met her gaze. "You're positive about this?" *About me?*

She growled. "*Yes*. Now stop talking."

That I could do. I licked her stomach again.

I sank further onto my knees so her pussy was right in my face. I pushed her thighs apart, admiring how wet she was, and licked her entirely. She arched off the bed like it had caught fire, and I held her down with my mouth. Humming against her, I flicked my tongue slowly, wanting her to burst with anticipation before I gave her the pressure she needed.

Her grip on my hair tightened, and her legs tensed around my face. With the flat of my tongue, I massaged her clit before sliding two fingers into her. She clenched around me, her muscles twitching as I fingered her, slowly, methodically. I couldn't stop watching her body as I brought her closer to orgasm. Her hips jutted up and down, her lips parting open as her moans got louder. Her long blonde hair was everywhere on the bed, and her tits bounced as she rocked against my mouth. Her brown eyes lit up as she stared back at me.

She was a dream.

"I'm so close, Cal," she panted, moving her hands to the sheets. She gripped them and arched her back so high her pussy almost suffocated me. *What a way to go.*

I went harder, both with my tongue and fingers, and she fell apart. Like shattered glass. She cried and bucked and said my name. I smiled against her center, finally knowing what she sounded like when she came. Glorious. Better than the buzzer after scoring a goal with two seconds left of a game.

I kissed the inside of her thighs softly as she caught her breath. Her large eyes were filled with heat and pleasure, and I smiled. There was so much I wanted to say, but my horny-ass mind just came up with, "Damn, Elle."

"Shh." She pushed up onto her elbows, her eyes flaring with

passion. "If I don't feel your hard muscles and body weight on top of me, I'm gonna die. I need you, Cal. Right now."

What an invite.

My lips parted when she put her hands under my arms and tried hoisting me onto her. It made me laugh. "I'm heavy."

"I know." She slid her fingers into my shorts and gripped my shaft. *Goddamn, fuck.* My eyes almost crossed when she spit into her hand and stroked me. Carrying a hard-on for her for months had been torture, and this was my sweet reward. "You're so thick."

I bit back a moan and buried my face in her neck. I licked her skin, the salty combination fueling my fire. "You're perfect."

She continued stroking me, my cock like steel and ready to burst. It didn't matter that I'd jacked off an hour ago. Her touch? Her sounds? Her body? I shivered. I had to kiss her again.

This kiss was slower than at the bar. More exploratory. There was no rush, just tasting and teasing. I could feel her heart pound against mine, the sweat pooling between our chests. Her breaths came out in little pants, and she stroked faster. "Condom," she said, letting go of my cock and breaking apart our kiss.

"Where?"

We were at cavemen status of speaking. She pointed to her side table, and I leaned over, found an unopened box, and took one out. I pulled my shorts all the way down, kicking them off to the side and sliding the condom on. Elle looked at me with flushed cheeks and hooded eyes, her glorious naked body shaking. All from me.

How could I turn this down?

"You're fucking beautiful." I climbed over her, caging her face in between my arms. I kissed her lips softly before glancing at her. "Are you absolutely sure?"

She nodded, her hands coming around to dig into my ass. She groaned. "Fuck me, Cal. Please."

I lost my breath at her demand and met it. I thrust into her carefully, making sure she adjusted to it before letting my head hang on her shoulder. *Perfection.* She hugged my cock hard, her legs wrapping around my waist as I fucked her. It started slow, each of us feeling each other out. She let out a little gasp as I held onto her, and I wanted to bottle up that sound. She stared up at me, her wet lips parting as desire flared in her beautiful eyes.

I rarely held eye contact when I hooked up. Made me feel weird, but with her? I wanted to see everything she felt. I slowly rolled my body in and out, watching, waiting, needing to see her reaction. "Good?" I asked, holding myself up onto my elbows so she wouldn't be crushed by my weight.

She nodded.

I placed my hands on either side of her face, touching her any way I could, and tried to find the words to describe the feelings in my chest. None came out though. Instead, I had to *show* her what she did to me. I kissed her forehead, then her nose, then her mouth. She moaned, loudly, as she nipped my bottom lip. That sent a shot of lust through me, and I thrust a little harder into her.

"I taste myself on your mouth."

"Then you know my favorite flavor now."

She laughed against my lips, the sound the best thing in the entire world. "You're not gonna break me, you know."

I paused and lifted my head to stare down at her again. I frowned. "Hm?"

"You're going slow and being gentle. I don't want that. I want you *unhinged*. So, stop worrying and *fuck* me, please."

Holy shit, she's perfect.

"Yes, ma'am." I swallowed, hard, before doing what she said.

I went harder. She breathed louder, her nails in my lower back now. She bit my fucking shoulder as I picked up the pace. I needed to own her, make her scream in pleasure. I slid one hand under her body, lifting her up to let my cock drive deeper. My muscles tensed as electricity danced along my spine. I couldn't get enough.

Elle sucked my skin, her greedy hands touching me everywhere. I forgot time existed and pounded into her, holding her in place as the bed rocked against the wall. She bucked, grabbed my face, and kissed the shit out of me. She growled as I sucked her tongue into my mouth, needing every part of her I could touch. Our teeth clashed, and sweat dripped between her chest and mine.

I wanted to taste it.

I stilled, broke apart our kiss and licked where our sweat combined. She groaned, and I swirled my tongue around her nipple before sucking it hard. I wanted more. I wanted to see her tits bounce while I fucked her. "Ride me," I barked out, full sentences not something I could do right now.

Her eyes lit up with pleasure, and she wiggled from beneath me. "On your back, Cal."

My body heated with need as she shoved my chest down with one finger.

"Good boy," she said, her smirk about killing me.

I grabbed her hips and helped her sink onto me. My eyes about rolled into the back of my head as she rocked back and forth, taking me deeper and deeper. Propping onto my elbows, I leaned forward to suck her other nipple into my mouth. Teasing the pebbled tip, my entire body shook with aggressive desire. "I want every fucking part of you."

"Then take it." She gripped my hair hard and rode me faster. She was wet as fuck and tight and found a rhythm between us that would kill me from lust alone. Her sweaty skin and vanilla lotion combined to the best smell in the world, and I inhaled it, her, everything.

I saw stars when I closed my eyes. I arched my hips up, going deeper into her, and she growled. *So fucking hot.*

"Elle," I panted, needing *more*. She got it. She read my voice or my eyes or whatever because she grabbed my hand and put it on her pussy.

"Come for me." I massaged her clit, applying pressure as she ground harder against me.

Her eyes half-closed as her face softened with pleasure. Her thighs tensed, and she let out the sexiest, deepest moan before shouting my name. *"Cal!"*

I couldn't get enough of her. Her sounds and body and voice and heartbeat. I used my free hand to hold onto her hip, my other on her pussy. She clamped around me, her large eyes opening and staring at me with so much heat. I bucked.

Her release set off my own, and I spilled into her, the pleasure numbing me from head to toe as she watched me, full of fascination. It was unlike any other orgasm. My soul floated out of me. My mind was foggy and my head in a daze as I came to. Elle's eyes were closed, her chest heaving, and I rolled to the side to lay on my back.

Each beat of my heart radiated through my body like thunder. That was incredible. The best sex I'd ever had. Life-altering, honestly. I blew a breath through my nose, grounding myself. I was in Elle's bed, her sweet vanilla scent mixing with sweat. Her hair tickled the side of my face. After a few beats, I sat up and disposed of the condom.

That was when it hit me.

The severity and reality of what we did. I didn't cuddle. I didn't stay the night. I fucked and left and maybe saw the woman a few more times. There was no talk about what it meant because I handled that all beforehand. With Elle? I'd forgotten all about my rules. I stood at the edge of her bed, naked, awkward, and coming down from the best high ever.

What did I say?

Something like a laugh came from her. "Oh, Cal."

"W-what?" I cleared my throat, determined not to let her see me freaking the fuck out. "Did you laugh?"

She rolled over, her feet dangling over the bed. She got up and walked to her closet, putting on an extra-large shirt that covered her to her thighs. She then tossed me my shorts with a half-smile. "I can feel you about to lose it. Put these on and go back upstairs."

"I'm not…freaking out." I slid my shorts on, glad to not be naked anymore. The air was tense again, and I tried reading every expression on her face. Her cheeks were still flushed and her hair wild, but her eyes were distant. *Fuck.* "I just—"

"I know." She did another fake smile I'd seen at the bar. She used it on patrons who were annoying her. "I knew what this would mean to you and what I was getting into. There's no agenda or secret plot to change you. I wanted you. We both had fun. This can be one of your three nights, right?"

Fun seemed too simple of a word for what we'd done. But I didn't know what else to say. Her words were what I *should* want to hear. A free pass. No drama. Three nights only. Yet, it seemed wrong and off. I didn't understand how to cope with that, so I nodded. "Yeah. Fun."

She chewed the side of her lip, glancing at the door before yawning. "I'm beat."

"Right." I was being *dismissed.* "Well, good night."

She did another tight-eyed smile before opening her door and walking me out. I wanted to kiss her again, tell her this was different than my casual fucks, but I wasn't sure what *different* signified for me. She did say one of three nights, so maybe that meant we could definitely do this again. I knew I didn't ever want to hurt her, and I probably already had. I knew she made me feel things I hadn't in years. But more importantly, the worst thing was that I knew I could never be who she deserved. I couldn't be the guy to give her swoons and romantic gestures. One her brother approved of.

I lifted my fingers in a wave, headed upstairs, and tried to come up with a plan to save my relationship with Elle. Because if I lost her…as a friend, co-worker, whatever she was, my life would lose the best part of it.

CHAPTER
NINETEEN

Elle

"I slept with Cal Holt." I stared at my bowl of cereal but felt Daniella's eyes on me.

"We can call him Cal. I know what Cal we're referring to."

"Cal Holt sounds more official."

"Is this a fancy conversation?" she quipped back.

I looked up to see her smiling. "What?"

"I'm not surprised at all. Y'all had this weird chemistry last year when we had that dinner. Remember? He stared at you the whole time and you with your Holt posters…so how was it?"

Gratitude for my friend made me want to hug her. "You're not gonna lecture me like my damn brother?"

"First, we've been besties way longer than me and Van have been together. And frankly, he can fuck right out of this." She leaned onto the table, her eyes going wide. "Sure, I'm worried Cal could hurt you, but you don't seem broken, so I want details."

"It was…" I trailed off, my face heating. The way he touched me, looked at me, spoke to me… "Hot."

"Love that for you." She did a little Alexis Rose shimmy. "Glad I stayed at Gabe's last night."

"If you were here, I probably would've sent him home when he knocked on the door at one am."

"Sexy." She wiggled her eyebrows. "Tell me everything."

I filled her in on the almost moment at Gabe's, the kiss at the bar, being interrupted and then last night. I still hadn't grasped what we did. We were friends. Bad for each other. Yet the sex and chemistry were… chef's kiss. It made every single interaction I ever had with a past guy seem… laughable. Dull. Nonsignificant to my life in any way. They were all black and white films, and he was the high definition 3-D version of movies. Even thinking about Cal had my skin tingling. "He stood there as soon as we were done, looking panicked as hell. Like he had no idea what to do, and that part sucked."

"Well, he's used to one-night or two-night stands." Dani shrugged. "I'm glad you finally got some, and let's be real, you've crushed on him for years. But… here's the question. What now?"

"Don't know." I rubbed my temples. "We see each other all the time. Every day. But I want romance, and he wants a few fucks and no emotions. This broke both our rules."

"Rules are stupid. I wasn't supposed to really date your brother, but here we are."

"Dani." I leveled my gaze with her. "You've always loved him."

"Pot, you've always had a thing for Cal."

"You're the worst."

She laughed. "You love me."

She was right, I did. But none of this chat helped with the fact that I had to see Cal later that day. Did we talk about it? Avoid it? Do it again? Technically, I should get two more nights with him. My body hummed at the thought of sleeping with him two more times. God, I wanted it. I wanted it bad. But how could I enjoy him that way and protect my heart? That was what had gotten us into this mess. Seeing his affection with Lizzie and how he'd opened up to her.

Dani stood up and put the few dishes in the sink into the

washer. We always agreed to keep the kitchen clean, but I itched for something to do. To get out this nervous energy. My budgeting homework.

Ugh, another reminder that Cal and I were intertwined at this point. I'd have to see him all weekend, then get together for another budget-book date Monday. *Not a date.* Meeting. I played with the end of my hair, completely lost as to what to do. There wasn't a romance guide for these things with messy emotions. Sure, friends with benefits could work, only Cal did three nights, and I already knew I had some feelings involved.

We could agree it was a one-time moment even though I didn't love that.

What did I want?

"I need to do something." I rose, fast, and Dani shot me a look. "I'm tired and confused and terrified I'm gonna get hurt."

"Answer me this. What is the worst that could happen?"

"I fall for him, and he treats me like all the others, ditching me. Then I see him with other women and know who he is on the inside, but he won't let me in." I swallowed, damn near afraid this was already happening. Of all the people for Cal to open up to, why would it be me, someone…normal and boring? Someone who grew up in her brother's shadow and preferred living inside books? "I like who he is, grouchy and angry at the world because it makes his smiles all the more meaningful. But he'll never be what I need."

A romantic partner. Someone to do brunches with and laugh and dance under the stars.

"Then can you have fun?" She scrunched her face. "I know you want romance. I love that and think you should never settle, but hear me out, you're single. Not attached to anyone. About to attend Central State with me, and we're going to have the times of our lives. Why not have a fling? Keep emotions out of it as much as you can. He's not your forever, happy-ever-after guy, but he could be your 'let's bang like rabbits for a bit' guy?"

"Yeah, maybe." My shoulders felt weighted, like the extra tension had taken root there. "Might go for a walk."

"I'm here for you, always. Only you can figure out what to do, babe. Trust yourself. You're pretty great."

I smiled at her before heading into my room. I had eight hours before seeing Cal again, and I wasn't sure if I was excited, nervous, or afraid of what he'd say.

The Bulls were in another round of playoffs, facing off against the Phoenix Suns tonight, and it was packed. I preferred to stay busy cause it made time go by faster, and I was glad to have endless tasks to do. Refill drinks, add them to tabs, wipe counters, clean glasses, get orders ready for Alex on the floor and repeat. It kept my mind and eyes from wandering to Cal in the corner at the door.

Thankfully, Alex had already been there when I'd arrived, so Cal and I were never alone. There were some looks, but like normal, I couldn't read him well. He had yet to smile, and his famous frown lines were right there.

He did get tense when some of the hockey guys showed up to bus tables though. Ty was one of them, but we'd left off on great terms. Just friends and definitely writing buddies. The hipster athlete was a fun combination because the gruff men at the bar had no idea what they were getting into when chatting with him.

Overall though, it was a great Friday night with easygoing patrons, the Bulls ahead at half-time, and tips coming in hot. I might take a little bit of the cash and buy myself a new swimming suit. There was a huge party at the lake for the Fourth of July that Gabe and Daniella had invited me to. It'd have former hockey players, dance team members, and some football players and cheerleaders too. I wondered *twice* if Cal was invited but tried not to worry about it. I was going either way.

I stretched my arms over my head as Cal came behind the bar. My pulse instantly raced, my skin tingling at his proximity. He smelled damn good, like laundry and aftershave, and huh, he had shaved. His jaw looked real smooth as he ran a hand over it, his frown line on full display. "You eat dinner?"

I smacked my forehead. "No, I forgot."

He bent down into the fridge with the Trulys and Whiteclaws and pulled out a small box. "I made this for you."

It looked like trail mix.

"It has protein and sugar and carbs. I snack on it all the time on the road to make sure I have enough nutrients. I figured you might forget to eat, and it'll be a long night here. Please, have some when you get time." He set the container down and took a step back.

My throat got all tight. "Thanks, Cal."

He nodded and returned to his post at the door. He'd made trail mix for me. It wasn't romantic in typical terms, but it was ridiculously nice and caring. I washed my hands and grabbed a handful, welcoming the sweet and salty combination. At the taste of food, my stomach growled with delight. *Feed me, woman.*

It was delicious and gave me a little hope. He wouldn't have made this for me if he was cutting me loose. Right? Unless it was a goodbye trail mix? No, he wasn't the type to do that either. Fuck. Even more confused than before, I kept busy throughout the game. It was cool to see my body forming muscles that weren't there weeks ago. Hoisting up a rack of glasses was no big deal, and I could carry a tray with ten drinks balanced on it. Look at me, growing and living life.

"What's with the smile, Barbie?" Alex asked, their voice dripping with innuendo as there was a break in orders. "You and beefstick take your party upstairs last night?"

Shit. My face drained of color. "Wait, what?"

"I left something back here and returned." They looked from me to Cal. "Surprised the table isn't in shreds."

"Alex, shh." I moved toward them, embarrassed that Alex had seen us. "I don't know… let's just…"

"Speechless? Interesting." They reached over and tugged at my braid. "I'm teasing you. Honestly, I'm not surprised. He's always watching you."

I turned, and sure enough, Cal's attention was on me. "Okay, fine. Yes, but dear god, I don't wanna gossip about it."

Alex laughed. "Fair enough. Gotta say, I think you suit him. Known the kid for three years, and he needs more… you in his life."

"What does that mean?"

"Annoying. Happy."

"Wow, that was almost a compliment." My own lips curved, and I wanted to ask more about their comment. I never got the chance though. Cal headed over, a wild look on his face. "What is it?"

"A party bus just arrived. At least twenty people." His face darkened. "Once I check IDs, I'll help behind the bar."

"I'm sure I can—"

"I know you can. But these tend to get rowdy." His eyes pleaded with me, and I nodded. I didn't get the worry when we'd had even double that amount a few weeks ago, but I trusted Cal's judgement.

Alex sighed. "Fuck, I hate those party buses. You get entitled drunks mixing with our regulars, who are generally blue-collared workers here to relax, and there's always a fight."

"Really?" I stood straighter, a prickle of worry edging itself down my spine.

"Yes." They rolled their shoulders back. "Once the shots start, it's bad."

The noise was the first clue Cal's reservations were spot-on. The group of partyers were loud as hell. Chanting and cheering as they walked in. Ridiculously obnoxious. They wore polos and goofy hats and beads, and Cal's stare bored into me. *Be safe.*

The group of men, all very large, tanned, and halfway drunk came up to the bar.

"Oh, hello, beautiful. My god, look at this angel."

"She's gorgeous. Come here, honey. Let me see you up close." One pushed onto the bar and leaned over the edge.

My skin crawled. I took a step back and pointed to the tap. "What can I get you to drink?"

"All business, no play, no fun." One guy pouted his lips at me, like a baby. It was horrid. "Twenty shots of whiskey, top shelf. Surprise me, baby doll. Papa's got some cash, and he wants to give it to you."

I swallowed down the gross feeling. Both Alex and Cal neared the bar, their bodies tense. It wasn't that the men creeped me out, but it was the amount of them. Their size. Sure, they were creepers, but ugh, I could feel them ogling me, and I regretted wearing short shorts and a crop top.

"I'll help." Cal appeared next to me, putting his hand on mine as I tried opening a second bottle. Twenty shots was a lot. I set up the glasses, my skin turning red at the attention. They screamed and shouted, earning complaints from the other guests.

I didn't blame them.

I had the glasses set up and poured the first ten before the bottle ran out. Cal did the second half, and we slid them toward King Bro. "That'll be hundred and twenty."

The guy tossed two hundreds at me. "Keep the change, baby, but give me some sugar."

"Take the shots and leave," I said, my voice growing louder.

"Oh, feisty thing." He pounded the shot and tried to move closer to me. I could smell the alcohol on his breath, and I cringed.

"Sir, back the fuck up." I raised my voice, and one of the regulars at the end of the bar noticed. Big Ben worked as a mechanic and never said much. He came here to unwind before going home to his sick mom and three kids. If Cal was big, Big Ben was double in size.

"There a problem?" Big Ben asked, King Bro smiling wide.

"Complimenting the lady, sir. But damn, you look like a tank."

Cal moved next to me, angling his body between me and the asshole. Heat radiated from him, and I was beyond glad he and Alex were there. The sense of entitlement around these guys was the scariest part about them.

"Why don't you boys head out before things get ugly? Leave the girl alone."

"The *girl* gave me a look. I know when I'm wanted, so mind your business, fatso." The dude looked at me again, his eyes moving down my body. "I'll throw in another hundred if I can take a shot off you."

"No." My voice shook. Fear rooted me to the spot. They could overpower me, easily. I had no muscle or weapons.

The guy reached over the bar, attempting to grab my forearm, when Cal punched him in the face. The sound was unlike anything I had heard in real life, just movies. Flesh on flesh. The gross sound of squishing. The scream. The thud. Blood.

It happened so fast and so slowly at the same time. Cal's left hand pushed me behind him as he retracted his fist from the guy's face. "She said no. Get the *fuck* out of here."

The party lost it. Shouts and shoves and pushes, and oh my god, it was a bar fight. Glass shattered, and I stood there, terrified and stuck in place. One of the party dudes shoved Old Jim, the seventy-year-old who always drank a Moscow mule. Panic clawed at my throat. *What if he's hurt?* Then Gregg with two g's fell off his stool. It was a madhouse.

The police! I had to call them!

"Police are on their way," Alex yelled, their voice angry as hell. They disarmed two of the bros and shoved them through the door. Big Ben took a punch to the gut before knocking one of them out. My entire body hummed with fight or flight, but I did neither, just froze and watched.

"Get in the office, now." Cal picked me up and carried me. "Lock the door."

"What about—"

"Lock the fucking door. Take this just in case." He handed me a knife and shut the door in my face. I locked it and gripped the weapon hard.

What the fuck was my life?

I crumpled into a ball, not wanting to be seen as everything trembled from my fingers to my toes. My eyes watered from the rush of emotions. Fear, anger, fear again. What if that guy had touched me? What if I'd been alone at the bar?

God, the possibilities of it were endless, and I swallowed. My mouth was completely dry, and I took some calming breaths. The police... Cal...holy shit. Cal had *punched* that guy in the face. Worry for him took over, and I snuck a look outside. It was still madness. Chairs were flipped, and *fuck!*

The window shattered right above my head. I screamed as shards fell on me. My skin stung from the glass, and a hand reached into the window and unlocked the door. *Oh my god, oh my god.*

"It's me." Cal was there, his gaze hardening when he found me sprawled out on the ground. "*Fuck.* You're bleeding."

"The window shattered." My voice trembled, and he bent down. "I don't understand."

He carefully pulled a piece from my face, his fingers gentler than I would've thought, and his frown deepened. He took out a few more shards before the sound of the cops stopped him. "Thank Christ."

"Charlie, the bar...." Having Cal with me, near me, provided me a much-needed relief. Being with him meant I was safe.

"It'll all be okay." He cupped my face, his eyes softening as he said, "I promise. I got you."

Someone gave me a blanket at some point. I wasn't cold, but the escape of adrenaline made me shiver. Charlie stood off in the distance, talking to the police as Alex explained what happened for a fourth time. Cal, Big Ben, Gregg, me... everyone told the same story because it was the truth. Even if the fucking asshole intended to press charges against Cal for the punch, every witness account said it was to defend me when the guy grabbed me.

My stomach ached for Cal. *If* charges were pressed, I didn't want that to affect his hockey career.

"How you doing?" Cal joined me on the bench, his arm coming around me. I snuggled into his warmth and fought the urge to cry.

This had been the most stressful day of my entire life, and my emotions were spiraling. "I don't know. Terrified, exhausted, concerned about you."

"Don't worry about me. My hand is fine. Just a little sore."

"Your hand is sore?" I moved and took his right one. Bruises had formed on his knuckles, and there were scabs. "Cal. I'm so sorry."

"Stop. You did nothing wrong, and I'd punch that guy a million times if he touched you again. I'm glad you're okay. Your face is covered in blood."

"The shards." I touched my cheek, and his fingers replaced mine. Our eyes held as he traced along my jaw and toward my forehead. A different kind of shiver overtook me, and I swallowed, hard. "Thank you. For punching him, for getting me to safety. The whole thing."

"Of course. It's my fault it happened. I knew better than to let them in. I ignored my gut, and now look at the place."

"No, you couldn't have guessed it'd be that bad."

"I had feeling." He tilted my face to look at him, his eyes moving over my forehead and cheeks. Then my mouth. "I need to stay with you tonight. Charlie wants to talk to me but then we're going home."

Stay with me? The guy who'd bolted last night after having sex with me?

The same guy who'd protected me and looked at me with so much warmth, like he'd slay every dragon that came my way? My throat tightened, and I knew my feelings were past the point of no return.

He traced his thumb over my bottom lip and left me there, but not without glancing back at me with a soft smile that had my heart skipping a beat.

CHAPTER **TWENTY**

Cal

I deserved a fucking award. My insides burned with the need to track down Todd Farmington and beat the shit out of him. He'd touched Elle. He put his greasy hands on her arm after she said no. What a piece of shit. Hours had gone by, and I still couldn't get the image out of my head—his hand on her skin, the fear in her eyes, the silence of the bar watching it happen.

I'd snapped.

My right knuckles hurt, but I'd come out ahead in that fight. Todd had fallen to the ground, already drunk, and then chaos started.

"You alright, kid?" Charlie put a hand on my shoulder and waited until I looked at him. I shrugged.

"I'm not mad at you, for what it's worth." He squeezed before letting go. "I see guilt written on your face, but from what it sounds like, you were defending Elle."

"He *touched* her without permission."

"Yeah, he deserved it."

"I'm not sorry about hitting him." I knew I'd have to deal with Coach Simpson and my agent, and hell even the Philly team's PR people would need a quote. The weight of everything should've had me freaking out, panicking.

I only felt anger.

"Wasn't asking for an apology."

I sighed, finally understanding Charlie wasn't about to yell at me for causing a scene at his bar. I quickly checked on Elle, who rested her head on her wrist as she sat on the bench. Her gaze was unfocused, and my stomach boiled. She was shaken up, and I needed to comfort her. "I do regret letting them in. Something felt off, but I didn't take action."

"You couldn't have stopped patrons in on your own. Not twenty of them. It might be time I hire security for the weekends." Charlie exhaled. "Believe it or not, this isn't the first nor the last bar fight I've had."

"No lie?"

"I'll tell you about the others sometime. I gotta head back to Lizzie though. My neighbor is there, and I don't want Lizzie worried if she wakes up and I'm gone."

"Sure." I waited for him to move, but he just stared at the bar, then Elle.

"I'm glad you stood up for her. She can clearly handle herself, but fuck that guy."

My lips quirked, and Charlie headed toward his car. Red and blue police lights lit up the street as people gawked at the scene. It had been a few hours already, but cops lingered, getting statements. I'd given mine, and I'd deal with it if that guy pressed charges. For now? I wanted to be with Elle.

I put my hands in my pockets as I neared her, resisting the urge to hold her tight against me. My mind kept replaying the start of the fight, the fear in her eyes. I'd needed to get her to safety. And then when someone threw an entire bottle of tequila at the office door, my stomach had just about fallen through my body.

Her brown eyes softened at my approach. "Charlie furious?"

"Surprisingly, no. He almost seemed amused? I couldn't tell." I rocked back on my heels and held out a hand. "Want to head back?"

"Yeah." She stood, her legs shaky, and I pulled her under my arm. She rested her head there, and god, she felt good. "My body is still trembling."

"Mine too. The adrenaline can take a bit to wear off, then we'll crash." I hadn't fought a lot in the past but enough scuffles to know the process. Alex stayed talking to Gregg, giving me a nod as we headed toward our building.

So many injuries, so much damage. We'd all agreed to let it sit tonight, and tomorrow, after good sleep, we'd go back in. It'd be a shit show, but with four of us working together, it wouldn't take long.

My main concern was Elle and maybe my own need to make sure she was all right. People called her Sunshine and Barbie for a good reason. She was upbeat and maybe a little sheltered, so tonight had been a totally different world. My throat felt too dry as we walked inside. "Your place or mine?"

"Yours. I don't want to explain anything to Daniella or my brother tonight. They might be there."

I nodded. Elle and I hadn't talked about sleeping together and what it meant, so seeing her brother was the last thing I wanted to do. I guided us toward the elevator, and we waited. "What's in your head right now?"

"Exhaustion. When it settles though, I replay the moment the fight started. Or when your hand came through the broken window. I thought... I thought it was that guy." She trembled again, and I wanted to kill Todd.

"He'll be charged. He won't come back."

"I know." She gulped and brought her hands tight against her middle. "I'm glad you were there, Cal."

Me too. I couldn't speak, the combination of relief and anger making my voice box break. I brought us into my place, and after locking up, I tugged her toward the bathroom. "Come on."

She followed, questions in her eyes as I hoisted her up on the counter. Blood flecks covered her face and neck and arms from the shards, and I wet a towel with warm water. I started at her forehead, carefully wiping the blood and making sure there was no glass.

Once I was done with her forehead, I got her cheeks and jaw. She sat there, quiet and watching me. I finished her face, and with shaky hands, I cleaned her neck and shoulder. I couldn't stop myself, and I pressed a soft kiss where her neck met her shoulder. "I'm sorry this happened."

"It's not your fault," she said, her voice hoarse.

I moved my face to stare down at her long lashes fanning against her cheeks with each blink. Her full lips pulled in a pout. God, she was incredible. I sighed, eyeing the blood on her black tank, and I grabbed the edge. "I'll give you one of mine."

She nodded as I lifted the shirt over her head and tossed it on the floor. She wore a white lacy bra that had my blood pumping. She was gorgeous, and her small cleavage was inviting, but it was not the time. At all.

I found an old hockey shirt and carefully put it over her head. She drowned in it, and if I was a sentimental kind of guy, I'd have taken a picture of her like that. "Water?"

She nodded.

I got two glasses and found her removing her shorts in my room. Good. I wanted all reminders of the bar gone. "Drink this. I'm getting out of my clothes too."

"Okay, thank you."

I moved to the bathroom when she said, "Cal?"

"Yeah, baby?" *Shit*. The term slipped out.

"Keep your shirt off. I can't seem to warm up."

"Okay." I smiled at her and did as she asked. I got ready for bed and climbed in next to her. She wasn't lying—her body was freezing. "Come here."

I positioned us so her entire back was against my chest, my arms wrapped around her middle. She sighed and relaxed into me, her little sounds adorable. The image of her fear was still rooted in my mind, and I squeezed her tighter. "I thought something was gonna happen to you. It terrified me."

"Me too." She snuggled deeper. "My mind is racing, and I can't relax. I don't know if I'm gonna cry or pass out, but it's overwhelming. That was fucking scary. The glass, the violence. What if someone had a gun?"

I could barely swallow. Those thoughts were in my head too. "What would help you relax?"

"Reading, usually."

"Want me to read to you?"

She tilted her head up so her forehead hit my chin. "Would you?"

"Sure." I smiled and kissed the top of her head. "I have my blind date right here. Only a few more chapters left."

She settled into me more as I picked up the book where I'd left off. It had been fucking years since I'd read out loud. Brief flashbacks to high school had me pausing, but I let that go. If reading helped Elle relax, then I'd do it.

I finished one chapter, then another. My throat was dry, but her muscles started to softened as I spoke. It felt surreal to be reading a book to the sister of a former teammate, a girl who'd hated me for months. But somehow, it felt right. Perfect, even. I was always the one causing others to be angry or upset, but to be the comforter? It was a nice change of pace.

After thirty minutes of reading, Elle's breaths slowed down, and her head leaned back on my arm. I checked, and she was asleep. Her lips had parted slightly, and her hair hung in her face, the image so strikingly cute I stared a little longer than appropriate. When I was satisfied that she was okay, deep in sleep, I set the book down, shut off the light, and moved us so I spooned her. I didn't want her to wake up cold, so I tucked her in tight.

We could worry about the bar, hockey, and what was happening between us tomorrow. For now, I was going to enjoy the moment because I knew more than anyone that moments like these wouldn't last forever.

A worried cry woke me. Like a whimper. I bolted up, searching for the sound when I remembered everything. The bar. Elle. *Elle.* "Hey, hey." I moved her so she fell into my lap. Her heart pounded, and sweat covered her body. My poor girl was having a nightmare.

"Wake up, let me fight your demons for you," I said, kissing her temple. She let out another pathetic sound, and it gutted me. I never wanted her to make that whimper as long as I breathed. My chest tightened, and I gently shook her. "Baby, hey, I got you."

She slowly blinked her eyes open. Her pulse raced at the base of her throat, and she clung to me. "Cal?"

"Hm?" I pulled her closer to me so I cradled her entire body. I liked her there, where I could protect her from everything but myself.

"I just... I can't..." she trailed off, her voice going high. "Kiss me."

The day I denied her that was the day I saw my parents again.

I tilted her neck up, holding my hand gently on her throat and brought my lips to hers. She let out a cry, but this time it was pleasure. She crawled onto me so her legs wrapped around my waist, and fuck, she was warm. "Elle," I said, kissing down her neck. "We should sleep. You're tired."

"I want to forget. Please." She tugged at my hair, her eyes desperate. "I need you, Cal."

God, I couldn't turn her down. Not when she said those words and wore that helpless expression. "Tell me what you need, and I'll do it."

"Touch me."

I roamed my hands over her skin under her shirt, removing it and tossing it to the side. Our chests touched, and I grazed my fingers over her spine, her ribs, her the edge of her panties. "I want to see your tattoo."

"Okay." She crawled off me and spun, letting me view her back. I traced the cursive letters, enjoying how her skin broke out in goose bumps.

"Write, don't think," I said, pulling her against me. "It fits you."

She hummed in response, and I dipped my hand in her panties. She was already wet, and I sucked in a breath. Fuck, this girl. She was everything.

"No." She stilled, and I froze. *What the fuck was I thinking?* She needed comfort.

"I'm sorry."

"Cal," she said, getting onto her knees and sliding her underwear off. Her flushed cheeks and wide eyes didn't seem like she was mad. I breathed easier.

"What are you doing?"

She reached over toward the table, grabbed a condom, and jutted her chin toward my shorts. "I want to see your face."

"Oh."

"Yeah." She smiled, a little bashful. "You make me feel…safe."

I closed my eyes, my chest breaking apart at her words. "Baby." I cupped her face and kissed her again, slowly, tasting and teasing her perfect little mouth. I lifted my hips a bit as she tugged my shorts down. In a twisting of limbs, we got them off and onto the floor so it was just our bodies.

I kissed her collarbone, nipping it as she ripped open the condom and slid it on me. I hissed, the pleasure of her hands making me jolt. "You're fucking perfect."

With my legs on either side of her, she took my cock deep inside her. We were chest to chest, our mouths a breath a part, and my soul hummed. I'd never had sex like this before, with prolonged eye contact. I had to watch her though, to make sure she was okay. "Cal," she said, closing her eyes as I thrust into her. She arched her back, and we found a slow pace that took me deeper and deeper. I couldn't stop touching her. Her throat, her chest, her back. When she opened her eyes again, they were hooded with pleasure and lust and *feeling*.

"This is what I wanted. You. Us." She leaned forward, her forehead resting against mine. "I'm so glad I have you."

Fuck.

I needed more of her. Desperately. No more space between our bodies. Just us. Her body and mine. She made a sexy ass sound again, and I held her tight against me as I fucked her. She'd somehow worked her way into my life and mind, and I wasn't sure how to ever let go.

"Cal, I'm… I need more."

I held onto her with one hand, using the other to stimulate her clit, and it barely took thirty seconds before she trembled and fell apart against me. Her sounds, her body, her greedy hands running all over my skin had my own release building up too. I kissed the base of her throat, and she somehow tightened her muscles, and *fuck*. "Elle," I groaned, my own orgasm knocking the wind out of me.

My ears rang, and my skin beaded with sweat as we remained there, forehead to forehead with our breaths coming out in pants. Had never been like this before. There had never been a girl like *her* before.

"Thank you." She kissed me quickly, softly, before pulling back. "That's what I needed. Just, thank you."

I'd do anything for you. I wanted to say it, but my words got tripped up as my heart tried to figure out what was happening. A burning sensation formed and grew, and my mind panicked. "I'm gonna, uh, toss this out."

I tied off the condom and threw it in the trash, desperate to get back to her but also confused. Why wouldn't I say those words to her when I felt them down to my core?

Because I'm scared. That was why.

I curled up around her, thankful she didn't say anything, and fell asleep.

I woke up with my entire body enclosed around Elle. She smelled like sleep and vanilla, and I inhaled her scent before slowly rolling away from her.

I'm so glad I have you. She'd said those words to me.

Last night had been about comfort. Being there for each other. We'd gone through a traumatic moment together. That was all. She'd wanted sex as a distraction. I'd done that before too with lots of women. Distraction from life. I got it.

That was all it was.

Eggs. I should make breakfast for her. She'd barely gotten to eat the trail mix I brought, and I bet she was hungry. I could make coffee too.

Yeah. The sleepy, emotional sex wasn't anything more than comfort after the fight.

I would've been just as upset if Alex had been threatened. *No.* Not true. Alex was a black belt and could kick my ass. I wanted them safe, I wasn't an asshole, but the emotions were not the same when I compared the two.

But what did that mean?

I cracked eggs of the pan and put bacon in the microwave over paper towels. Did Elle like bacon? Most people had to, right?

Why didn't I have bread for toast? Ugh. I shut the fridge, annoyed that I couldn't prepare a real meal for Elle. We had to clean all day, and we'd burn a shit ton of calories. Okay, I had yogurt and fruit. She could eat that too.

Good. Content with my meal, I made sure the eggs didn't burn. Now the coffee. I didn't know if she liked it strong or mild, so I went with medium. That was safe. I stretched my arms above my head, my pulse racing. It was essential this breakfast was perfect. I didn't know why, but it was true. Pacing until the eggs and bacon were done, my gaze kept going to my room. She'd get up soon, probably. What did I say to her besides good morning?

I'd never had anyone spend the night before, and I wasn't handling it well. Not at all.

Juice! Elle might like juice. I checked the fridge, and fuck. No orange or apple juice. I might have time to run out and get some if I was quick.

"Morning."

"You want juice?" I fucking yelled at her.

She blinked in surprise, sleep lines covering her face as she hesitantly walked toward me. "Um, I feel like I should say yes."

"I don't have any."

She blinked again. "That's alright."

"Good. Great."

Jesus, pull it together.

"Food?" I gestured to the table, like a fucking butler. Elle pressed her lips together, her eyes dancing with amusement.

"Cal, are you okay?"

"I don't know." I shrugged, hard, and let my hands hit the sides of my thighs in a real dramatic way. "I'm freaking out because I've never had anyone stay over before, and I want to make sure you're fed to help clean today, and I don't know what this means."

She took a breath, padding one foot in front of the other before sitting down at the chair I still held onto. She pressed her lips together, keeping her face blank. "It doesn't have to mean anything if you don't want it to."

"What?" It totally meant something! I felt it in my chest. But I was a twat who couldn't express it.

"We lived through some wild shit last night, and I really needed… a friend. That's all. You helping out a friend." She offered a real Elle smile and looked at the counter.

Was that all it was? Me helping out a friend? *Sleeping* with a friend?

I frowned and shrugged, anger working its way up my neck. *I'm so glad I have you.* That *could* be said to a friend. Fuck. I closed my eyes, my heart racing because I felt like I'd missed my chance with Elle before I even had it. "Well, sit. I'll cook for you."

I finished the eggs and toast, already getting the yogurt and fruit ready, and placed the dishes on the table. "How are you feeling?"

"Eh, pretty tired." She took a bite of eggs and put them on her jellied toast.

"What are you doing?"

"Oh. I love eggs and jelly together. Is that strange?"

"Yes."

She laughed and finished making her weird egg jelly sandwich. "Yum"

My lips quirked, and I relaxed. If she could be this chill, why couldn't I? *Right*. We still hadn't talked about what happened. How come she hadn't brought it up? Didn't *she* want to figure it out too?

Unless she already told me with the *friend* comment. Fear of being rejected kept me quiet. I wasn't sure what I was even asking for, but I knew it would hurt if she said no. And…I couldn't lose her. I'd rather watch her be with someone else than not have Elle in my life. That was how much she'd worked her way into my soul.

I gripped the back of my neck, my entire body a ball of nerves. She ate her food in silence, letting out a sigh of pleasure every so often. There were a few cuts on her face from the glass but no blood, thankfully. She narrowed her eyes at me as I stared, and she pushed her hair out of her face.

That was when I saw it.

The bruise on her forearm.

It was a handprint that stretched a good six inches. "Fucking *asshole*." I jumped from the table, kicking the chair to the side. I wanted to punch him again.

"Cal!" She stood too, frowning as she stared at her arm. "Oh."

My jaw hurt from how hard I clenched, and I wanted to throw my plate across the room.

"Hey, it's okay." She frowned and walked toward me. My temper caught me off guard, and I took a few deep breaths.

"Do you... need ice?" I managed to say in a normal voice. "I might have some."

"No, I didn't even feel it until you saw it." She reached out a hand but let it drop. She looked like she wanted to say something, but she hesitated. She seemed nervous.

"I'm sorry I snapped. I just," I paused, pinching the bridge of my nose. "The thought of you getting hurt *physically* pains me. Give me a minute."

She remained quiet as I caught my breath. I had to get it together. Between sleeping with her, spending the night with her, and the bruise? My mind was a fucking mess. My phone went off, breaking the tension, and thank god for that.

It was Charlie. The clean-up party would start in thirty minutes.

Elle finished her food, put the plates in the dishwasher, and thanked me. "I'll give you your shirt later."

I nodded, not caring about that. I wanted to be alone to figure out what was wrong with me.

"Thank you, Cal." She stood on her tiptoes and kissed my cheek. "I'll see you in a bit."

My skin tingled from her kiss, and as soon as the door shut, I went to my plants. I needed to escape my own damn head before seeing her again. I'd tried so hard for so many damn years to not feel anything but the high of playing hockey. It was easier. Lonely and sad and miserable as fuck but easier. This mashup of terribly loud and unhinged feelings were so unfamiliar. And weird.

I'd only known her a short time, but the thought of something happening to her terrified me. If I fell deeper and it didn't work... would I recover? Could I?

I didn't fucking know, but we had to talk about this thing between us. She meant too much to me to avoid hard conversations. So, I'd help with the bar and then get my shit together because life with Elle made living *off* the ice worth it.

CHAPTER
TWENTY-ONE

Elle

One night. That was all it had taken for me to cross the line into *really* having feelings for Cal. Sure, a lot had happened. A shit ton had happened, but I was eighty percent in love with Cal Holt. The way he defended me, the care afterward, dressing me and cleaning my wounds. The fact he *read to me.* The guy who didn't like reading, had read to me for an hour. His voice had gone hoarse, and I knew he'd been tired, but he'd done it anyway.

Then when I had a nightmare and he held me and took my mind off it?

Then the breakfast after?

Fucking shit. I had it bad.

I showered quickly, keeping my hair up in a pony, and dressed in old jeans and a Central State tank top. Today was going to be rough. Not just because my emotions for Cal were confusing and he didn't seem to have a handle on it either. But because of the bar and everything that happened. That had been fucked up. Really, really fucked up. I could've been seriously hurt—hell, any one of us could've been. The fact no one had more than some bruises and chipped teeth was incredible.

Todd probably had a concussion, but that fucker deserved it. I shivered, replaying the crazed look in his eyes. Drunk guys without consequences were the worst humans of all time.

I made as little noise as possible before leaving a note on the door. *Something came up, be back later!* Daniella and Gabe would flip out when they learned what happened, but I wasn't ready yet. I had enough mental things to sort through before talking to them.

Cal...the bar...the fight...my feelings...*his* feelings. Yeah, before telling them, I needed to process everything on my own.

Cleaning relaxed me, and maybe getting the bar back in shape would be closure for last night. I locked my unit and almost jumped at seeing Cal's tall frame leaning outside my door. "Jesus."

"Sorry." He looked it, his face all pale with bags under his eyes. "I waited for you and tried to keep distance to not scare you."

"Some people text."

"I'll keep that in mind." His mouth almost curved, and for a few seconds, everything returned to normal. Elle and Cal, buddies.

Then memories of what happened all came back. "Guess we should head there?"

He nodded.

We walked in a comfortable silence. I was stunned at the scene in front of the bar. There were at least ten people. Gregg and Big Ben, and a bunch of other regulars who were there last night too. "What's this?" I asked.

"Huh." Cal walked faster, and I kept pace. Gregg saw us and smiled.

"Glad you're both alright. Last night was a bitch, huh?"

"What are you doing here?" I asked, waving as they turned to look at us.

"Helping clean, of course. Charlie's place has been a second home for years. I'm not letting him deal with this alone."

"Plus, you shouldn't be the ones cleaning up when they were the fuckers that started it. How are you feeling, Sunshine?" Big Ben asked, his eyes moving toward the bruise on my arm.

My eyes welled up at the display of friendship. "Better now."

"Good. Now, let us in. Albert put a post on social media, so we got a good crowd."

Cal smiled, a real one, and held out his hand. "You're a good man. All of you are."

"Don't let Cindy hear you say that. She's here too."

Cindy waved, her cigarette hanging from her fingers. I couldn't believe it. This was incredible. All these people. Here to help Charlie, us. My heart fucking soared. I'd wanted to find my own place at college, and despite my family and Gabe thinking the bar wasn't it, it was. People who had each other's backs no matter what. My eyes prickled. "Cal, let's get a plan going, and we can divide and conquer! Oh, this is amazing. I thought this would take days."

"Charlie's a loyal motherfucker." Cal laughed as I unlocked the door. The smell hit me first. Then Cal muttered, "Shit."

"Horrible."

I flicked on the lights and winced at the scene. Glass, beer, tables, shoes? It was a hot ass mess and smelled even worse. "Give me two minutes, then we start."

Cal held everyone off as I found a path toward the bar. I got sticky notes and divided the bar into five categories: trash, items to repair/wash, bar area, back area, and main area. "Three people per section, then we need an assembly line to get shit out in the dumpster."

"That was fast." Cal stared at me with warm eyes. "And impressive."

"Cleaning is my love language."

He smiled and held my gaze for a beat before opening the door. "Okay—here's the plan."

Everyone got to work and cleaned their asses off. Sweat dripped from every part of my body, and my muscles ached from lifting and scooting and shoving things back to their rightful spot. Even with the air and a fan on, the summer heat had snuck in, and oof, it was gross. Cleaning was therapeutic to me. I thought I'd be scared to be back here, but I felt at home just as much as I did in the apartment. With Gregg and Big Ben and Cindy shooting the shit, with Cal directing and thanking everyone, with Alex complaining the whole time but working their ass off, it felt like a different sort of family.

All the glass was cleaned up, the trash taken out, and the chairs and tables righted. Cal swept the floor, and Alex followed with a mop. I wiped the bar top a million times with bleach and then moved to make sure every bottle of liquor was cleaned. No evidence of the fight remained, besides my bruise.

Charlie handled all the press and nosey neighbors, and he whistled when he walked in, his bushy beard moving side to side. "This place looks better than before. Damn. Maybe we need to fight once a month to actually clean this shithole."

Everyone laughed, and Charlie ran a hand over the bar. "Thank you from the bottom of this grump's heart. This place is my home, and I'm lucky to have y'all as family."

Charlie shook everyone's hand, promising them a drink on the house when they returned. Alex, Cal, and I hung back by the bar as Charlie said goodbye, and when the last helper left, he faced us. "You three."

"Don't lump me in with these two." Alex pointed their thumb at us. "They're newest."

"True." Charlie clapped Alex on the shoulder. "Thank you. All of you. For keeping this place running, for taking care of it. My life turned upside down, and having things be the same here means a lot."

"Sure." Cal nodded. "Where's Lizzie?"

"She's with my neighbor who has five dogs. She's happy." He beamed like a proud parent. "I don't know what it'll look like now that I have Lizzie. I can't work every night, and if that means I hire more people, I will. Cal, you can stop helping anytime you want. Elle, if you're still interested after all this shit, you can pick your schedule."

The thought of not working with Cal made me want to throw up. I *loved* seeing him every day. Our little glances, the walks to and from the place. His snacks. I sucked in a breath and tried not to react.

"And me?" Alex asked.

"When have you not gotten what you wanted?"

We all laughed, and Charlie tapped his knuckles on the bar. "We're closed tonight. I'm making the call right now. Go out, have fun, do what you need to move on from last night."

"Are you sure? We can handle it," Cal spoke up.

"I'm sure. Tomorrow, I'll come around lunch to create a new schedule. All of you get lost, go be young."

Alex didn't wait a second before bouncing, and I, too, wanted to shower from the sweat and enjoy a night off. I got to the door and paused, feeling weird. I was so used to heading home with Cal that it was strange he wasn't with me. I glanced around to spot that he hadn't moved yet. He spoke to Charlie in hushed tones, his back toward me. Charlie frowned.

Must be serious.

I couldn't very well ask him to walk with me, that'd be weird. It was broad daylight at three in the afternoon. His comment about alone time that one day… I bet he needed that. I waved. I didn't want him to feel uncomfortable, so I said, "Bye, you two!" and left fast.

I pushed open the door, breathed in the humid air, and walked home. It amazed me to see such support from everyone. That kind of found family was so important and honestly got me thinking about my future. I loved writing but knew the reality of it was tough. What if I owned a book bar?

My insides got all tingly with the idea, and I was dying to get to a pencil to write it all out. One wall could be all used books and others featuring books people brought in, like a trading post. We'd serve food, wine, beer. Have good hours to accommodate students and late-night workers. Oh man, what if we had cats too? That'd be sick! We could have 'blind date with a book' nights, speed dating for book lovers. My usual fantasy included a nerdy guy with glasses and sweaters, but now... Cal showed up in my visions. No glasses but definitely the sweaters hugging his muscles.

"Elle, what the fuck?" Cal ran up to me, his eyes pissed.

My heart leapt in my throat about him interrupting my daydream. "Um, hi?"

"You left without me."

"I thought you needed time alone." I frowned, feeling bad at the worried look in his eyes. "You know, when you're playing hockey games, I'll be working the bar and walking home by myself. It will happen."

"I'm already worried about it. Look." He dragged a hand down his face, running it along his jaw as he bit out, "Are you sure you should work here still? There'll be other places that'll open once school starts."

Something flared in the back of my mind. "Is *that* what you were talking to Charlie about?"

He looked guilty. "It doesn't matter."

"Cal." Anger flared. "You and Charlie don't get to decide what I should or shouldn't do."

"I know, but the fight, your arm... it's all a bit much. What if you got seriously hurt? He could've done real damage, and what if I'm not there next time? You could find somewhere else that's safer."

"I appreciate your concern, but I love working at Charlie's." It had been a second home with people who cared in their own way. I loved Gregg and Big Ben and Cindy. The smell of beer than never quite went away. The lingering humidity in there. The sound of a game always being on the TV. It was beautiful.

"But—" Cal started.

"Enough." I held up my hand in a stop sign. "I understand you're worried, but this is my decision, not yours. Do *not* try to get me fired."

"Fired? No, just not working weekend nights." He gripped the back of his neck. "I don't mean to upset you, please. I just don't want anything to happen to you." His deep voice went even lower. "Elle, I'm sorry."

Some of the anger left at the despair on his face. He looked really upset, more than his usual frowning. His cheeks were red and his jaw tight.

"I overstepped."

"You did." I crossed my arms, staring up at him.

He swallowed and looked helpless. I refused to help him out though. He had to talk his own way out of this. He sighed and hung his head before meeting my gaze again. His feet moved side to side, and he gently lifted my forearm with the bruise. He trailed one finger over it, his breath coming out harder. "Seeing this all day really upset me. I wanted to fix it, and the only thing I could come up with was you not working there."

"It's just a bruise."

His eyes flashed. "It was just a hailstorm."

"What?"

"My parents died from a rainstorm. A simple, Midwestern rainstorm with hail. There wasn't any damage to houses or crops, yet their car swerved, flipped, and they died. *Just* a bruise is still a lot." His eyes went wide, and he dropped my arm.

Oh my heart. I put a hand on my chest, sucking in a breath. "Cal."

"I should take a walk. Yeah, I need a minute." He squeezed his eyes shut and spun the other way. His shoulders were about up to his ears as he walked away, leaving me in a pile of feelings.

I was still rattled from the night before, upset about his chat with Charlie, and overwhelmed by his admission. We'd never talked about how his parents died. I'd never asked because it wasn't something you pulled out of someone. They shared it on their own. But like this? In the heat of an argument?

I rubbed my chest as a pang radiated up my neck. It explained his reaction so much though. How angry he'd gotten this morning when he saw it, how he'd hung around me all day, protecting me. My anger dissipated at him trying to get me to quit—sure, we needed to talk it out, but I understood his motivations. He struggled with emotions, and he had so many today. Fuck, I fought with my own, and I could generally handle them.

I thought about going after him but decided against it. I'd wait for him to come back. Yeah, I could make him some dinner and bring it up to him. Until then, my fingers twitched with the need to write my heart out. Writing was my escape, my therapy, and I dashed upstairs.

Cooking and writing would keep me at peace until Cal and I could talk.

I tried ignoring the telltale signs my male main character's traits were starting to morph into someone I knew in real life. Jackson struggled with emotions after losing his wife years ago. He used work as a way to escape and acted out when things got serious. The emotionally damaged hero didn't expect to run into his high school sweetheart with a daughter. The features on Jackson shaped into Cal's—big broad shoulders, soulful eyes, a deep voice meant for radio, and a jawline delicious enough to distract a nun. Amanda, the female lead, knew he'd be tough to crack but worth the wait.

Shit. Was I Amanda? Was I delusional enough to project me and Cal into my writing? I shut my laptop and pushed it away. Yes, I had feelings for him. I wasn't sure they were love, and I knew better than to think he reciprocated all of them. He felt *something* for me. The guy's love language was gestures, and he'd done so many things for me that I'd lost count.

But love? Romance?

He said over and over he didn't do that, that he was a three-nights-only guy.

I doubted I, who was exceptionally average, would be the one to change that. I wanted to, hell, my heart ached for him, but I'd be a fool to think it would happen. Putting my hopes out there that I was enough or that he'd change for me would be naïve. Gabe said he'd bolt at the first snag of something going wrong, and sure enough, he'd stormed away after he mentioned his parents.

That's not the same thing. I groaned, annoyed at my indecision. I wanted to be with Cal. I did. But…mentioning it to him and ending up like Sherry? He'd never promised more than friends, and I knew if I asked his face would get all tight and his gaze hard, and I wouldn't survive him icing me out. Fuck. This was difficult.

I made a lasagna since it was my comfort food. Carbs, cheese, meat. I pulled it out of the oven right around six. My outfit wasn't fancy, but I did spend more time on my hair than normal. I curled it and added two layers of mascara. Then lip gloss. I looked good but not too good.

Oh my god I had it bad. I had to check to see if Cal was home though. If he wasn't, I'd leave it in front of his door. It would suck not to see him, but I'd go to the bookstore at the strip mall instead. Get lost in a book and use last night's tips to buy a journal.

Elle: are you home?

Cal: yes, busy though

Good. Nerves exploded all throughout my body, like Pop Rocks lived under my veins. I wasn't sure why it felt different between us. His admission? Last night? Sleeping together? Surprisingly, out of all the things that made our dynamic shift, us having sex was the least of my worries. That was… explosive.

With the lasagna in hand, I headed upstairs and tried to settle my stomach. He could send me away, which I'd respect. He could say no thanks, which I'd take. My consolation prize was eating it myself and going downtown. I could live with that.

I exhaled, knocked on his door, and waited. Thirty seconds, forty-five. *The handle!*

He opened it, his eyes widening in surprise. "Elle."

"Hi." I smiled. "I brought you dinner, if you want. It's lasagna. My favorite. Lots of cheese. I even added red pepper flakes, so there's a kick if you're into that." Oh god, my word vomit had lost control. "I think we should talk. About anything! Food or not."

He pressed his lips together, his gaze sweeping over my head, face, legs. He inhaled loudly and frowned. "Now's not a great time."

"Sure, of course." My stomach sank. He'd told me he was busy, but it still hurt. His eyes didn't hold the same spark or warmth I'd seen earlier. They looked…cold. Back to the original Cal. The brick walls around his heart. The place I *never* wanted to be. Fuck. "I understand, right, yes."

Maybe he needed to be alone still, to think. He was an introvert. A grumpy one. I could give him space. No problem. Or maybe the conversation about his parents still upset him. He needed time. My mind created scenarios that would help protect my damn heart as to *why* he looked at me like he wanted me gone. But then…

A laugh carried through the door. A female laugh. Throaty and happy and *oh* fuck. *This* wasn't a scenario I'd planned for. Him having another girl in his place. He stared at me, his eyes widening with what I assumed to be guilt.

He wasn't going mention he had a girl over. He was going to get me the hell out of there and not tell me.

I blinked back the shock, my eyes watering. I had to leave. "Here." I shoved the lasagna in his hands.

"Elle," he said, almost dropping the pan. He fumbled with it, but I was already at the door to the stairs.

"Enjoy the food, please. Eat. I made it for you." My back was toward him, thank the lord, because tears came hard. I jogged down the stairs, my feet not moving fast enough because fuck, this hurt. Badly. Sprinting into my place, I locked the door and dove into my bed.

And the thing was, even as I cried into my pillow, I *knew* better. He technically had done *nothing* wrong. We weren't more than friends. We both said it all the time. Sure, we'd slept together, but did that actually change a single thing? He could sleep with whoever he wanted.

I was just the idiot who'd fallen in love with the guy who would never return my feelings. Either by choice or because I wasn't special enough to change the great, grumpy Cal Holt.

CHAPTER
TWENTY-TWO

Cal

The door to the stairs slammed shut, echoing in the empty foyer of the fourth floor. I saw the second she thought she knew what was happening. It was clear as hell on her face. Michael and *his sister* and his girlfriend's sister were over to talk about proposing to Naomi. Ryann Reiner was a fucking hoot and someone else who gave Reiner shit. I loved it—but that was the extent of my relationship with her. And Cami…she was a gorgeous spitfire who cared a lot for her sister. Michael had invited the three of them over without asking me. He never gave me a warning.

The absolute crushed face of Elle would stay in my head, but honestly…it was for the best. I needed distance. The bruising, her working at the bar, the fight, sleeping with her *twice*. I was too involved with her, and I didn't do that with *anyone*. I shut the door to my place and forced the ache in my chest away. Michael was here.

"My neighbor brought me dinner."

"You're friendly enough with neighbors to do that? How? Jonah and I are so nice, well, I am, and no one has ever brought me dinner." Ryann eyed the dish and clapped her hands. "Pasta, yes, please."

Michael narrowed his eyes at me. "What neighbor?"

"Yeah, who is she?" Ryann asked.

"I have an idea." Cami's gaze sparkled. She was a dangerous one who knew too much, and I narrowed my eyes at her.

"Settle down, Reiner clan. One of you is enough. And Cami, shut up."

They chuckled as I set the dish on the table. Elle had made this, for me, and looked so beautiful. She'd done her hair, and her lips were all red. And I'd let her think the laugh was a hookup. She assumed that of me because I hadn't given her a reason to know it wasn't true. Guilt ate at me. God, I was the worst. I rubbed over my ribs as Michael, Ryann, and Cami joined me. Compartmentalizing was a weakness of mine, and it was the perfect time to practice it. For a guy who'd avoided emotions for years, there were so many bubbling up that I couldn't sit still. "So, what's your plan?"

I needed Michael to talk so they'd stop asking me questions. My pulse already raced at thinking about Elle downstairs. Was she crying? I swore her eyes had welled up with tears before she ran away, and fuck, I didn't want to make her cry. I just needed to turn down my feelings for her because it was too much. She deserved more than me. Someone who didn't lose their mind over a bruise or run away when the conversation got hard.

"I found this guy online—"

"This sounds weird. What does that mean?" Ryann interrupted.

"Yeah, like a weird sex thing?" Cami asked.

"Shut up, my god, let me get to it." Michael grinned, looking a little wild. His hair was disheveled, and his eyes had a glint that hadn't been there before. "He does data for a living. I don't know what or how or care, but he's going to help me come up with a code or problem that Naomi will have to solve. And when she does... bam. It'll say, will you marry me?"

"Interesting... so what's the story though? Like, hey babe, solve this riddle for me?" Ryann leaned forward and grabbed a fork. "I love the creativity, but I need more of the plan."

"Hm, I can almost see this." Cami nodded.

"Okay, so we often work at home after dinner, have drinks, watch TV. I figured I'd get a weird email. Ask for her help since she's all techie. Then, when she's working through it, I'll get the ring out and wait for her to figure out the message."

"Not bad." Ryann grinned, her side smile matching her brother's. "Okay, I love it. Cami, what do you think?"

"This has Naomi written all over it. Yes." Cami grinned wide and hit the table. "This plan is fucking perfect."

"Yeah?" Michael smiled back and hit me in the shoulder. "Holt, what are your thoughts?"

From what I knew about Naomi, she'd appreciate the fact he was using her language to ask her. I nodded, my throat getting tight as I my mind wandered to Elle. What would she think? Very romantic. She could write about it. "It's great."

"Man of many words, this one." Ryann jutted her finger at me, winking. I'd celebrated a couple holidays with Michael and his sister, and every time she teased me, it used to make me upset that I didn't have a sibling. But now, I had a cousin. I could tease her when she got older and make sure anyone she was with treated her right.

God, whatever human fell for Lizzie would have to deal with Charlie *and* me. God bless the poor soul. I smiled a little bit, and Michael saw it instantly. "Thinking about your neighbor?"

Cami wiggled her eyebrows. God, she was a pain in the ass. I felt for Coach. Twin daughters? Jesus.

"No. My cousin."

"Charlie's newfound child? How's that going?" Michael took his own plate of lasagna, and we all ate Elle's dish. It was fucking tasty, and another wave of self-pity hit me. I'd intentionally let her hurt because I wanted space from my emotions.

The worst kind of asshole, even if it was best for the future.

I focused on Lizzie and told them all about her, her room, how Charlie was already an amazing dad. Michael looked really pleased for me, and it felt good to have him on my team. He was one of the two people I liked, well... four now with Elle and Lizzie. *If* Elle talked to me again.

"That's incredible. He didn't know?" Ryann had a hand over her heart. "Wow, that's a real story right there."

"That's wonderful she has you guys." Cami's normally flirty face softened to sympathy. "What a brave little girl."

"I know." I sighed, the ache in my chest getting larger and larger. "Sorry to distract, Lizzie's just been on my mind."

"Dude, no worries. It's awesome you got a new family member." Michael held out a fist, and I hit it. "I got a question for you both. Cami, you already know you'll be involved somehow."

"Go for it." Ryann took another bite of the food and nodded. "God, this is good."

"Can you call Jonah?" Michael asked.

"Oh, shit." Ryann nodded, pulling her phone out of her pocket and putting it on speaker. Her boyfriend answered on the second ring.

"Hey, Ry."

"Hey, sunshine, so Michael asked me to call you. We're sitting with him, Naomi's sister, and Cal Holt."

"Alright." His tone sounded as confused as I did. Ryann and I shared a look before glancing at Michael.

"I want the three of you to stand up with me at my wedding."

"That wasn't a question," Jonah Daniels said, almost making me laugh.

"J.D., I swear to god," Michael said, chuckling. Jonah laughed too, and Ryann already stood up and hugged her brother.

Cami looked on, her eyes a little wet.

"Of course, I will. I'll find the cutest tux ever and be your best man," Ryann said.

"I'm in too," Jonah said.

Then they both stared at me. My heart beat fast, and my palms sweated, and the hope in Michael's eyes was almost too much. He wanted *me* to be in *his wedding?* Those photos were forever. "Are you sure?"

"Dude. We've celebrated holidays together. Get drinks once a week. We're family, man. Our weird little crew. I'm not gonna be your coach forever. We love you."

My throat constricted, and I took a shaky breath. I gripped the sides of the table as wave after wave of emotion plowed through me. *We love you.*

We're family.

I closed my eyes for a second. No one had told me those words since my parents died. We love you.

I knew Charlie cared for me, but he wasn't one to say that. And besides him, there hadn't been anyone else. A soft hand landed on my shoulder and squeezed. I opened my eyes to see Ryann smiling at me softly. "Hey, I know it's a lot. Jonah is a bit emotionally stunted too, and us Reiners broke through."

"I'm still on the phone, Ry."

"I'm aware," she said, laughing but not taking her eyes of me. "Michael talks about you like you're the brother he never had. Jonah and I watch you play almost every game. Come, join the circus."

"It is a circus, Holt, but it's worth it," Jonah said. "I say that reluctantly."

I rarely cried. I'd kept it in and shoved it down all these years, but my eyes prickled. I ran the back of my free arm over my face and nodded. "Jesus Christ, fine. I'm in."

Cami beamed.

Ryann clapped my arm, and Michael nodded at me, the absolute joy on his face somehow a comfort. These two had no idea what this meant to me. There was no way. To be included, and called family? Even when I'd been a total asshole?

"This means... a lot, Reiner."

He nodded again as Ryann hung up the phone. We finished eating dinner, but the thing I kept thinking about was how badly I wanted to tell Elle. She'd be so happy for me and smile and do the squeal thing she did when something sparked joy. I forced myself to not freak out that I'd just hurt the person who had somehow worked their way up to the top of my list.

I might care about more people now, but Elle was at the top. Even if I was bad for her, I could work to be better? Michael liked me, somehow, and didn't think I was a piece of shit. I'd learn. Grow. Study whatever book Elle needed me to so I could be enough for her. To prove to her and Gabe that I could be good.

Elle deserved the world and maybe I could be the person for her?

So, after Michael and Ryann headed out, I made a plan.

First stop Sunday morning was to finally get a tattoo for my mom and dad. *Take Off Your Pants and Jacket* from 2001. My dad had been obsessed with this album. The stoplight represented so much to me—almost like my life. I'd come to a complete stop when they died, danced in the yellow as I slowly figured out next steps, and yeah, it had taken years but I finally felt like I was in the green now. Ready to go.

Ready to stop being so fucking mad all the time.

My mom's favorite was Incubus's *A Crow Left of the Murder*, and the red flowers on the artwork would be perfect. Plus, she loved flowers. My dad had always bought her some for no reason, and it put a huge smile on her face. Once I decided on the two designs, I had a sense of peace. I wasn't angry at my life as much.

I printed both out after reading the shop's requirements online and headed in. Neither were large but would take two hours or so, and I texted Charlie that I might be a little late to the bar. He didn't care since I told him what I was doing.

Learning I wasn't a fan of needles was fun, but the whole time I was there, I wished Elle was with me. She'd hold my hand and laugh at the way I winced. They bandaged up forearm and gave me care instructions, and I left a generous tip. The artist combined the flowers with the stoplight, and now, I carried a little part of my parents everywhere I went.

My lungs felt lighter, like they didn't have to work as hard as before. If I'd have realized a tattoo was all it took, I would've done this years ago. Even though deep down, I knew I hadn't been ready. I ran a hand over my chest, smiling up at the sky. Pain was a symbol of a deep love, and even though my parents were gone, I'd experienced what it felt like to be loved. Not all kids had that. I'd gotten eighteen years with them. Lizzie had gotten four with her mom.

Michael had gotten twenty.

As I drove home, I made a quick stop at the store to grab snacks. Even though I was sure Elle was furious at me, she needed to eat. I bought cookies, fruit snacks, and almonds and quickly headed to the bar. It was only an hour later than I'd planned.

My gaze searched for Elle the second I walked in the door. She wore a red bandana in her hair, tied at the top, and a white tank top. Her cutoff shorts were darker than normal, and she didn't look up at all as the door swung shut.

"I want to see it." Charlie stood from the table, Alex nodding at me as I entered. Charlie met me halfway, and I carefully peeled the bandage off my arm. "Wow, they did a great job. You should post something online and credit the artist."

"For sure." Alex joined him and whistled. "This is great. What does it mean?"

Elle slowly turned around, her curled hair hanging down her back as she finally looked at me. There was a quick flash of hurt in her eyes before she grinned. "Did you get a tattoo, Calzone?"

Wait, what?

Her smiled looked genuine, her eyes filled with warmth. I didn't understand. I shook my head and cleared my throat. She wasn't... mad? What did that mean? "Uh, yes. It's for my mom and dad. It's based off artwork from the bands they listened to. Figured it was time I carried them with me."

Charlie smiled and patted my back before returning to his table. Alex followed him, and Elle stared, her brown eyes taking in the design. She was so pretty it hurt. She made me want to try to open myself to feeling again. I wasn't sure the hows or whats, but I knew I wanted *her*. But…she stared at me the way she used to, before we kissed, and everything changed. My breath hitched in my throat.

"This is beautiful." She reached out her fingers, like she wanted to touch it, before letting her hand fall down. "How bad did the shading hurt?"

"It wasn't fun."

She scrunched her nose. "I couldn't stomach the shading. I only got lettering, and that was bad enough. You'll have to give me the artist's name so I can have a person down here. It's been about six months, and I'm itching for another."

She went back to her seat, across from Charlie, and that left the open one next to her. I was confused as fuck. I was prepared for her to ice me out, to block me, to *hate* me. But this indifference? It was worse? Like maybe I'd made up the tears in her voice. Maybe she didn't care about me at all?

The thought was sobering and sent a wave of panic. *This is why I don't feel.* This feeling coursed through my veins, making my fists clench.

"Okay, team." Charlie pushed out a sheet of paper with our names on it. "I plan to open back up for lunch on the weekends *and* hire security. After Friday night, I don't want any of you to deal with that again. I've already reached out to a buddy who owns a company. Starting Thursday, we'll have someone at the door at all times."

Then what can I do? Not be here with Elle? If I didn't work at the bar, how would we see each other? Would she even want to? My pulse throbbed at the base of my neck, and I ground my teeth together to prevent myself from freaking out.

Charlie looked at me, his gaze narrowing. "You can stay on during the week if you want, Cal. But unless you wanna bartend, we don't need you anymore."

"I'll do the weekdays." Desperation made me sound needy. I didn't care. This bar would mean Elle and I were connected. Weekdays were enough. Plus, once hockey started, my weekends were shot. "I can bartend too, if needed."

He nodded, then turned to Elle. "Alex's schedule hasn't changed, but you don't need to be here six days a week, Elle. Pick four."

"Thursday, Friday, Saturday, Sunday."

The weekend. I gulped, trying to catch her gaze, but she focused on my uncle.

Had she intentionally picked days I wouldn't be here? Fuck. Or was it because she made more money then? I didn't know. She wrote her name on the paper and passed it back to Charlie. The only day we'd both be here was Sunday—if I chose to work it.

My gut churned like I'd drunk sour milk. It happened once, made me throw up. Elle was being so chill that it drove me mad. We needed to talk… to figure out this dynamic.

"I'm also hoping Tina comes back from maternity leave soon. Once she's back, she works every weekday, and we can finally get a balance. Now, I can't do nights past six. Lizzie understands I need to work, but I want her feeling comfortable."

"If there's ever a night you need to be here, I'm happy to watch her for you." Elle smiled at him. "I live two minutes away, and my roommate is on the dance team. We have more pom-poms and glitter than anyone should allow."

"Thank you, Elle. I might take you up on that."

"The offer is the same for me," I blurted out, annoyed that she volunteered herself and not the two of us. "Anytime."

Charlie frowned at me but nodded. My insides were going wild since Elle had gone off-script. I planned everything to say if she was furious at me, but this? She hadn't looked at me since we sat down. Why? I really fucking needed to know.

"Tonight, I need you three here since the crowd might be bigger than normal. But after this week, the new schedule will take place."

"I wasn't sure if you closed for the Fourth, but I was hoping to be off." Elle tapped her nails on the table. They were purple now, different than yesterday. She must've done it last night or this morning…when she thought I was with someone else.

"I'll shut down. Lizzie wants to go to a pool party in our neighborhood." He hit the table and laughed. "Look at me? Never thought I'd want to close for a day for a kid."

"Your life is different now," Alex said, a rare smile on their face. "Priorities change. Your wants change. Doesn't take more than a moment."

Charlie and Elle kept talking about the fourth plans, but Alex's words hit me in the center of my chest. *Doesn't take more than a moment.* My life had changed multiple times in a single moment. Losing my parents, meeting Elle, seeing Lizzie the first time. I wanted to be someone who Elle deserved. But now? I wasn't sure if she'd ever want me. I ran a hand over my forehead, groaning.

"Late night?" Alex said, wiggling their brows and looking at Elle.

She shook her head, her lips flat. "I went to a bookstore, alone, and was asleep by nine. Wild animal over here."

They all looked at me expectantly, and I felt pressured to answer. "Had friends over." That was the truth, but Elle just stared at the back of her hand. It'd be tough to talk to her with Alex and Charlie hovering around, but I had to. Even if I didn't have my emotions in check, I knew I couldn't lose her, and for some reason, I felt a countdown ticking down, like I'd miss my one tiny chance to be with her if I didn't try soon.

CHAPTER
TWENTY-THREE

Elle

The Oscar belonged to me and me alone. I was a badass bitch who didn't show one ounce of how sad I was on the inside. Not even a little. I applied my best mascara and midsummer outfit. Did my hair. Wore my favorite Chucks. Put on my battle gear –perfume and hoop earrings, and I refused to show Cal how upset I was.

One, for my own ego. But two, so he didn't need to feel guilty. That was what I'd learned from him all these weeks was that he acted out of what I assumed was pain and then felt like shit about it. He didn't want to hurt me. He hadn't paraded the woman around me intentionally. He'd asked for space, and I'd showed up unannounced.

It was a real kick in the crotch to know he'd done nothing wrong while crushing my foolish, romantic heart. It'd be easier if he was an asshole about it, flaunting another hookup or promising me something and breaking it. He'd done NONE of those things.

How did one get over something they did to themselves? If anyone had the answer, I'd pay money. Big monies. I wiped down the bar with a towel as more patrons came in, and I felt his gaze on me. I gave him a quick smile and wink before tending to the guests. It'd be great to not have to stare at him all the time here. I refused to quit or change jobs. I loved it too much, but not working with him on the weekends would be a start. A little distance right now would help. I could piece my heart back together before we hung out again.

Sleeping with him had changed everything, like I knew it would, but my ding-dong heart had made me fall in love with him anyway. Jealousy wasn't a feeling I got too often, but thinking about the owner of that laugh had my insides turning green. Did *she* know about his past? His soft heart? His fear of being alone? His plants?

Okay, settle down.

I poured a glass of gin and tonic just as I heard my brother's voice.

"A fight? I read about it in the news?" Gabe plopped down at the end of the bar, his face lined with anger. He looked me up and down, his frown growing. "What the hell? Didn't want to tell me?"

"Not really. And this is why." I gestured to him.

He deflated, his eyes closing. Gabe loved me. I knew that. But we still were figuring out this new dynamic between us. He sighed.

"Are you alright? Did you get hurt?"

"I'm fine." I held my bruise and found Cal watching us, his brows drawn together. I refocused on my brother. "It could've been significantly worse if Cal wasn't there though. I'm thankful he was."

He twisted around and nodded at Cal. "Is he okay? What did he do?"

I gave Gabe the replay of what went down, and I swore he was gonna break the glass of water I'd given him. "Dude, it's fine now."

"You shouldn't be working here. Find a new job. I can help you."

Irritation had my jaw tightening. "Not again. Cal said the same thing, but you're wasting your breath."

"Yeah, well, he's right." He huffed and frowned. "Never thought I'd say that, damn. Glad he kept his word."

"What *word*?"

"Told me he'd take care and look out for you." Gabe narrowed his eyes. "Y'all are just friends still, right?"

Clearly. "Did you come here to scold me, Dad?"

He stared me down, his shoulders losing some of the tension. I raised a brow, my own pulse racing at the mini confrontation.

"I'm sorry, really." He sighed. "I'm adjusting to having you here, alright? I want you safe, and reading about a bar fight? With arrests? At the place you work at? It fucking scared me. You should've told me. Dani and I could've stayed with you."

"I stayed with Cal, *not* that it's your concern. We lived through it together, and he protected me numerous times. He's a good person buried beneath his tough exterior. I'd appreciate if you stopped acting like he was a piece of shit."

"Whoa, Elle, I didn't—"

"You did. You insult him all the time and make sure he knows it. Don't you think that's hard enough?" My temper flared now. I quickly glanced to make sure Cal stood at the door, but his back must've been toward me. "He donates more than you earn a year to charities. Did you know that? Takes care of plants that are half-dead to try and get them back to life." My voice remained a whisper, but I felt people watching us. I took a breath and took a step away.

Gabe stared at me, eyes wide, before he blushed. "I don't want him hurting you."

"I understand your intentions, bro, but leave him alone. I can take care of myself."

"He bothering you, Sunshine?" Big Ben asked, nursing a large glass of Guinness.

I shook my head. "Just my brother."

"Ah, carry on. Let me know if he needs thrown out."

I winked at him, Gabe watching the exchange with fear and amusement. "They take care of me here. It's… a second home. You had hockey as your family at school. I have Daniella, obviously, and you're around. But this place feels like home."

Gabe's shoulders slowly relaxed as he stared at me. "You might be right."

"I am."

"I like this version of you. It's… different, but you're braver. Growing into yourself." He smiled big now. "Never would've thought Elle back home would befriend guys at a bar. Not my sweet dorky writing sister."

"Surprises come in many forms." My gaze briefly moved to Cal before returning to Gabe. "I love you and am so glad you're my brother, but you got to experience college without family. That meant making mistakes and learning and being dumb. I want that too."

"I understand." He patted my hand, pulling me across the bar into a hug. "I'm proud of you, and I'll work on not being an asshole."

"You're not an asshole per se, just extra annoying."

"I'll work on that too." He released me and frowned at the bruise on my arm. "This from Friday?"

"Yup. Cal punched the guy right in the face, so don't worry."

"Good for him." He glanced back at him again. "I'll see you later, alright? Dani's gonna freak when she hears about it, so maybe tell her before she reads about it online?"

I winced. "Fair point. I should've told you both. Next time."

Gabe did not like my joke, but I laughed.

"You're fucking irritating. I'm leaving."

"Byeee!" I waved and couldn't stop smiling. I was lucky to have Gabe as a brother. I loved him, and most of the time, we got along well. I considered him one of my closest friends. But this was an adjustment, and I couldn't take another person in my life wanting to decide things for me. Or thinking I made poor choices just because *they* wouldn't choose the same ones.

"Elle, hey." Cal appeared at the end of the bar, his tone gentle. He leaned onto his forearms, a distant look in his eyes. "I brought snacks if you need them."

He set a bag down.

Still bringing me food. Where they out of guilt? A truce snack? My entire body hummed from him being near me, like it knew he was my person.

But he wasn't. Not really.

I couldn't meet his eyes. Not without my face giving away how much I cared for him. The urge to throw my arms around him and not let go dominated my mind. I needed to act chill, cool, unhurt so he didn't feel guilty. My plan sucked though.

"I'm good, but thanks." I flashed a smile, hoping it worked, and washed glasses that I was pretty sure were already clean. He stepped closer, his cologne and laundry smell almost too much. *Scrub, rinse repeat.* I focused on the glasses.

Friends. He can sleep with who he wants. I love him, but he doesn't want that.

A light touch came to my lower back. "It's been hours since lunch. You're probably starving. Are you sure?"

"I'll eat later, Cal." Shit. My voice came out sharper than I intended.

"Okay." He let go and stepped back, lingering a beat before leaving the bar. *Phew.* I came out all right in that exchange. Gave nothing away. My pulse skyrocketed, but I hid my neck from view. Only two hours left until closing time.

It went by slower than I liked. The Sunday crowd was steady but never enough to keep me busy every minute, which meant more time to think about Cal. It was clear we needed to talk. If anything, I wanted to ask about his parents. Him sharing how they died last night, then the tattoos…we could discuss as friends. I'd make it clear that was what we were. After I finished my side work for the night, I quickly darted off to the restroom and shut the door. The mirror was foggy, and the bathroom smelled, but I took a second to breathe.

Cal would walk me home, and we'd discuss the elephant in the room.

I'd insist I was fine.

Then I'd go home and write until I cried.

I washed my hands and put on the best face I could. He waited for me by the dart board and had his signature frown line in place. His jaw was tight too, almost looking like a younger version of him but angrier.

"Ready to walk home, partner?" I asked.

Partner? Oh my god.

He blinked in surprise. "Sure, yes."

"Great. See y'all later!" I waved, overdoing it but whatever. This was brutal. I deserved cookie dough. We stepped outside, the air a bit cooler with the sun setting. It was still humid as hell, and I struggled to take a deep breath.

Cal grabbed my hand, stopping me. He spun me around.

He scanned my face, glancing between both eyes as he ran a thumb over the back of my hand. "Are you... are we alright? You and me?

He seemed nervous, his voice all tight, and his forehead filled with lines.

I let go of his hand and crossed my arms, nodding. "Of course, why wouldn't we be?"

"Look," he said, causing my alarm bells to go off.

Fight or flight! Save your heart! Protect yourself!

I *couldn't* survive him trying to explain last night. I wouldn't. It'd shatter my heart into more pieces, and two large ones were enough to deal with.

"Cal, it's okay." I squeezed his forearm without the tattoo. My throat ached from withholding emotion, but I powered through. "If you were worried I was upset or had gotten too involved with you, I didn't. I knew you were a three-night guy, nothing more." I faked a smile, hating the pull I still had toward him. "There is no need to feel weird about hooking up with someone. You and I are friends who slept together twice. Nothing more. I didn't catch any feelings. I'm a romance girl, remember? I want a hero to sweep me off my feet, not a three-night guy."

His throat bobbed. "Friends," he repeated. A muscle in his jaw twitched.

"Yeah. And, as your *friend*, I want to ask about your parents but will follow your lead on that."

He worked his jaw like he chewed gum, his eyes going dark. His nostrils flared as he clenched his fists. The subject of his parents must've upset him. "What about them?"

"You mentioned how they died and took off. I was worried about you, hence the lasagna. Oh! Did you get to eat any of it?"

"We finished it, yeah. It was delicious. Thank you."

We. I winced, wanting to throw up that him and his lady friend ate the food I made to comfort *him.* "Cool. Keep the pan forever."

He ran a hand over his face. "Are you sure you're okay?"

"I'm great."

He looked like he didn't believe me, which let's be honest, I didn't believe me.

I blurted out, "I need to go. Got plans later. Big ones."

His eyes looked so sad, but I refused to be swept up into them. We needed some space, time to figure out the new dynamic. That was all. He could continue his flings, and I could move on. I skipped to the left, completely abandoning all dignity since my heart and brain were apparently broken. "Chop-chop."

His long strides caught up him to me, and he stopped me again, gently holding my elbow. "Elle, please, last night—"

"Don't, okay? You've done nothing but be honest with me. Maybe we shouldn't have slept together because it slightly changed things between us, but you can be with whoever you want. You should!" My voice sounded manic. "I'm glad you enjoyed yourself."

"You're not…were we not kinda seeing each other?" he asked, his voice low, low, low.

Oh my god. My heart ached. This confused me even more. Were we seeing each other? I didn't know. I wanted to see him. Be with him. But he didn't do that! He said he didn't! He never told me he wanted more! I knew from the start we weren't more than friends. We'd continued to point out how different we were from the beginning, so why would I ever assume we were more? I'd fantasized about it but never assumed it would be a reality.

"No! Of course not." I smiled again, the gesture so fake and painful. I was going to throw up. Cal would beat himself up over this, so I tried to be as direct as possible so he wouldn't feel bad or guilty. "I knew exactly what I was getting into with you. Now, we've said all we need to. I really can't be late, so I gotta go."

With that, I left him on the sidewalk and almost sprinted to the building. I didn't wait to see if he followed as I ran into my apartment. I might've thought I had it together, but I didn't. I really, really didn't. My eyes stung, and I slid against the door, wrapping my arms around my knees. I loved him. Of all the people in the world, I had to fall in love with the guy who'd run away from me at the mention of his parents, then slept with someone else. The guy who didn't do *feelings* when that was all I did.

"Oh fuck." Daniella stepped out of her room wearing a baggy shirt and hot pink shorts. "What did Cal do?"

"How do you know it's Cal?" I sniffed.

"Because, honey, it's clear you have it bad for him." She joined me at the door and pulled me to my feet. "What do you need? Ice cream, popcorn, alcohol?"

"Cookie dough."

"Then let's get some."

Without missing a beat, she grabbed her keys and dragged me out of the apartment. "There's a place Cami showed me that has the best dessert. It's hidden, but it's what you would say *romantic.*"

"Can't think of a better date than you."

"Aw." She intertwined our arms and guided us down the road toward campus. I couldn't help but scan the area for Cal. Was he upstairs? Was he out with her again? Was he walking around worried about me? It sucked to still care so much for him.

"Now, explain everything."

"Well, to sum it up in a logline, hopeless romantic tries to not fall for the emotionally damaged athlete, who had been nothing but upfront about what they would be the entire time, and fails miserably."

"I wouldn't see that movie. Sounds too dramatic."

I snorted, and Dani put her head on my shoulder. Thank god for her. I could pretend I'd be fine at work but for how long? We'd intertwined our lives so much that it'd be impossible to ignore him. "Shit, we're supposed to meet up tomorrow for our tutoring sessions."

"I think you can cancel."

"But I don't want to let him down, I do care about him as a friend too."

"Babe, text him that you're not feeling well, go a day without seeing him. It'll do you both good."

She was right. Probably. My soul hurt, and the question swirled around my head over and over. How would I ever move on from him when I saw him all the time? Was I destined to love someone who refused to love me back? What happened next?

CHAPTER
TWENTY-FOUR

Cal

Something wasn't right. Even though Elle's words said one thing, her eyes said another. Her posture had been too rigid and her voice slightly off. Then she cancelled our meetup, saying she didn't feel well?

I called bullshit, but I didn't know why? If she was upset with me about thinking I slept with someone else, why didn't she tell me that? She said it was fine. That I could be with whoever because we weren't anything but friends, but fuck, that hurt. Was *she* sleeping with other people? God, the thought made me feral.

After the way she'd defended me to her brother, did she still want to just be friends? I'd heard every word and couldn't recall a time someone had defended me. My mom and dad would, but I was happy back then.

So why stand up for me?

Because she was kind, thoughtful, and wonderful.

The pain in my gut wouldn't be settled by food or drinks or going out. It was deeper than that. I tossed a stress ball up and down as I lay on my bed, unsure of what to do. If she was legit sick, that could explain her weird mood. I could bring her soup!

Yes. My dad always got soup when my mom was sick. Unless... she was on her period? That was a logical explanation! I could get chocolate and a romance book, but what if she already owned it?

I could attach the receipt. Yeah. That'd work.

I couldn't sit here and do nothing when I knew something was off. I missed my old Elle, the one I'd left when I ran after talking about my parents, when emotions had overwhelmed me. Watching that bar fight and knowing one tiny little accident could've hurt her had made me think of my parents. I avoided thinking about their death so much that it had caught me off guard. My initial reaction was to rebel and push away any feelings, to isolate myself into my lonely world until I could breathe again.

But then Michael's visit and Elle's unannounced visit happened, and somewhere along the way, my Elle changed. After she heard Cami's laugh.

Because she has feelings for me.

Hope was a bitch because I wanted that to be true so fucking badly, but she'd never said a word. Ugh, why had I let her think Cami was another woman? I should've invited Elle in! Made Ryann and Cami introduce themselves. Stopped Elle from running away. But I hadn't done any of those things because I was an idiot and wanted her to think poorly of me in a low moment of terrible self-protection. If she hated me, then I'd stop wishing for more.

My phone buzzed, and my agent's name popped up. Peter was a nice guy for a sports agent, and it had been a few months since he'd called. "Hey, Peter."

"A bar fight?"

"Shit." I sat up. "What do you know?"

"News article saying you punched some guy? He's in the press saying he wants to press charges when he learned who punched him." He clicked his tongue. "Todd Farmington, local business owner and alumni of Central State, says Cal Holt was overly aggressive with him and assaulted him after a joke. *The guy swung out of nowhere. It's clear his aggression and anger doesn't stay on the ice. I say, leave it on the rink, bud."*

"Jesus." I hissed. Bad press was the last thing I needed for the team or my future. Worry wedged its way between my shoulder blades, and I put the phone on speaker to stretch them out. Tension in my back affected my play, and life without the NHL? I couldn't even imagine it. It was my future, the thing that had held me together all these years. "That's not what happened, by the way."

"I figured."

"Wait, really?" My voice rose.

"Yeah, you're an asshole, not an idiot. You wouldn't punch unless triggered. So, what did happen, so I can help squash the BS?"

Asshole, not an idiot. That should be my next tattoo. I laughed. "He grabbed my girl, the bartender. She has bruises, and it's all documented. He was being a complete dick too, but him touching her after she said no multiple times was what set me off. She looked terrified."

Just thinking about it got my blood pumping again, the fear, the way I'd pushed her away and regretted it two seconds later.

"Got it. Good for you then. So, *your girl*?"

"Oh, no, the bartender. We're friends."

"Sure. Your voice is strange."

"No, it's nothing. I'm… it's fine. Just more complicated than I thought."

"Alright. I'll stop bugging ya. If you get charged officially, let me know. I think this guy is wanting his three seconds of fame."

"Will do."

"How's school?"

We chatted for fifteen minutes about hockey, the path to still finish my major, and exploring the option of finishing early. If I took online classes *and* a full load, I could graduate junior year and then head to the NHL. The thought intrigued me more than I would've assumed. But Elle's face came to mind…could I leave her? Did I want to?

"I'll come down once the season starts, and we can get a drink. Glad to hear you're doing well, you seem… different. Good, but different."

"Bye, Peter."

I hung up as he laughed and, I digested what he said. I did feel different, but I blamed that on getting the tattoo. Reframing how I thought about my parents. But realistically, I knew it was Elle. God, I had to fix things.

Even if that meant admitting to her how I felt. Michael could throw feelings around without breaking into hives. His sister, too, didn't seem scarred and messed up. Maybe I could get that way also? Being rejected by Elle though… I wasn't sure I could survive it. She looked at me with warmth and love one second but then glacial indifference the next. The same nagging feeling returned, that I had a narrow window to prove to her I'd be worth it and that it had already passed.

The same pressure built behind my ribs, and I exhaled. Sitting here in the apartment would make me lose it.

Keeping busy eased my mind, so I went to the store to get stuff for Elle. I'd leave something outside her door in the morning. Then, when she was feeling better, we could talk. Really talk. That'd buy me time to figure out what I wanted to say because I had no idea.

Just that I wanted her around me all the time and to touch her and hold her and feed her. I enjoyed her laugh and expressions and wanted to make her world the best place ever. I bought chocolate, flowers, soup and crackers, and two romance books the lady at the desk recommended. I put each in separate bags, depending on *why* she didn't feel good, and paused at the cards.

She was romantic, and I was the complete opposite. I could write her a card? No, I sucked at writing. What I could do though… an idea hit. A not-terrible one, probably. Reading and writing were really important to her. I could donate money to a local business that helped kids learn how to read! Or to the library! They always needed donations.

I bought the items and went back to the apartment. After some research online, I found two centers near campus that could benefit with a few extra thousand dollars. I used their online portal for donations and hit submit. I smiled, finally feeling like I'd done something right. Instead of cards, I found a pale sticky note and wrote two of them:

If you're sick, here's soup and crackers and a book.
If it's the time of the month, here's chocolate and romance books.

Then, I added a third note. *I donated money to the reading centers in your name.*

I put them together and would set them outside her door tomorrow morning.

Not five minutes after eight am, Charlie called me for help with Lizzie. He had to go meet with his lawyer about custody issues and was freaking out. Two hours, max, he said, before dropping her off at the apartment building. He'd barely set her outside the door before hugging her and driving away. I'd just woken up, was grumpy after a shit night of sleep, and the last thing I wanted was to be upbeat and chatty.

And Lizzie was both of those things. Majorly.

We stood in the lobby, waiting for the elevator to arrive when the door to Elle's place opened. *No!* The gifts were still upstairs. I scanned her, seeing if she was pale or gave any indication she was sick. She seemed okay, just flushed cheeks. But her eyes. God. They were sad. She hadn't seen me yet, but her shoulders were slumped, and I wanted to hug her, to fix everything. I didn't know how though. There wasn't one thing that would mend what had changed—she'd said we were just friends. I was Mr. Three-Nights and her the romantic. She wore a white dress that landed above her knees, and her hair hung down in curls. She looked gorgeous, and my heart stuttered in my chest.

Where is she going? With who?

"Cal, Cal, please?" Lizzie said my name, pulling me out of my Elle trance.

I didn't even hear what she'd asked, but Elle must've heard Lizzie too because she spun around so fast. Her eyes widened, and she took in the scene. Her pouty lips were turned down, but when she realized Lizzie was there, she grinned. "Hi, Lizzie!"

"Elle!" Lizzie gave her a hug, still holding onto her stuffed unicorn. Elle squeezed her back, getting onto her knees to be eye level.

"What are you doing here, sweetie?" Her gaze landed on me. "Hanging with your cool cousin, Cal?"

"Dad had a meeting."

"Ah, I see." Elle stood, her cheeks reddening as she glanced at the floor. "Well, enjoy what—"

"Come play with us!" Lizzie tugged her hand, clearly not picking up on the sad vibes from Elle.

"Oh, she's busy." She wanted space from me, and I fucking hated it. I'd respect it, but it killed me. I shook my head. "She doesn't feel well, Lizzie, another day."

"Please?" Lizzie pulled Elle's hand toward the now open elevator doors. "We're gonna watch TV and color."

Elle glanced at me, a frown on her pretty lips, and instead of putting up the shield I'd seen the last two days, she let me see all of her. Sad, worried, vulnerable. "I don't know, hon. I don't think I can today."

"Are you feeling any better?" I asked, wanting her to continue talking to us.

She glanced at the floor, moving her left foot side to side on the tile. She wore a toe ring, the bling charming me even more to her. "A bit, yeah."

She wouldn't look at me. It hurt. "Elle, I'm not…if you want to hang out with us, you can. I thought you needed space."

"Please!" Lizzie said again, grabbing Elle's hand.

"I can get doughnuts or those croissants you love," I said, needing her to agree to this. If she said no and turned Lizzie down, I was screwed. "But only if you want to. You look busy."

"Oh." She glanced at her outfit, like it surprised her. "I was gonna meet up with some writers because, uh, I was feeling better." She shuffled her weight side to side, head hung low. She was the walking definition of guilty.

So, she felt *fine* but was avoiding me. The truth punched me in the gut.

She didn't want me. Plain and simple.

"See, Lizzie, she can't." My voice came out louder, my irritation and worry at her avoiding me taking over. "I'm *glad* you're doing better."

"No, I can. I can." She righted her posture and smiled at Lizzie. "Let's go color. I bet your dad would like some pictures to hang up at work."

She beamed at her, then marched into the elevator. Elle followed, her perfume reminding me of home. The tension was thick enough to cut with a knife. I stared at her, daring her to admit she'd lied to me about not feeling well. I knew she needed distance, but *why*? If nothing had changed and we were just friends, why did she want space from me?

Elle and Lizzie chatted about their favorite animals, Lizzie's being horses and Elle's obviously an owl. For whatever reason, it fit Elle's personality perfectly. My pulse raced all the way through my fingertips, and I was desperate for Charlie to get back so we could finally have a talk. A real one. Because she was avoiding me but felt guilty enough about it to come up with Lizzie.

"Flowers! I want to color flowers." Lizzie sat on the ground near my couch, her legs crossed in her dress as Elle joined her. She sat on her knees, pushing her hair over her shoulder as she bent down to color. She hadn't looked at me since we'd walked into my apartment. This was worse than when the team had been pissed at me. Like I'd let her down even though *she* evaded me. I didn't get it.

I itched to do something besides stare at the two of them. Elle pushed Lizzie's hair behind her ear, and for one second, I saw Elle as a mom. Warm, comforting, patient. The idea of having a family and future with her made me happy and desperate for it to work. Wait. *What the fuck.*

Sitting on the other side of Lizzie, I grabbed a piece of paper and crayon. Drawing wasn't a skill I had, but Lizzie didn't care. She pointed to my paper and tapped it. "Color space, Cal. Elle is doing flowers."

"Okay."

Elle met my eyes for a second, her signature smile quickly in place before she went back to drawing. "What colors should our flowers be?"

"Pink. Black."

"Definitely Charlie's daughter," Elle said, laughing at herself.

"He told me she wanted a tattoo after seeing all of his," I said, earning another quick grin. "I found a bunch of fake ones, and I plan to prank him with it."

"That's a great idea." She chuckled, smiling at me. "We could do it now? Do you have them?"

"I do." I paused my terrible rendition of space. Earth looked like a marble. "Lizzie, want some tattoos?"

"Yes! A skull!"

I laughed and pushed up. "They're in my room. Be right back."

"I'm thirsty." Lizzie set her crayon down.

"I'll get you water when Cal gets your tattoos. This will be awesome." Elle went to the kitchen, and I grabbed the tattoos I'd tossed on my dresser. There was a barbed wire one that would be funny as shit to put on her arm. Charlie would die. Smiling, I came out in the room with Elle standing near my phone, her face pale and her eyes accusatory.

My stomach bottomed out, like it knew shit was bad before

my mind did. I went through every single thing I had ever done wrong, trying to piece together why the dread from her expression grew each second. Her jaw tightened, the usual spark in her eyes dulled as she pressed her lips together tight.

She shook her head, her hands at fists on her sides before she gave me a forced smile. "I need to go."

"Wait, Elle—"

She was on her way out, and I had no idea what I'd done. But I knew I fucked up somehow. It was who I was.

CHAPTER
TWENTY-FIVE

Elle

"Wait, please!" Cal shouted, his long strides walking up to me as I was out the door. I did not stop. It would be too much. Too soon.

That fucking text!

I hadn't meant to read it. His phone was right there, lighting up. My eyes just glanced at it because it was bright. Who even let their texts show on the home screen anymore? There should've been a password!

It was my fault that I saw it. It wasn't like he showed me his phone and said "Hey, read this, Elle." But there was a box of chocolate with a sticky note saying ELLE on it on his kitchen table. I wanted to investigate because food, but then the damn phone buzzed right next to it. Fuck. He was leaving. Going to the NHL to escape *me*.

I made it back to my unit and slammed the door. The words flashed in my head like a neon sign in the middle of the night.

Peter: Not poking my nose in, but an easy way to get rid of the problematic bartender "not your girlfriend" situation is to leave. Looked into your online classes, and you could be training in Philly by next week. Talked to the org, and they love your idea LMK.

Problematic bartender. *Not your girlfriend.* Me. I was that. Online classes…training next week…leaving campus. He promised he'd tell me if he was doing that! But maybe that had changed when he hooked up with someone else. I saw how he'd reacted to that cute girl at the nursery. When others became too involved, he got rid of them.

My breath got heavy, and my head buzzed, and I couldn't do anything about it. I wasn't supposed to see the message. It was his business! Sleeping with someone else meant he didn't want me getting attached but *leaving* because of me? That hurt so much more. Our friendship meant something to me, even if he'd never have real feelings for me. I didn't ever refer or think of myself as his girlfriend, and problematic? I'd told him everything was fine, that we were good. I'd tried to be less dramatic. I'd aimed to be zero drama. Even though my own fears held me back from speaking it out loud, I didn't understand this. If I was an issue, why didn't he tell me about it? Call me out?

I'd seen his face, pale and guilty. His eyes gave him away though—they'd gone dark, worried. He had the signs of someone who'd done something they shouldn't. He hadn't even looked that ashamed about the girl in his apartment.

Why had I fallen for him? Why couldn't I have kept my distance? I knew this would happen. He basically told me it would, yet I couldn't stop. Thought I'd be okay. That maybe I was different and exceptional and made him *want* to try love again.

I'm a fucking lovestruck idiot.

Dani was gone, Gabe was at work, and the writing group had already started thirty minutes on the other side of town. There wasn't anyone I could talk to about this, not that I wanted to pour my heart out. I sniffed, the tears coming stronger now, and yanked my keys off the rack. This pain was horrible. It was as if someone took a fist around my ribs and squeezed. *Heartbreak.*

I'd read about it countless times as the dark moment, which

always led to a happy ever after, but this wasn't a book. I wasn't different. Cal wanted to escape me because I was *problematic*.

Writing. I needed to write. To get past this. To bleed out my thoughts and worries where I could dive into my head. Normally, my daydreams were a fun place to be, but right now, they were all dark and cloudy. No sunshine today. All rainclouds and thunderstorms. I shut the apartment door and took off toward a coffee shop. I ignored the buzzing of my phone. Cal had called three times, but I didn't want to hear his excuses. He could've talked to me. Clearly, he'd mentioned me to whoever Peter was, probably his agent or coach or something.

There wasn't an excuse that had that text message making sense besides the fact he was running away.

When I found a shop that I hadn't been to before, I ordered a cold brew with oat milk. If I was gonna write to escape, I needed my drug of choice, and I even went wild and added sweetener. Opening up my draft, I scowled.

My character Jackson, who'd started to look like Cal, was getting a makeover in this story. Because right now, I hated the emotionally damaged character who upset people around him even if he didn't intend to.

Because that was Cal. I hurt, but he hadn't done anything wrong. We weren't together or dating or even casually sleeping with each other. It had happened twice. I'd had a one-night stand before. It didn't mean anything. Yet, I'd fallen for Cal with his silent gestures and tough exterior all on my own.

I changed the scene with Jackson opening up to the heroine, where he'd be willing to try a relationship because she made him happy and he couldn't imagine not seeing her every day. Instead, he pushed her away. Wanting her to feel the pain he carried.

Okay, not great romance right there. I rubbed my temples, eager to get some words down. Anything to distract myself. An hour went by, then another, and I barely got three hundred words. In all my life, writing had been my one escape, but now I couldn't do it.

I felt defeated. Let down by my own feelings. Instead of writing, I opened my budget spreadsheet. The least I could do was finish the assignment Cal gave me, even if I'd lied about not feeling well. I jotted down the things I'd spent money on and pulled up my bank account to document the previous items. I categorized them by type: fun, rent, utility, food, clothes, books, etc.

There were trends, for sure. I spent almost all my money on rent and food, the other items significantly less. If I bought more in bulk, I could save a few hundred dollars a month. And, as long as I made a thousand a month in tips, I'd be fine. I wrote down all my findings and got an urge to share it with Cal, to thank him for the help and wish him luck. Yeah, I could email him. That'd be way better.

I could hide behind my words and exclamation points, using the keyboard as a block between admitting and showing him how upset I was. He'd hate to see me cry, and hiding this emotional rollercoaster from him was best. Even though each breath hurt and the only person who could comfort me was the one causing the pain.

I rubbed my eyes, smearing the mascara, but I didn't care. I refused to abandon Cal as a friend. It would hurt like hell, but he'd let me into his circle, and I'd always be there for him. I loved the sad idiot, but *right now* I was in self-protection mode. Eventually, someday, maybe we'd be pen pals who sent emails or FaceTimed once a month. Yeah, we could do that. Okay. I cracked my knuckles and hoped my words seemed joyful.

Calzone,

Sorry for running out—hope you and Lizzie drew forests of flowers! I think I ate something at lunch that messed with me. I'm doing better now and finished up your $$ assignment. I attached my notes My trends are interesting, and I'll be able to cut spending too much if I buy more food in bulk. I even made a couple of slides with graphs.

Next week we can dive deeper! I have three blind books for you to choose. I embedded a form with the options. Let me know what you pick!

See you soon!
Elle

Totally chill. That was me. No crying over what could've been at all. Sending the email felt like closure, almost. I shut my laptop and headed home, hoping to watch disaster movies until Dani got home and I could cry with her. She'd know what to do.

"This might be wild, but I think you should sleep with him one more time. As a goodbye."

We eyed the gifts Cal had placed outside my door. Even after running out on him, he'd left things for me. Romance books, chocolate, soup, crackers…a sticky note with his choppy handwriting.

I bought these for you yesterday. I'll stop by tomorrow to make sure you're okay.

"Dani, where's your brain at?" I poured myself another glass of wine, glancing at the stuff he brought me. It was so *kind*. I couldn't help but feel like they were remorse gifts. Like he knew he'd hurt me and wanted to apologize with presents. But then again, he was intentional and thoughtful…one of the reasons I'd fallen in love with him. "Why the fuck would sleeping with him be a good idea?"

"Because." She crossed one leg over the over. She jutted her chin at the gifts on the coffee table. "You've talked about nothing besides how much you'll miss him. Even with a broken heart, you love the guy, and he hasn't left *yet*. He obviously cares for you in some way. No one would get you gifts like this if they didn't. I love you to death, and all I'd do is get you chocolate."

I swallowed the ball of emotion in my throat. She had a small point, but it didn't ease the turmoil and hurt. "They're guilt purchases."

"No they're not." She scoffed. "He knows you're upset and

wanted to make you feel better. A great *friend* who has at least one feeling for you would do that."

"But he called me a complicated girl problem."

Even saying it aloud, my excuse seemed weak. My stomach tightened with the truth of the matter—I'd avoided talking to him about everything. Coming up with excuses was fine but deep down, the truth ate at me.

"Emotions are complicated." She shrugged and gave me a look that said *get it together, idiot*. "Do you love him? Look at how messy you are."

My shoulder deflated. The fight left me. "I hate when you're correct."

She beamed, the words clearly going to her head. "I love hearing it from you, your brother. Does the ego well. So, tell me, why not appreciate a few more nights with him if you *love* him? Enjoy every second you can. Life's super short, girl. Y'all already talked about it not going anywhere, right?"

My cheek twitched. *No. I'm avoiding him because my poor heart.* I swallowed down the ugly reality check and instead focused on her words. Enjoying a few more nights with him would be… mm.

My body hummed at the idea of sleeping with him again. To feel his arms around me and his mouth. To experience his intensity in the bedroom. I squeezed my eyes shut, my pulse racing. "So, I go up there and say *sleep with me?*"

"No." She frowned. "I'm suggesting that you're the one making it weird between you. You're the one more invested and upset. Not him. He probably knows something's off with you, but this was his MO. To be friends. To go to the NHL. To not get involved. You're talking like you're cutting off all ties with him, like a breakup. You're not breaking up. You just fell for a guy who doesn't love you, but he *does* feel something. The gifts show that. Everything he does shows that."

"Ugh, it makes me sound pathetic. I should know better." I fell onto my back, hitting the couch and groaning. "I suck."

"You don't suck, and we can't help who we develop feelings

for." She patted my leg. "I didn't want to get feels for Gabey Baby, but I did."

"Yuck." I cringed at the nickname girls from high school called my brother. It was horrendous. "But he had them back."

"True, but I knew it was gonna hurt when it was done, and I dove in headfirst. To me, it was worth the pain because being with him was everything. Are you happy around Cal? Does he get you to smile?"

Yes. "Maybe."

"Liar." She pinched my elbow, causing me to yelp. "You gotta do what you feel is right, and if that's cutting him out of your life, then great. If you want to make the last few days longer, do it. Plan to remain friends when he goes to the NHL? Or not? That's your choice. But I wouldn't want to miss any time with the person I loved."

"He's leaving and didn't even tell me." *And* probably slept with someone else.

But how would you know, dumb-dumb, because you're avoiding him?

My conscious was being a dick to me.

She chewed the side of her lip. "You technically don't know that's true. He could've planned to tell you, but you never gave him the chance. You saw a text that sure, is suspicious, but from everything you shared about him, he cares about you as a friend. Friends don't leave without telling each other. And those gifts are really nice. I love you, but I think you're letting your feelings for him cloud what's going on."

"I hate that you might be right." I rolled off the end of the couch and fell to the floor. "He's called a few times."

She arched a brow. "I understand you're hurting, but he might be too? In his own way? His circle is small, Elle, from everything you said. You avoiding him isn't cool."

She's right, goddamnit. Yet, I still fought it. "I wanted sympathy and to cry."

"You have it and can, but I'd be an asshole to not point out some things. You need to talk to him. Whether you share what you're going through or not, you owe him a conversation."

"Yet you told me I should sleep with him again."

"I'm saying...enjoy your time with him and don't ice him out. He doesn't deserve it. Take care of yourself, but when or if he even leaves, your pity party can't start until then."

I ran my fingers through my hair a few times, the curls still there from earlier, and I glanced at my phone. He'd be at Charlie's until midnight, and it was only ten. I *could* go there to talk to him. He'd called four times and texted more. Apologizing, asking to see me. I owed him this.

Dani was right. His small circle of people included me, and that was precious. I'd never take that for granted, and even if it ripped my heart out, he deserved me always being on his team.

His team. An idea struck. A goofy, romantic, *heroine in a love story* idea.

"I'm heading to Charlie's." I dusted off my shorts and adjusted the hem of my yellow tank top. "He's working, and that way I'll keep my hands to myself."

"Seems less fun but good." She grabbed my hand, her gaze getting intense. "I feel like our roles reversed right now, and it's weird. But don't count him out yet, alright?"

"Is it dorky that I daydreamed about us having heart-to-hearts living together?"

"Not at all. I love this!" She grinned hard.

"I don't know what I'll say when I see him, but I can at least thank him for the gifts."

And admit everything to him. Lay it all on the table. Shout that I love him.

"It's a good start. Then do what feels right."

That I could do.

I loved Cal Holt, and even if he didn't say it back, he could take my love with him wherever he went. It was about time I took the reins of my own romance story.

CHAPTER
TWENTY-SIX

Cal

Maybe graduating early and heading to the NHL wasn't the worst idea. The daily workouts and competition would keep me busy enough to not feel this terrible stomachache. It was like the night I'd heard about the accident. An unknown number had called twice, and between that second and third call, my senses went into overdrive. Like my body knew something bad was gonna happen before it did, and it was a miserable place to be.

I ran my fingers over the tattoo, trying not to itch the irritated skin. Seeing symbols that represented my parents comforted me for a bit but then my mind returned to Elle. The hurt look in her eyes. The way she'd left without turning back.

I wasn't sure what I'd done.

She saw the gifts? But that wouldn't cause that reaction. I rubbed my chest, wishing the night would end already so I could go watch a YouTube video to numb my brain. Business was slow, and Alex handled all the drink orders. I sat on a stool at the door, occasionally bussing a table when more than four tables were dirty with glasses. I missed Elle's laugh at the bar, the coy looks she'd give me across the place. Even if we weren't talking, knowing she was close reassured me. I could make sure she ate, keep an eye on any fuckers messing with her...

Why was she ignoring me?

I scrolled through my phone, bored out of my mind, and my heart skipped a beat seeing her email. *Elle!*

I read it, proud of her trends and the fact she completed the assignment. But her words felt off. Awkward. Not *her*. I wanted to reply with a million questions, but she hadn't texted me back. She could be writing, lost in her head, or maybe with Ty? Or ignoring me.

I wasn't sure what was worse, Ty or intentionally not responding to me. My temples ached, my jaw giving me TMJ. With less shifts at the bar, that meant more free time. More free time meant more time in my head, and I wanted to escape my mind.

The opposite of Elle who lived in hers.

It was barely ten o clock, and we'd start shutting down soon, but it wasn't like I was bursting to get out. Nothing waited for me. My knee bounced up and down, and a table left. I jumped to pick up the glasses, desperate to give myself something to do. The glasses clinked together as I stacked them in my left hand. I held the tray of nuts and napkins in the other. I'd wash them for Alex and maybe sweep the floor.

My back was to the door when it opened, the bell chiming. It was a dull, low sound, but it was nice to know when someone came in. I set the glasses in the sink, tossed out the trash, and lifted my head to nod to the patron. My breath caught in my goddamn throat at seeing Elle *here.*

She had on a Central State Wolves jersey with *my* number on the front. My breath caught in my throat as I eyed the rest of her outfit.

Her white shorts flirted with the tops of her thighs. The material hugged her curves, and she wore matching orange shoes.

She was a breath of fresh air, the epitome of joy in a human form. How could I *not* see her every day?

The glasses rocked back and forth on top of the sink, slipping from my grip. "Shit." I righted them, my face heating. I had to fight the urge to run over to her and hug her, to apologize for whatever had her running from my apartment, to tell her the feelings I had that wouldn't settle down.

I forced a breath as she padded toward me. Her hair was up in a bun, her face clear of makeup, and her mouth pressed in a firm line. She waved two fingers, her eyes losing some of the warmth. She chewed her cheek and glanced at the ground.

She looked *nervous.*

She approached the bar and pushed her hair behind her ears. "Hey."

I smiled at just seeing her, her presence calming me. All day, turmoil had soured my stomach, and it went away with her being *here* in front of me. I wanted to kiss her. All the time. Not just for three nights.

I wanted to be the romantic hero she'd dreamed about.

"Could we talk for a second?" she asked, her voice lacking her usual luster. "If you're not too busy."

"Yes, yes." I eagerly came around the bar and sat at one of the tables. Alex met my gaze and nodded, like they knew this conversation was important. Elle joined me, her floral perfume settling my nerves. She didn't look happy nor sad, and I readied myself to be prepared for whatever she wanted to say.

The nerves worried me a bit, but she was here.

She cracked her knuckles and set the palms of her hands flat on the table. "Cal, thank you for the gifts."

"You're welcome." I cleared my throat.

She'd admitted as much that she'd lied to avoid me, but I hoped they helped her anyway. My muscles tensed, bracing for the worst news as she wrinkled her brow. She could say that she hated me. That she was moving. That she never wanted to see me again. Each thought made me want to throw up.

"I should apologize." She gulped, moved her hands to her neck. Worry danced behind her eyes, and I grabbed one of her hands, intertwining our fingers. She sucked in a breath, and I ran my thumb over her wrist. I was being *that* guy, the PDA one. She clutched my hand, her finger digging tight into mine.

I used to think anyone showing PDA was a fool. But the thought of not seeing her again hurt *worse*. "What's going on?" I asked, my voice hoarse.

She stilled my thumb—not a good sign. Then she sat up straighter. Her eyes blazed with heat and warmth. "I bought this jersey tonight. It's yours."

"Yes." My lips quirked. "I noticed my number on it."

She gulped and used her free hand to push some flyaway hairs behind her ears. She didn't have any earrings on tonight, and I missed them. She blinked, and I squeezed her hand. "I really like seeing my number on you."

Her tongue wet her bottom lip, and her cheeks turned pink. "I'm going to say a lot of things, and you can't interrupt me. Okay?"

I nodded, every muscle in my body tensing, waiting.

"Wherever you go, I'm always going to be your biggest fan. You could play in freaking Antarctica, and I'll still wear your jersey and watch every game. Nothing will change this. I will lo..." She paused, closed her eyes, and my mind finished that sentence.

I will...love you? Look for you?

When she opened her big brown eyes, she smiled. "I love you, Cal. And even if you leave for the NHL next week, that love goes with you—"

Holy fucking shit. My body came to life, tingling and buzzing with a happiness I had never experienced in my entire life.

"Elle—"

She held up a hand, silencing me. "I'm not done, Calzone. Please. If you ever read a romance book, this is my grand gesture."

I swore the colors in the bar deepened, got brighter. The dark walls seemed...prettier. The sounds of laughter were better. The light overhead didn't irritate me. She loved me. Elle loved *me*. She said those words, with her mouth, and I could fucking fly.

"I've been avoiding this chat for a while because I was scared. I've lived in Gabe's shadow my whole life, so I didn't think I would be enough to be an exception to your three nights only rule. That I wasn't exceptional enough. I might not be, but I don't care. You might've slept with someone else and want to escape to the NHL to get away from me, and that's fine, but you have me for life as a friend, if you want me. I found out I can stream the games for the farm team, and I figured I could drive out for a game if I schedule a weekend off from Charlie's. I could take Lizzie with me and we'd watch you play. Gabe said I could borrow his car. I asked him."

Her eyes watered, and her palms sweated against mine. She sniffed, loudly. "I thought I wanted some fictional hero from a romance book, but really, I just want you as you are. Grumpy and sad and the softest soul I've ever met. You." She sniffed again. "Are the best person I know, and I want to tell you every day how amazing you are. If you let me. I'm asking a lot." She hung her head, tears spilling down her face. "You might not even want this. You probably don't."

How could she possibly think I didn't love her? That seeing her cry physically hurt me? We had some things to clear up, but fuck, my soul sang. This beautiful, joyful girl wanted me *as I was*. I couldn't imagine anything better?

"Hey, can I say something yet?" I asked, my voice gentle.

She nodded.

"I love you too."

She whimpered, and I moved fast to her side of the booth. She crawled onto my lap and wrapped her arms around my shoulder. She kissed my neck and cheek and face and then my mouth. Her warm soft lips were like coming home after being away for months. I hummed against her, my damn heart fluttering like a bird in the wind. The sounds from the bar faded away, and it was just her and me. She smelled like flowers and sunshine after a rainstorm, and I held her tight against me as I kissed her. My skin tingled with lust and love and fear because even though I wanted all she said, the fear still lingered. But I wouldn't give up a shot with her because I was scared. Not anymore. I groaned into her mouth, our tongues sliding together slowly and needily. She dug her fingers into my shoulders when I deepened the kiss.

She pulled back and whispered. "I'm sorry if I hurt you by running out."

"You did, but I hurt you too." I cupped the back of her head, smiling so wide it felt strange on my face. The spark of hope doubled, then tripled in size. She made me feel this way, like my life wasn't going to be a storm cloud forever. "Two things. I *never* slept with anyone, and I'm not leaving to go to the NHL yet."

"But I heard a woman, and the text..." she said, her voice small. "It doesn't matter. We weren't *together*."

"Baby, we're together. It's you and me now, yeah?" I kissed her forehead. "Reiner and his sister and his girlfriend's sister came over. He's going to propose and wanted us to approve his plan."

"Oh." Her lips made a perfectly pretty oh.

"Yeah. That's who you heard. I was freaking out about my overwhelming emotions for you so I let you assume the worst in a terrible attempt to protect you from myself."

"Cal, you idiot."

I laughed and kissed her again. One, because I could and two... because she tasted so good and made me happy. "I'm sorry I did that. I'm never going to be a perfect romantic guy for you. I'm a fucking mess most of the time."

"I don't want a *perfect* guy. I want you." Her brown eyes got serious, and I kissed her again. She put a hand on my chest and stopped me. "I've never done distance before, and it scares me, but we can figure it out together. I promise."

"Distance?"

"I didn't mean to spy," she said, gulping. "The text about...

escaping me and going to the NHL early. It popped up on your phone—"

"*That's* why you ran out." I sighed and rested my forehead against hers. I breathed her in before continuing. "I thought you saw the gifts and I'd done something wrong. I'm new at all of this but—"

"The gifts are amazing, Cal. Everything you've done for me is. You might think you're new, but you've shown me you've cared for weeks now." She nodded, her eyes sparking with hope. "You've shown me your soul, and I'm sorry it took me so long to figure it out."

God, when she said things like that, my heart fluttered in my chest. I smiled at her, unable to stop it. She made me *happy*. "I love this, you, us."

Her lips curved up, but a nervous, hesitant look crossed her eyes. The joy dimmed slightly, and I tensed. "What is it?"

"Could you explain that text? Please? I trust you, I do, but," she paused, swallowed loudly. "It messed with me a bit. I don't want to be problematic."

"Fuck, no, you're not. I am. I'm the messy one." I closed my eyes and exhaled. It was exhausting to spill your heart out after learning you still had a functioning one. "My agent learned about the bar fight online and wanted to come up with a game plan for the press. He picked up on my feelings for you before I did, and I said the attraction was problematic. Not you. I swear. He's always been upfront about my options, and there's an opportunity for me to go early and finish school online."

Elle blinked and sucked in a little breath. "But you're staying?"

"Yes." I grinned again. "Mainly, because life here has been more fun and happier since I found you but also because I made a promise to my parents that I'd get a degree. I want to graduate in honor of them."

"Oh, Cal." She placed her hands on my face, gently rubbing her thumbs over my cheeks and jaw. Her eyes got all watery and warm. "I want our love story so badly."

"You'll have it."

Then, I kissed her again.

She tasted like red wine, and I wanted to drink her in, her sweet floral smell, the little moans she released as I deepened the kiss. She grounded me and made me feel like I could fly. I ran a hand along her spine, pulling her closer to me and kissing her softly once, twice. I pulled back, staring down at her, and her brown eyes were crinkled on the sides in a smile. "I'm selfish to ask this, but the bar closes in an hour. Can you wait for me?"

"Of course, Cal. You're worth waiting for."

Somehow, those words felt deeper than surface value. The intonation of her voice, the way her gaze heated at me. I kissed her forehead and forced myself to take a step back. The last thing I wanted to do was stop touching her, but I was at work. "One hour, then you're mine."

CHAPTER
TWENTY-SEVEN

Elle

He *loved* me. Cal Holt said he loved me, with his mouth. My insides went bananas, dancing and hollering and freaking the hell out. He wasn't leaving. He hadn't slept with someone else. He wanted to be with me.

I should've been chill as hell and beyond happy. Never in my dreams had I thought he'd say those words to me? That he would feel the same? That he wanted to do romance? He was adamant that we'd never be that, so while the immediate joy was amazing, my nerves still held on tight. It felt too easy? Too good?

Our relationship had all the signs: he'd said he loved me, I'd said it back, and we'd go back to his place and get naked. My heart raced, and my palms sweated. He smiled at me across the bar, and my stomach did a swoopy thing. The story should be over, but nerves crept into my mind, messing everything up.

I texted Dani a quick recap, and her answering fire emojis weren't the least bit helpful. For once, I wasn't sure Dani could help me with this. It was my own head in the way.

For a girl who daydreamed about big gestures and wild declarations of love, I should've been settled, happier. Instead, my insides twisted with worry, and my leg bounced, and I couldn't figure out *why*.

"Almost done." Cal walked by, running a hand over my neck and gently squeezing. Goose bumps broke out over my body, tingling from his touch. I nodded, hiding behind a shy smile.

He looked so happy. How could I burst that bubble with worries I couldn't explain? His smile was less forced, and in the time I'd known him, his frown lines had become less…frowny. He deserved all the happiness in the world after the things he'd been through. But was that my reservation?

That I was afraid he hadn't really changed? I'd spent every minute the last few weeks reminding myself he wasn't a relationship guy. That he moved on after three days and didn't get involved. My mind was incredible, and I could convince myself of anything if I tried hard enough. (For real, I'd convinced myself I was pregnant from a toilet seat once and made Dani buy me a test)

Had I trained my mind not to trust Cal with my heart?

I watched him and Alex joke around, their banter making me smile because they were both grumpy and mad at the world, but they'd found their people. Finding your people was the whole point of life.

So, was Cal my person?

Yes. He was worth waiting for, but were we like Gabe and Dani? I chewed the side of my lip to the point I had to reapply lip balm four times. The final time, Cal stood in front of me and held out a hand. "Ready?"

I nodded.

My palms were damp with sweat, but if he noticed, he didn't say a word. He intertwined our fingers so our palms had no space between them, and he guided us toward the door. I waved at Alex who rolled their eyes, mouthing *finally*.

Cal walked so quickly I had to move twice as fast to keep up. I almost tripped on a crack in the sidewalk, my shoes making a scuffing sound.

"Shit, you alright?" He stopped and glanced at me feet.

"You're in a hurry, couldn't keep up." I forced a smile, which he returned at first. But then, the smart guy he was, he frowned. His gaze moved between my eyes, his hand coming up and resting on my collarbone.

"We don't have to do anything when we get upstairs, okay? We can talk, eat, watch a movie. It doesn't matter. I'm in this for the long haul, so we can go as slow as you need."

My lip trembled. "I'm so sorry. I don't understand what's wrong with me."

"Hey, whoa." He moved the hand to go over my heart. "Nothing is wrong with you. You're the best person I know."

"Then I shouldn't be worried right now."

"You're allowed to freak out whenever you need to. There's not a rulebook on feelings. Trust me... I know."

I snorted at his attempt at humor. He stared back at me, his eyes filled with warmth and support and love. It gave me a little more confidence. For a moment. "When I convinced myself you'd never want to be with me, it was easier. Safer."

He nodded. "It's terrifying."

"We could hurt each other."

"Yes, we could." He smiled softly, gently. "But what if we don't? I've hated the idea of hope because it was fickle. Fleeting. Dangerous. *Hoping* for things didn't make them true, but since you came into my life, I don't fear it as much. You make me wish for things. I'm going to fuck up, often. I've never been a partner before, and I'll struggle with voicing how I feel. But I'll try really hard, all the time."

His voice went deeper as he brought his hand to my hip. "I hope I can be a partner you're proud to be with."

"Goddamn it, Cal." My eyes pooled with tears, and I hugged him hard. "I'm already proud of you."

"This is a good hug, right?" he asked, picking me up so he held me entirely off the ground. His muscles hardly tensed as he started walking toward our building.

"Yes. A very good hug." I breathed in his clean scent, knowing he was right. It would be terrifying, and for a girl who'd dreamed of romance, I'd frozen when it happened to me. His warmth radiated to me, and I held on tighter. "I can be a good partner to you too. I'd never come between you and hockey. I'll give you space when you need it. Even when you do go to the NHL, I'll stay with you."

I could picture it now, Dani and Gabe and I watching his games. Cal and I FaceTiming when he returned to the hotel room. Laughing and saying how much I missed him. Him coming back to me after a road trip. I could envision it all and wanted it so badly.

He squeezed my thighs. "I know."

"You mean so much to me, Cal. God." I snuggled into his neck, breathing his soapy scent in. Then I pressed my lips to his skin. He shivered, and it hit me that I'd *made* him shiver. Cal Holt.

The guy I'd crushed on for two years from afar. The guy who loved his parents so much that he'd become lost for a little while, and I wanted to bring him back.

He hoisted me onto one side, opened the door to the building, and walked us in. The cool air blasted us, a break from the humidity and heat of the bar. He pushed the button, calling the elevator, and then we went in. It was just us, and the ride was short, but Cal pressed my back into the wall and looked down at me. Everything was heightened. The smell of the elevator, like damp carpet. The cold press of the wall on my back. The heat of his touch and warmth of his gaze. The feel of his breath on my face before he bent low and kissed me. Oh, *baby*, he kissed me, slow, long strokes of his tongue and gentle touches of his lips. His heart thudded against mine through his chest, his hand moving to cover my throat. "No one," he said, kissing down my jaw. "Has impacted my life like you."

God. I shivered. Those words meant everything from him. I gripped his shoulders and slammed my head back into the wall when he nipped my earlobe.

"You're the best part of my day."

"Cal," I said, panting at this point. His words were a comforting hug, reassurance I hadn't known I'd needed. He could crush me, totally destroy me, but if the guy who lost so much would take a chance on us, so would I. He wasn't the textbook version of a romance hero, but he was mine.

The guy who brought me snacks.

The guy who held me all night, without expectations.

The guy who bought me plants and gifts when he thought I didn't feel well.

The door opened, our eyes meeting for a beat with the same heat. The genuine warmth and trust on his face had me grinning. My heart raced with emotion while my skin burned alive from how much I wanted him. My nerves were gone, replaced with excitement. Excited to be with him, everything on the table. To explore the chemistry with a lens of love. I'd never slept with someone who I cared so much for, and the thought made me buzz with anticipation. There was so much trust with Cal, and we'd seen each other at our worst and *still* wanted to do this. I'd never been so attracted to another human being before, and it wasn't just looks.

It was who he was and who he made me want to be.

"I thought I'd lost you before I even had a chance with you," he said, opening his door and guiding me in with a hand on my lower back. He spun me around, his large hands on my hips as he turned me. "I'm a lucky bastard that you'll have me. I won't blow it, Elle. I need you to know that."

I nodded, my heart doubling in size. I cupped his face, my hands trembling as I kissed him. His jaw was hard lines, a soft layer of scruff covering it. He leaned into me as I said, "You have such a soft heart, Cal. I'm lucky you're sharing it with me."

He smiled at me, his lips curving up so high my stomach swooped. It was pure joy. I wanted to give him reasons to smile like that every single day. I ran a finger over his neck, along his shoulder and down his forearm. He sucked in a breath when I pulled the edge of his shirt up. He reached behind his neck and took it off, tossing it to the side. His chest was incredible, all muscles and lines. I kissed the center of it, right above his heart. I wanted to savor every minute of being with him.

I explored his pecs with my fingers, tracing the outline of his nipples as he shook beneath my touch. I brought my mouth to his stomach. He tasted like sweat and smelled like soap. "I love how you take such good care of your body. You're so passionate and dedicated and wonderful."

He hoisted me up with his hands, lifting me off the floor and walking us to his bedroom. "I want your skin on mine," he said, almost in a growl. He set me on his bed gently, lifting my shirt off and helping me remove it. He kissed my neck as he reached around to undo my bra. Chest to chest, he lowered us onto the bend, kissing me in slow, meaningful strokes. There was no rush if we were *really* doing this. None at all.

I arched my back, clinging to him as he bit my bottom lip in a playful nip. Our gazes met, his eyes softening on the sides, and I nipped him. Laughing, I rolled us over so was on top of him. "So, you're gonna tease me today, huh?"

"Possibly." He ran his hands up my sides, across my ribcage before settling over my nipples. I sucked in a breath, the feel of his palms on my breasts sending shots of lust straight to my core. "I've thought about your body every second of every day since we were together."

He pinched each nipple, pulling them. I tilted my head back, my pulse racing from his words and touch. I ground my hips on him, letting all the worries fade away.

Foreplay had never been like this before, maddening to the point I wanted to go wild. He sat up, keeping one hand on my lower back and pulling me tighter. He closed his warm mouth around my nipple, kissing and sucking it before moving toward the other one. He hummed against my skin, the vibration making me pant with need.

"Cal," I begged. Rocking my hips harder, he chuckled and slid one hand down my body and between my thighs. He didn't go in my waistband. He moved his finger inside my shorts, pushing my panties to the side. "Fuck," I hissed, the fact I still wore bottoms somehow making this hotter.

"Keep rocking."

I did as he thrust his middle finger, then two fingers into me. I moaned, enjoying the buildup to what would be an amazing orgasm. There was no doubt. My body was attuned to his in a way that was hard to describe. Each breath I felt, each beat of his heart. When he moved to reposition us, my body naturally went with him.

"I want you to let go, Elle," he said, his voice raspy and deep. "Come over my fingers before I fuck you slow."

I shook at the heat of his words. I grabbed his face, kissing him hard as he used his thumb to rub my clit. The sensations of everything were perfect, almost too much. The feel of his tongue on mine, his fingers inside me, his other hand fisting my hair behind my back. Sweat fell down my chest as my muscles clenched. He thrust harder, the orgasm seconds away.

Right before I came, he broke out kiss apart and watched me. It was hot as fuck to have him observe me losing it. I bit my lip, the pleasure making it impossible to keep quiet. A moan escaped. I arched my back. I held onto him tighter, desperate to lengthen the orgasm. "Cal," I cried. "Yes!"

His eyes singed me with the heat and love and emotion swirling behind them. Instead of being self-conscious, it boldened me. This man *loved* me. I fell forward, resting my forehead against his, and he exhaled just as hard, like my orgasm made it tough for him to breathe. "Never getting sick of that sound," he whispered against my neck.

"Of me coming?"

"Yup." He cupped my face and kissed me slow, moving his hand to undo my shorts' button. "Need you naked, now."

I laughed, the desperation in his voice matching mine. "Yes, sir." I hopped off him and removed my shorts and panties as he did the same. He reached over to his side table and pulled out a condom. I took the wrapper from his hands, ripped it, and slid the rubber on his cock. He was so thick and hard and ready for me. Crawling over him, I kissed his jawline, his neck. Then I bit his shoulder before lowering my body to his. "You're amazing," I said, needing him to understand how much I meant it. "Your dedication, your mind, your heart. I'm lucky I get a part of it."

"You own it." His voice was more intense, aggressive. "You own my heart, Elle. Be careful with it, please."

My soul hummed as I reached down to guide him inside me. I sucked in a breath, adjusting to him, and rocked my hips. "Always," I said, holding his gaze. I'd never *made love* before because it sounded cheesy. Having sex was hot and fun and dirty, but this? With him? I ground on him slowly, enjoying the way his thighs tightened and his abs clenched. His lips parted, and his eyes were on fire as I slowly came down to kiss him. He gripped the back of my head hard, digging his nails into my scalp as he thrust up into me.

It was hot as hell. My nerves exploded around us. Pleasure and love and ecstasy.

Sweat pooled between our chests, our breaths mingling as the kiss went deeper and his thrusts got harder. I'd never come like this, but I didn't care. This was about us, about our bodies enjoying each other. I nipped his lip, and he grunted. "I'm flipping us over. I need more."

He slid out, held onto me, and rolled us so I was on my back. He yanked my legs down to the edge of the bed, and he stood, pulling my ankles at his ears. "Fuck, you're gorgeous like this, Elle."

He pounded into me now. The slap of skin, the sounds of him groaning, the beat of my heart in my ears. I thrashed on his bed, his scent surrounding me. He used one hand to play with my clit, and I tightened my legs around his head. "Yes, Elle, give me one more."

My back arched, and I held onto the sheets and yelled, "Faster!"

He obeyed, and the tingling sensation burst from my core, my muscles clenching around his cock, and I fell apart. Stars burst behind my eyes, my heart hammering against my ribcage as my orgasm knocked the wind out of me. Cal's grip on my thighs tightened, and he barely let me come back to earth before going harder. His jaw was set in determination, his eyes burning. He grunted before completely losing it. He groaned, his head going back as he thrust a few more times.

Watching him lose control was the best transformation of his face. No more hard lines or frowning. His skin was smooth and relaxed and even a little red. When he caught his breath and stared down at me, I smiled. "You're sexy."

One side of his lips curved up, and he kissed my stomach. "Don't get me started on you." He went to the bathroom and quickly came back, the condom gone. He crawled into bed, pulling my back against his chest, and rested his nose on my neck. "I want this every night. Breathing you in, having your hair on my face. I've never felt this way about someone before, but I know you're the one for me."

"Cal." I swallowed down the emotion in my throat. That was an intense thing to share with someone after agreeing to be together five seconds ago.

"Don't say anything back. I'm just letting you know you can count on me to be around a long ass time. I'm gonna work every day to stay in your life." His arms tightened around me. "I'm not a romance hero like in your books, but I work really hard at what I love. And that's you."

I kissed the back of his hand, my eyes welling up. "I don't know. That's a very romance hero thing to say."

He laughed, the wonderful sound making me smile. He pulled me tighter, and his breath hit my neck, his pulse slowing down against my back. I relaxed into him. All this time, I'd convinced myself he wasn't like the guy in the stories, but he was in his own way.

He showed love through actions, and I used words. He was gruff and rarely smiled, but I brought out the joy more and more each day. I smiled, snuggled deeper into him, and let my daydreams go wild. Us in a year, us at holidays. Us living together even. Traveling and me sitting in the stands while he played. Me wearing his jersey at his games and texting pictures to Charlie so he could show Lizzie. Us going to Lizzie's dance recitals or school shows. Him and I visiting bookstores or greenhouses or decorating *our* place someday. I saw a future with us, with our friends and family, and I was a fool for thinking he wasn't my happy ever after.

He definitely was, and we were only in the beginning of our story.

EPILOGUE

17 Months later, Thanksgiving
Cal

Snow covered the entire backyard, leaving no sign of the grass that was once there. It fell silently, the cold winter air unforgiving for an Illinois winter. It wasn't even December, and it was already brutal.

My cheeks stung from the wind, but the moment of solitude was needed. Even just for a few minutes. My life was filled with people and noise now, but every so often, I escaped to the quiet for me. To reflect and think about my parents. Therapy helped, with Elle and Michael's insistence that I continue, and they were right. I refused to tell Reiner that because he'd feel all proud, but I shared that with Elle. She was my other fucking half, and knowing she'd be by my side after graduation was the only thing keeping me sane. My wonderful, kick-ass girlfriend scored writing gigs online, was working on her second novel to be published, and was mentoring high school students who dreamed of being writers. Writing, she said, could be done anywhere, and she planned to travel wherever the NHL took me.

How had I gotten so fucking lucky?

"Hey." Elle's soft voice had me glancing to my right. "I figured you'd be out here. Can I join?"

"Of course." I smiled, held out a hand, and pulled her to me. She leaned her head onto my shoulder, her shampoo tickling my nose. "It's a madhouse in there."

"Yeah, but it's our people. It somehow makes it better?" She laughed and moved to stand on her tiptoes. Her hair was down today, straight and long. It blew in the wind around her face, her cute note and red lips so damn perfect. "I'm so happy you came."

"You're here." I pulled her toward me and kissed her. She tasted like red wine and whipped cream. "You and Lizzie get into the desserts before dinner?"

"Desserts after dinner is really more of a suggestion, Calzone." She used her thumb to wipe under my lip. "Red is a good color on you but maybe not smeared on your chin."

I smiled, pulling her into a hug. She fit against me perfectly and patted my ass.

"I can't believe this is happening," I said.

"What? This snow? I know." She glanced up and cupped my face. "Your skin's cold. We can find you a nice quiet corner to hide in? I'm sure Naomi and Michael wouldn't care if you sat in a closet."

I shook my head. "No, not the snow. The people. Having a loud holiday. I spent three Thanksgivings alone, drinking, hating every second of every day. Now look at where I'm at?" I gestured toward the patio doors. I sucked in a breath, my emotions getting the best of me. "I'm lucky. That's what I'm saying, but I'm shit at expressing it."

"Thank goodness I wrote the Cal-Emotional-Handbook then." She kissed me again, softly. "Come inside. Have a drink. Take in the fact we're all family now, in some way or another."

I nodded, grabbing her hand and letting her lead me back inside. The second we opened the door, warmth spread through my body. Lizzie, Charlie, and Alex sat at the kitchen table, playing some kid game. Alex laughed and even wore a sweater that wasn't black. It was gray, but that was improvement.

Michael and Naomi looked like the happy newlyweds they were. She beamed as she showed Cami and Cami's incredibly tall boyfriend Freddie their photos on the wall. I was *in* the photos. My face hung on someone else's wall on one of the happiest days of their life. Michael's sister Ryann, and her fiancé Jonah were visiting that week too. Jonah hadn't wanted to steal Michael and Naomi's thunder, so he'd proposed the day after they got married. They wanted to come see Michael coach and tag along for the holiday. Ryann sat on Jonah's lap on a chair, the two of them discussing the best Thanksgiving movie.

It was *Planes, Trains, and Automobiles,* and no one could argue differently. Coach Simpson was there too, nursing a beer and chatting with Elle's parents. Elle had insisted on having her family come down so I wouldn't miss a holiday with Lizzie, and sure enough, the Van Helsings were here, at my assistant coach's house. Gabe too.

Hell, I never thought I'd be *friends* with Gabriel Van Helsing, but we got together every few weeks. Even now, he laughed with Daniella in the kitchen as they finished making a green bean casserole. Gabe met my eyes and nodded before tickling his girlfriend. We'd double-dated a lot since his girl was my girl's best friend.

Again, my life was almost like a movie. There was so much joy and laughter. All aspects of our lives blended together. It was messy and sometimes annoying, but fuck, it was…wonderful. Elle tugged my hand, dragging me toward the garage. "Let's get a beer before Gabe challenges everyone to a game or something. God, that guy needs more to do since he's bored at his job."

"He could coach hockey."

"Huh." She smiled, her eyes lighting up. "That's a great idea. I'm surprised he hasn't thought of it. You should tell him the next time you have a bro-ment."

"A bro-ment?"

"Yeah, you getting brunches and shit. It's like a bro moment. Bro-ment." She winked and handed me a cold can of beer.

"You're ridiculous." I grinned.

"Yeah, but you love me." She opened her can, and I did the same. We clinked our cans together. "To Thanksgiving!"

We took a sip, our gazes holding. "I love you, Elle."

"I love you too," she said softly. "Promise me even when we're traveling the country during your hockey career, we always find a way to come back here for the holidays."

"Done." My throat got tight again.

The door opened, and Reiner's smile grew when he saw us. That fucker was always smiling. "Yo, you getting beers for everyone or what? Come on, Holt."

"Only a few more months and then you're not my coach anymore."

"How excited are you for that?" he asked, laughing and clapping me on the back. "I'm ready to watch you go big. Bring Central State some clout, you know?"

Elle met my eyes, nodding, like she understood I needed that little gesture of support. I shrugged at Reiner. "I have you to thank for this." I held out a hand. "So, thank you."

"For what?" He eyed it, tilting his head to the side.

"Saving me from myself freshmen year." I swallowed. "Now look at my life? It's one I didn't know I could have."

"Dude." Michael Reiner was a hugger, and I should've known better. He pulled me into an embrace, patting me on the back *hard*. "No thank you necessary. We're family, man. And family gets free tickets to any game, alright?"

He gave me the exit I needed, and for that, I was grateful. "Of course."

"Good, now we need beers before we fight for the TV. I want the game, but Cami knows some of the girls dancing in the parade, so we'll have to vote. I'm counting on you for support, Cal."

My lips twitched, and Elle took my hand again, interlocking

our fingers. With her by my side, I'd get my own version of a happy ending, and for the first time in forever, I was looking forward to more holidays.

Because I wasn't alone anymore. I had…all those people in the house. People who cared about me and people I cared about. Music blasted from inside, *Incubus* playing on the radio, and I knew it was a sign from my parents. I smiled and met Elle's eyes. Yeah, I was a lucky bastard. I'd do my damndest to make sure to enjoy every second of what came next because life was too short.

But with Elle, life didn't seem as hard. We had friends and family and each other to lean on when things got hard. I used to think I'd spend the rest of my life alone, angry and sad, and sure, I still got angry and sad but I was never alone. Not with Coach Simpson or Michael or Gabe or Charlie or Lizzie or my girl always there for me.

Central State used to be my own version of hell, but it was where I'd found my people, and I would forever be grateful for this place. It taught me how to live again. It gave Michael his second chance at happiness when he found Naomi, let Cami and Freddie learn they were worthy of real love. It was the place where Gabe and Dani crossed the line from friends to something more. All of us growing and finding love.

Now, I thought about my spreadsheet with all my research on wedding rings. I'd planned to wait until after we graduated together but I might not make it that long. I hadn't truly experienced life much until I found Elle, and while it was still strange for me, I was impatient to start *life* with her.

Our story might not be typical, but I'd spend my life making sure we had our happy ever after.

ALSO BY JAQUELINE SNOWE

CENTRAL STATE SERIES

The Puck Drop

From the Top

Take the Lead

Off the Ice

CLEAT CHASERS SERIES

Challenge Accepted

The Game Changer

Best Player

No Easy Catch

OUT OF THE PARK SERIES

Evening the Score

Sliding Home

Rounding the Bases

SHUT UP AND KISS ME SERIES

Internship with the Devil

Teaching with the Enemy

Nightmare Next Door

STANDALONES

Holdout

Take a Chance on Me

The Weekend Deal

ABOUT THE AUTHOR

Jaqueline Snowe lives in Arizona where the "dry heat" really isn't that bad. She prefers drinking coffee all hours of the day and snacking on anything that has peanut butter or chocolate. She is the mother to two fur-babies who don't realize they aren't humans and a two amazing kiddos. She is an avid reader and writer of romances and tends to write about athletes. Her husband works for an MLB team (not a player, lol) so she knows more about baseball than any human ever should.

To sign up for her review team, or blogger list, please visit her website www.jaquelinesnowe.com for more information.

Printed in Great Britain
by Amazon